# Advance Praise

Richard Martin's *I Inherited a Mixed Animal from Uncle Living in Woods* is strange, brilliant, unique, and hilarious. There are so many moments of brilliance in this book. By way of Lemuel, Shane, Yonder, and the ragtag citizens of Hmm, Martin draws us in to a place we don't recognize at all until we recognize it so completely we come to think of it as home. Somehow infusing beauty and humor into each page, if not every sentence, Martin reminds us the world is not to be taken lightly, except when it is. Simple and complex, ludicrous yet authentic, and utterly, painfully relatable, it reminds one of the old theatre of the absurd. Ionesco. Ibsen. A tale about finding our people in this often-lonely and messed up world, this book is nothing short of incandescent. I hope the Pulitzer folks take note.

> — Gae Polisner, author of *In Sight of Stars* and *Jack Kerouac is Dead to Me*

Brilliantly creative and utterly hilarious, Richard Martin's *I Inherited a Mixed Animal from Uncle Living in Woods* is a masterpiece. This wonderful novel is consistently laugh-out-loud funny, but in a loving way. The author through his sardonic narrator, Lemuel, isn't shy to point out that the human flaws and frailties we find amusing can be found in all of us if we look hard enough. The oddball yet incisive and warm humor make us care about Yonder and his bewildered keeper. Filled with colorful and memorably unexpected prose to match its characters, the novel's humor is reminiscent of T.R. Pearson's *A Short History of a Small Place*; its delightfully original settings and cast recalling Katherine Dunn's *Geek Love*; its gentle yet incisive satire resurrecting memories of the canon of Kurt Vonnegut; its homespun wisdom walking in the footsteps of John Steinbeck's *Cannery Row*. However, it is by no means derivative. This book, like Dunn's *Geek Love*, has no siblings. It is an only child.

— Steven Mayfield, author of *The Penny Mansions*

A rowdy, fast-paced and moving tale of unique surrealism, Richard Martin's *I Inherited a Mixed Animal from Uncle Living in Woods* is utterly original, unlike anything you have had the pleasure to read. This novel invites the reader into a world with its own dream-like logic, a constant feast of visual delights and hilarious dialogue that keeps the reader turning pages well into the night. Martin has successfully and joyfully created a world that hearkens back to a Pieter Bruegel-like sensibility combined with an astute sense of Americana, an Americana of the absurd. One of the great triumphs of the novel is the mixed animal himself, Yonder, who dwells in the realm of the inexplicable, and while remaining a mystery is also whole and tangible. How the author describes Yonder is a delicious literary achievement. Mixed Animal is a genuine madcap delight, a truly one-of-a-kind yarn. The reader is taken into that hyper spot at the end of a dream where the unreasonable somehow makes complete sense. You will laugh out loud and shake your head in disbelief. You will highlight passages and show them to your friends. Yonder will become a part of your own dreamscape, the ultimate surrealist creation who is both impossible to imagine, and yet real as can be. A marvel!

— Stephen Tunney, author of *One Hundred Percent Lunar Boy* and *Flan*

# I
# INHERITED A MIXED ANIMAL FROM UNCLE LIVING IN WOODS

Richard Martin

Apprentice House Press
Loyola University Maryland

First Edition

Paperback ISBN: 978-1-62720-578-8
Casebound ISBN: 978-1-62720-579-5
Ebook ISBN: 978-1-62720-580-1

Cover & Internal Design by J.P. Stromberg
Editorial Development by Rebecca Thompson
Promotional Development by Abby Szypula

Published by Apprentice House Press

Apprentice
House Press
*Loyola University Maryland*

Loyola University Maryland
4501 N. Charles Street, Baltimore, MD 21210
410.617.5265
www.ApprenticeHouse.com
info@ApprenticeHouse.com

"There is one small movement of the story that eludes your control, that you cannot even see, one alien thing with no purpose other than to teach you that in the darkest corner of the story dwells a wild force that is too much a part of you to see, a blind spot, just as you do not see your own eyes as they sweep the woods you walk through for danger."

—Wilbur Daniel Steele

to everyone and anyone who ever made me laugh from my heart

# 1.

Our Uncle Leonard was a hermit who lived in the woods his entire life. Unc had a sack of money stashed away, and when he went to meet his Maker he left every penny to my little sister Shane. Meanwhile, he left me, a full grown man, a rusty bicycle and a busted set of drums. I don't mean he *left* me a full grown man, I mean I *am* a full grown man. Therefore, why would he go and leave me a load of childish junk instead of cold hard adult cash?

Oh, he also left me some kind of a mixed animal, which turned out to be even more questionable than the junk.

*

The beast found its way to me here in Hmm in the middle of the night a barrelful of moons ago. Unc's woodsman neighbor Chuck woke I and Shane, pounding on our cottage door with his forehead because his hands were full. Chuck was a stalwart, self-reliant fellow in mud-plastered boots and Siberian greatcoat, but that night he had a real bad case of the heebie geebies.

He had drove four hours from the Unconscious Forest to deliver the news of Uncle Leonard's passing, along with the cash for Shane, and the bike, drums, and critter for me. He drug the goods in and spun to depart as though a ghost was on his tail, but Shane blocked the doorway and we managed to calm the big chap down enough to reel a few rambling incomprehensible facts out of him, first off how Unc had demised.

"Sudden natural causes," says Chuck. "Or so Doc said. That there—" (indicating the animal, who stood undescribable in the shadows, fur bristling and eyes of fury) "—is all that survived the fire and explosion."

"*Fire* and *explosion*?" says Shane.

"Yes, ma'am. Your Unc transformed hisself into quite a rampageous experimenter in them woods." Chuck glanced at the animal which in turn latched its gleer onto me for no known reason. "Leonard's death-bed wish was, 'Brang them these gadgets—them orphan kids, Shane and Lemuel, my bonehead blood.' I done as he ast, laid him to rest on the bluff under the Lights. Then I nursed that gasly thingum back to health. Oh!" He reached in his greatcoat and set a small burlap purse on the coffee table. "That there's a poultice for the stitches." He run a finger along his ribs area. "Good luck!" And at that he elbowed through us and out the door.

"What is this animal!" Shane shouts after him.

"Mixed!" Chuck explains. He climbed in his old Helms truck and got it roaring.

"What's its name!" I holler, but Chuck's Helms truck was already skreeching down our driveway and out of the village, leaving me and Shane to our minor grief and major bafflement.

"Did you follow all that?" Shane asks.

"I hoped *you* had," I say.

Slowly we lain our eyes upon the creature. It stood in the corner, blazing bad intentions our way. Size-wise, it was near to a long large turkey, a smaller wart hog, or about one and two-thirds emperor penguin. Simply standing there it disarranged your entire deductive facility.

I say, "What and the world was Unc up to out in them woods?"

"No good."

"It don't look tamed."

"I concur," Shane says. "It has retained its wilderness."

"What sort of a animal do you figure it could be?"

"Contradictory," says Shane.

We gandered at it from different angles.

"Part up there resembles mutt, but this over here calls pussycat to mind."

"You got you some pig right there, a dab of goat up around back."

The thing was, the parts blent so seamless you couldn't pin down where one left off and the next begun.

"Would you say a little monkey perhaps?"

"I would. And possum in the middle."

"Here's some fox up the spine, maybe raccoon over here, pinch of wolverine in that region."

Shane and I shook our heads in unbelief, and the dang thing shook *its* head in unbelief right back. Both it and us appeared no happier than the other to be seeing what they saw.

Out of nowhere the animal gave the lowest growl that ever been gave. My footbones felt it through the floorboards.

"So, Unc's gone on," I say, hoping the varmint would appreciate a change of subject from itself. "Our poor old Uncle Leonard."

"Fiddlesticks," says Shane. "He was mean and lowdown and loved it. We couldn't stand him and he couldn't stand us more. And him dumping this thingmabob on us only proves it."

"Well, you ought to respect the dead, even if you hated their guts."

"I respect the dead's inheritance," she says, scooping up her undeserved cash and flouncing back to her room as if our life had not just took a bad fork forevermore.

I sat in my rocker and commenced my to in fro, real reassuring and calm, keeping one eyeball on the sole remaining consequence of whatever Unc's lurid business had been out there in the Unconscious Forest. The thing kept a bead on me right back, not a blink in sight.

"I'm Lemuel," I say. "You could sit down if you want."

It declined with a snort. To act normal, I took a close whiff of the little burlap purse Chuck left and that stinkbomb knocked my olfactories back to Independence Day. I was not keen to slap no poultice on that thing's undercarriage. "I wonder why you went and got yourself stitches," I mummer.

From the corner shadows it glowered at me like I personally flang it out of the Garden of Eden.

"Don't blame me, fella," I say. "I'm just a link in some spooky chain I never asked to be no link in." But then I reckoned, why should I care *what* it thought? Was I my dead Uncle's animal's keeper? It looked like I was, for the nonce, but I didn't got to like it, did I.

# 2.

What infernal region could Uncle Leonard had plucked that savage mixum out of? Chuck's insinuatings led me to imagine Unc in his lab, splooshing genes up in a blender, or slapping mismatched rutting species together, or something unimaginable worse. Nobody sane would keep that thing around them day or night. You wouldn't trust it with all the tea in China. Trouble was scrawled on it from stem to stern, and I had all the trouble I needed as is.

The animal hadn't no visible license tag. I did spy a old tattered red collar peeping out of its funky overstuffed golden-orange and silver-red neck fur. But I wasn't reaching in that rat's nest with its curled lip and many splendored teeth nearby. Uncle Leonard wasn't the kind to believe in licenses, but if he was, what category of animal would he had told the clerk he needed a license for? General? Missileaneous?

This is what I told the brute: "I'm proud to be a fella that takes things in stride, but when it comes down to it, this is *my* cottage, *I* say what happens and what don't here, and if anybody has a beef with how I operate—except for my bossy sister—I won't be the one hightailing it for the exit." It listened but appeared thoroughly unconvinced.

On the other hand, I was leery about toting that hellion over to, say, Jinx's Pawn & Putt to hock it, or the Hmm Pound for unlikely adoption, or shooing it off on February Mountain to fend for itself. If it turned out diabolic, or even illegal, and got traced back to me, we'd both get oustracized.

Plus, Ma and Pa raised me and Shane to have a heart. I feared some greedy local would grab the thing and sell it to a city scientist to perform godawful tests on. I didn't need that anywhere near my conscience, which was shaky already from other things I done and hadn't done, not that that's any of your particular business. Any case, you never want science, the law, the newspaper, or morals involved in anything of yours if you can help it.

I ought to explain one or two things.

First, I happened to be the rebel kind, the grumpy young man, the Kafkaest outsider. I kept to the backroads on my house call fix-it rounds, often traveling by railroad hand-car, not for the romance of it, but because it's a mind-your-own-business style of transport. Suddenly finding a large hazardous uncultured animal under your wing did not fit my lifestyle, which was to do what I wanted when I wanted where I wanted how I wanted if I wanted. My motto was "Don't follow me, don't lead me, just be my friend and leave me the hell alone."

Second, my sister Shane, she bugged me galore, it was her mission in life, but she could take dang well care of herself. We split expenses and argued about everything, and it worked out fine. If I wanted more problems in my life I would have got me a girl friend. Don't kid yourself, there was a gaggle of village gals that would had loved to get their hooks in my modest untaxed income, my ever-expanding collection of *Reader's Digest Condensed World Literature*, and my invention-and-fix-it flair.

All of which goes to say that a primitive, smug, briny, mal-discontent animal that nobody even known what it was, roaming around your cottage—not my idea of a holiday.

The only other possibility was how could I make a little cash off it. The way it inhaled its first breakfast (a bucket of oats and bananas), keeping it fed would cost me a bundle, plus utilities. It would be a considerable investment that was only natural to secure a fair return from.

As unauthorized inventor/fix-it master in Hmm I had plenty of work, but who couldn't use the extra moo-la. I had repaired millions of appliances and invented gizmos both beneficial and interesting to Hmmkind, yet barely made a nickel overall, soft touch that I was, accepting payment in mustard seeds, busted bricks, promises, homemade underpants, and the like.

Shane ran a lucrative fortune-telling enterprise out of the garage (that she had to put in a blind trust during her mayorial campaign), so it weren't right she should land Unc's dough while I received a pile of broke-down crap, plus this hodgepodge animal that from the git-go didn't hanker to get took care of by me any more than I hankered tooking care of it.

# 3.

Uncle Leonard had always been a crabby, menacing fellow that me and Shane done our best to steer clear of. To be honest, we barely known him, but it wasn't our fault—old Unc went out of his way to not be knewn.

The last time we seen him alive was two years previous. We drove my Henry J three hours to his cabin in the mist of the Unconscious Forest. We was his only living relatives that we knew of, and we visited him for the purest of reasons: pity and guilt. We hadn't no idea of no so-call animal or any kind of experimenter business at the time.

You could smell Uncle Leonard's despicable pipe tobacco a mile away from his cabin. To get to the door we had to park in a big mud puddle and shoo away a gang of mangy sourpuss crows that lounged around on the porch like they owned the place. They cursed and mocked and grudgingly flapped up on the tin roof where they peeked over and continued gossiping about us.

Unc answered the door in floppy slippers and a foul lab coat. His white hair stuck up like a bunch of wires to nowhere. Ignoring our greetings, he gave us the once over like we was Bible salesmen. He left us on the porch, shuffled down the hall and locked the heap of locks on the door to the rear room that bore a gigantic "DANJER" in red spray paint. Then he come back and rudely gestured us inside like we was thieving bellboys.

The whole visit he sat there brooding at us from the skreechy chaise lounge that he kept adjusting to interrupt us, and smoking the dickens out of his stinking corncob pipe. We could of been a annoying program on TV that he was gawking at. You could tell where that animal learned to gleer at you like it did. Every once and a while, like a donkey, Unc spread his lips and shown us his corn-colored teeth as if they was pirate gold he had drug up from the bottom of the seven seas.

Unc's eyes had the combination of Peter Lorre, Ulysses S. Grant, and a snapping turtle in them. When he wasn't sucking on that putrid pipe, he was rolling his tongue in and out of his mouth like a demented yo-yo. He made his own pipe stuffings out of a raw blend of secret ingredients he grown out back in the woods. You could smell Taipan retchroot in it, and purple skunkcap, and night crawler weed, and beyond that it was anybody's guess. There weren't no mistaking that stank, there was only one, and you'd never forget it. The air also had a faint scent of toe jam to it that you tried in vain to not keep sniffing to see if it was still there, but then you got used to it and it submerged into the other stanks.

I couldn't see no radio nor TV nor record player. The only entertainment in town was them crows up there cursing and yelping and scratching that tin roof like the devil's sock hop. The sole reading material was a pamplet called "Ethics and Esthetics of Biotechnology At Home"; a handmade cardboard sign nailed to the wall that said: "If you reeding this sine you wasteing my time"; and a big white Bible that was so old and read-worn and coming apart I thought it was a pile of melting snow on the table.

On top of all that, Unc never offered us the first snack or soda pop.

Nevertheless, I and Shane tried opening up various and Sunday avenues of conversation.

"Uncle Leonard?" says Shane. "Have you happened to be

following any current events?"

Unc grunted and spat through a bullethole in the window.

Shane persevered. "Oh, speaking of current events, you'll be proud to know that your favorite niece is running for mayor of Hmm. My platform is 'A new shining face for a new shining Hmm upon a golden hill.' Even though it's not exactly upon a hill. Or golden."

By way of answer, Unc presented a turbulent clump of bewildering and inappropriate facial expressions.

Shane says, "Bro, it might be a good time to tell Unc one of your ribald man jokes."

"What ribald man jokes?"

Unc rocked faster with his bony stubble chin thrust out, eyeing us like a bullfrog eyes a couple fat horseflies.

I cleared my throat. "OK, well, Jinx told me a good one yesterday when I was hocking a sack of compost. OK, so, two antennas meet on a roof, see. And then they fall in love and everything, and so they go and get married, these two antennas. Well, the wedding weren't much, but the reception was great."

Instead of laughing, Unc stuffed his fingers in his mouth and gnawed them like French fries.

"It wasn't ribald enough," says Shane. "Hey, maybe he's going deaf. Do you get it, Uncle Leonard! Antennas! Wedding! It's a *double entendre* about reception!"

He gave her a growl of such astonishment you'd thought she made a *double entendre* about his long johns.

Another way we passed the time was Uncle's pipe kept going out. That didn't stop him from sucking away on it with a hideous whistling noise, till Shane or me rose exasperated and re-lit it up for him with big homemade matches that popped and sput like fireworks.

11

At one point Unc's woodsman neighbor Chuck (who two years later would brung the animal to me) dropped in to borrow a blowtorch. The woodsman wanted to touch up a plaque in front of his place that said, "CHUCKS' PLACE!" He was a hail fellow well met, but I didn't know who would even see his plaque except for Unc, who actually busted about one-tenth of a smile upon seeing his neighbor. Nobody else came within ten miles of that part of the forest but bears, lost French tourists, and Shane and me.

Uncle Leonard's rotten pipe went out one more time and we let it. After a while his head fell on his shoulder and he started snoring like three night watchmen. Shane and me snucked out while we could. We had to bat a whole jury of them obstriptruss crows off the car, and as we drove away, I saw Unc standing at the grimy cabin window wearing a big pumpkin grin, like he had really put one over. Or maybe it was one of them grimaces that sad and lonely people get when they think nobody's looking. Or gas. Either way, it was the last time we ever seen him, so to speak, and I'll always remember his pumpkin grin fondly, whatever it might of meant.

All that happened two years before the animal arrived in Hmm, in case you lost track of time, which happens to everybody now in then. It don't mean you're losing your mind, necessarily.

# 4.

With the monkey way it clumb, I feared the animal would scram over the 15-foot-high red brick privacy wall I and Dad built around the property, knocking off the potted petunias on somebody's head that Shane put along the top, and do untold damage to the village and its precious population. I don't mean she put *somebody's head* on the wall, I mean it's *petunias* she stuck up there.

I didn't want to be responsible for some Hmman losing a limb, say, not with medical bills the way they were. Plus you-know-who would get mixed up in it to his elbows and beret, namely, Ernie "Transplant" Anderson, the addled voodoo man and village doctor, who also owned the Hmm Drugstore & Casket Corporation.

I decided to keep it housebound until I figured out where to unload it.

Meanwhile, I sat on the porch swing and assumed the feathered camel posture. I needed a little homemade meditation to restore my pre-animal cool.

But that beast had got inside my head. I meditated on its numerous annoying qualities. It had the manners of a smug bum, smelt like a basement, and you could trust it as far as you could throw Shane. It closely observed your reactions as its expressions kaleidescoped from coy to frisky to dismissive to bullheaded. Every once and a while it let you pet it, but it kept a tension in its fur that let your hand know what a precarious situation it was in.

Before I could get any Oms going on the porch, I felt its wild presence rush by. Shane had charred a tray of rhubarb dumplings, cracked the door for air, and the thing made a break for it, jouncing down the stairs for the garden and the wall.

"Hell's Bells!" I say, but gave not chase. It eyed the privacy wall, casual as a convict, and began proudly browsing the garden like it had planted it. The winter ground lay hard as a councilman's skull, with a couple raggedy parsnips and jicamas sticking up, so there wasn't much destruction it could do.

It sidled over to the wall and got to gnawing on a brick. It went at it like a cob of red corn, back in forth, brick chips flying. I had no idea how it could do that, unless it tilted its teeth outwards, which you wouldn't put past it.

"Alto!" I holler from the balcony. "Attention! Animal! That is a privacy wall! Cease!"

It gnawed on, then shook the chips off its dome and ambled over to the compost heap. Rooting around in the steaming breakdown, it come up with a big fat brown snail in its paw, turned it one side and the other like a fresh brownie, and downed it in one nonchalant gulp.

"Ew! Sput that out!"

Instead it strutted around eyeing the height of the wall from different angles, as if calculating to make a run for it.

"Hey!" I call down. "I know what you're thinking. Desist!"

The beast squinted over its shoulder at me like Dirty Harry squinting at the police chief. I shook my head real slow-like, fearing how far I might have to escalate things to keep the upper hand around there.

After more enigmatic meandering, the animal strolled up the stairs, marched right past me, stepping on my toes, and curled up in a bookshelf that it first cleared out by bumping half my entire priceless *Reader's Digest Condensed World Literature* collection onto the floor with its nose and butt.

You might think we are a bunch of hicks, I and Shane, but we enjoy our literary delights. Mom was the Hmm librarian and somewhat of a thief, so our childhood was ripe with books in every nook and cranny. Dad was unliterate and liked to hear Shane and me read out loud because it put him to sleep, so we developed into deeply mental children.

I believe a fully rounded modern fellow has a duty to himself and his community to stay on top of world literature, but there's no reason to strain your eyeballs on condensable sections. If you read a book and don't notice the parts that got themselves condensed, they obviously hadn't been meant to be uncondensed in the first place.

My favorite author was Frank Kafka. European gentleman. He wrote about a bug, a castle, a trial, a panther, a hungry man, and much, much more, always starring somebody that was trying to figure out what was going on. I liked Frank because I'm interested in problems and I like to read and smile wisely as if you knew what was going on more than the dumbfloundering hero.

My other favorite author was Lao Tsu (pronounced Low Stu), a shy Chinese fellow, a bit of a loafer with one little book to his name, the *Tao Te Ching*, Chinese for "The Way of Getting Out of the Way." It was simple and complicated, like Kafka, and many of the stories in it wasn't fifty words long after *Reader's Digest* got through with them. If you slip a line from a Low Stu story into a conversation, such as, "Mystery and reality emerge from the same ground, therefore, the more you talk, the less you say," then everybody will suspect you're smart, plus they'll have the vague feeling they been insulted, but if they accuse you of it, you deny it with a hurt frown, and you win either way.

For her part, Shane adored questionable author Louis La'mour.

He is a French cowboy *not* covered by *Reader's Digest*, so she had to read every clump of windbag exposition that trailed off into obscure territory that must had amused the probably drunk author.

Whoa, it was a big old thing, to get back to this brute of a animal that I was getting my first, long, up-close gaze upon. It filled up one entire bookshelf with plenty hanging over. Must of weighed, oh, I'd say 25 to 45, 50 strapping pounds, offhand, likely more. It sported stiff fur that proved to be bushy, orange, and raven at times, and other times fluffy, silver, golden, and red, depending on the light, background scenery, barometric pressure, and your and its mood.

Its ample head dangled out of the bookcase gargoyle style. You couldn't call it unattractive in the conventional sense, for there was nothing you could think of to compare it to.

Out of its throat a noise issued like a hangman's rope getting drawn back and forth through a hole carved in a cardboard box. It sounded like both a little tiger, a flippant porpoise, and a angry nightingale. You couldn't tell if it was purring, growling, set to hack up a tennis ball, or deep in a state of wonder. It packed a lot into everything it did, even if it wasn't doing anything.

Its claws extended like a bear cub's that it allowed me to gingerly fiddle with, while its eyes fixated like little bowls of black radar upon my fingers. They had a unpleasant flexibility, like mud-encrusted gummy bears. Its claws, not my fingers. Under the tip of each pawpad sat a indented sort of octopus suction cup appendage that expanded and contracted as the animal inhaled and exhaled.

The tail was medium to short, spiky, reddish, fuzzy, prehensile, and cubular at the end, as if part got wrent off in a tiff.

It held one eye ajar, watching me, and the eye remained open even as it begun snoring like two lumberjacks sawing a icebox in two.

I remembered the stitches Chuck mentioned. I grabbed that stanky poultice and a roll of duck tape and poked around in the underbrush of its torso. I found a jagged stitched-up slice about a hand long that sent a shiver to my confidentials. I slapped the poultice on the gash, taped it down, and backed my hand out of there.

"Oh, in Heaven's name!" I say.

Two feelers popped between its sleeping lips. It was that compost snail! It was crawling out of its mouth! The emerging snail made the animal look like it was sneering at me, with that one eye open. It slept on as the snail crawled across its snout, wobbling from the snores.

The snail appeared nor the worse for wear. I plucked it off and returned it to the compost. It sat there a moment in dismay, realized it was back home in the rot, and slowly slud away, trying, I imagine, to forget the whole thing.

# 5.

Shane didn't care to have nothing to do with the animal. I told her the story about the snail and she fell out the window onto the porch.

Otherwise she sat on the floor in her room counting her inheritance over and over. Looking out the window at the sun setting melancholy behind old February Mountain, she mummered the list of stuff she planned to buy: "A telescope. Basketballs for the whole village. A scooper for my pond. A new wardrobe and extreme makeover for my mayoral campaign. And a hundred pairs of Japanese big-toe socks."

"That's a lot of stuff for $74.25," I say.

"Not if you know where to shop."

"Where do you shop, the twelfth century?"

"A girl doesn't need time travel to find things on sale."

"You won't find many basketballs in the twelfth century, on sale or not."

"How many will I find?"

"None. They didn't play basketball in the twelfth century."

"I doubt you know everything everybody did in the twelfth century."

"I know you won't be able to run no mayorial campaign in this century if you spend all your dough on frivolous items. Propaganda costs money."

"I'm going to run on the coin of my personality. However,

when I start passing out free basketballs I won't even need a personality."

"I think you just found your campaign slogan."

Shane didn't have a June bug's chance in Duckville of winning for mayor. Not against the ruthless, corrupt, intrenched, and sarcastic 93-year-old incumbent Mayor Buck "Shuffleboard" Humphrey and his shadowy entourage. Shuffleboard's perpetual campaign slogan was "It could be worse! A lot worse!" The thought terrified us, so we kept voting him back in. Still, I hoped Shane would pull off the impossible democratic dream, for her sake and mine, even if it brought the village down around everybody's ears.

For her sake, fortune-telling out of the garage wasn't no real purpose in life. Shane was born to be mayor or princess of somewhere or other. Although a boy friend is what she could have used the most. One time she had a lad picked out, namely, Louiscious Betts from Ambo, one village over. She had been gathering wild yams in the woods one moon-lattice evening and spied Louiscious lazing against a log playing "Old Buttermilk Sky" on a juice harp. Him and his twangy song snabbed Shane's black heart like a spider web snabbing a bumblebee.

Alas, she was too bashful to speak to him. Instead, she commissioned me to build him a oak Thereamen Electromagnetic Oscillator Box like the one she had admired on The Strange Musical Instrument Channel. She planned on giving it to Louiscious as a first meeting present, to kind of break the ice. I sent for the blueprint and knocked one off pretty quick. Unfortunately, before she could finagle a roundevouz, she found out he was married, had a girl friend, and was on parole over in Ballpeen County for pawning stolen haybales. So she broke up with him before he ever heard of her.

I tried to play that blasted Thereamen Box myself, but couldn't get the hang of it. The eerie screwball sounds hypnotized me and I forgot I was the one playing it. I guess you can't always master what you built. Shane said she'd eat a can of Borax if she ever saw the contraption again as it reminded her of the bad relationship she never had with Louiscious, so I stuck it up in the attic.

Winning for mayor would keep her lonely mind occupied with power, property, and prestige, and if anything was left over, the common good. She might even trawl a mayorial groupie boy friend out of it.

As for my sake, if she won, she would move into the Mayor's Royal Cottage, thereby establishing peace and quiet around the homestead at long last for once.

*

Shane wanted me to tie the animal up while it was inside, but I gallantly refused. First of all, I wouldn't want to be tied up myself. Second of all, I tried tying it up and it didn't pan out. We had a tether ball pole sticking up from the middle of our coffee table for a quick game during commercials. I took the ball off and went to hook the chain to its collar, and it give me a look like, "You sure you want to go down that dark road, Neighbor?"

I would let it settle in before I begun its training. If I'd got yanked out of my home in explosive circumstances, then shipped off to a distant village to live with strangers as missileaneous as Shane and me, I might be a bit surly myself.

Up to that point, diet-wise, it had aten anything we gave it. "Gave" meaning whatever it could fit in its mouth. From a whole orange to a family bag of Blazing Czili Vegan Cheeze Znakes to a stack of eggplant pancakes with okra syrup. Not so much aten as sniffed and gone. There was Billy goat in there that shaggy red goatee only hinted at. Once it was chewing extra earnest on a wad

21

of something tough and stanky. Just as I realized with horror it was that poultice and duck tape, it swallowed the whole thing, gulp.

Later, I and it sat in the living room ignoring each other as best we could. I was tinkering with a new invention, a mobius accordion calendar, which is all I'll say for now, for patent purposes. The animal was rubbing my bare ankle with the side of its head, which felt like a brush you'd scrape tar off with. It smelt like a potato that been in the bin too long and gone musty. It wouldn't gag you, but you'd have to hunt down the source. I would had liked to shave it and scrub it down with a SOS pad. However, I decided to bear its rude scent for the time being, due to its teeth situation.

That is, inside its head, which was rhomboid but roundish in the middle and corners, dwelt a remarkable set of chompers. Rather worked in and worn, it was a whole army of them, 50 if it was one. It liked to show me how they glinted and gleamed with a lazy-mouth menace, leisurely picking at them with claws and acrobatic tongue. The front ones were biggish, not quite rabbit's, and the rest had a amiable crookedness, all packed in vise-like jaws it enjoyed snapping like a trap. So I would wait till it got to know me better before giving it the scrub-down it deserved.

At that moment a imperial moth happened to fly out of the watchpocket of my Sir Guy bowling vest. The animal let its jaw hang down idle as it peered at the ceiling bulb where the moth begun doing loop-de-loops.

In some kind of slow-time the animal catapulted over the coffee table, up into the rafters, snabbed the moth in its mouth, spun on the tether ball pole, did a half gainer, landed on the rug on all fours hind-end facing me, and peers over its shoulder at me, like, "What?"

"Sput that out!"

Immediately it coughed out not the moth but hello and behold that gruesome chawed ball of poultice and duck tape, which flew across the room and stuck right on top of my barefoot. I finally got it kicked off while making disgusting noises, while the animal waited patiently, and then opened its jaws once more and the moth itself dizzily exited and twirled out the nearest window and into the unaten night.

I say, "I note your propensity to seize small living things in your mouth and then let them go, just to observe my horrified reaction. While not a crime, it makes me wonder if you're attempting a variety of communications with me."

The animal studied me with a sad insooshance, rotated its shoulderblades, farted gingerly, shrugged off my "Where do you think you're going?" and exited the very window the moth had took off out of.

# 6.

The rumor of the animal's presence spread across Hmm like a plague carried by my little busybody sister. During her morning campaign swing she blabbed about the "insolent odorous what's-it" that her brother had inherited.

Accordingly, half the village grabbed their ladders and clumbed up to gawk over our privacy wall. The beast responded by striking a conceited sidewise pose in the middle of the parsnip patch, as if it were a jaded prince lounging in the garden at Versailles.

The folks of Hmm commenced guessing what it was. They passed around the village encyclopedia, looking at pictures and calling out the names of animals.

"Could it be a lemur you got there, Lemuel?" says Justin Liloff, the village barber. He held up the picture.

"Perhaps a touch," I say, "but not mainly."

The animal stood sunbathing in the attention. Its eyes was almost closed as it made a slowly nodding smerl. I won't say anything, but it reminded me of a fellow known as Benitoe Mussolini. If that's how the animal was thinking, it would do itself a favor to read a history book or two.

Unlike the lemur, this animal had big thick floppy oblong ears with personalities of their own, like soft flour tortillas with crinkles and freckles and red blond fringe. Also, its legs was shorter, especially for its size, and appeared to stretch as it sauntered about, as though its bones was part bread dough or taffy.

The tail was not striped nor unsuitably long as a lemur's, and had small inverted golden polka dots playing along its wavularity, and seemed longer than the day before, perhaps a factor of the Northern Lights. Said tail shone black at the tip and was composed of donkey-maneish bristles that stuck out like a bottlebrush when it was startled or dreaming.

"Could resemble pinney martin," says Merle Eh, one half of the village weightlifting Chinese ex-scientists couple.

Pearl Eh, the best half, says, "I think he gots ya, Lem!"

I hadn't no idea what a pinney martin was, but I knew it wasn't one. Those unpredictable Ehs was trying to undermine my one moment of village authority. "Less than a dab at the most," I say. I suffered fools gladly, because there was always at least one wherever I went.

I picked up a bamboo stake from the garden and commenced to note stray features of the animal, who basked with a sly boredom in the limelight of my lecture.

"As you see," I begin, "it presents a flat face, except for nose, forehead, and chin, with a droopy mouth like a bloodhound, but turned up at the ends in a half-Buddha smirch. Its vigilant, glittering sea otter eyes are close together at times, at others farther apart, depending on how hard it's pretending to misunderstand your questions and commands.

"The shapely nose is good-size, ovular, plum black, boasting faint pinkish borders and a circle of oscillating copper-colored whiskers. Its nostrils are spacious, personable, moist, and active, sea anemone like."

The congregation hummed, wrapped in befuddled admiration of my rather moving impromptu seminar.

"Please note the long half-moon of red and white beatnik fur under its mouth. Its big black silver and green eyes are studious, sorrowful, and rude by turn, under long lashes of exuberant wit and mystery.

"Grand shoulders, handsome neck, slappy paws. Snout is somewhat bearish or foxly, emerging from its face at a petulant angle, tapered and tubular, like a Tibetan teapot. Fur of many colors, predominantly gold, orange, red, blond, black, white, silver, fuchsia, and zinnwaldite; texture of Kansas hay by day, Japanese rice grass by night."

"Chupacabra!" says Leona "Sting" Ray, the village beekeeper.

"No," I say, "but the sideburns are right."

"Looks dangerous," says Leona, "like a purseful of firecrackers."

"Yes, it's more wild than not, plus moody, forgetful, and glib, like firecrackers, so take precautions till I can sell him to a traveling circus."

The crowd gasped and flang threats:

"We'll sell you to the circus!"

"That critter was give you to live in Hmm!"

I say, "It was give me to have dominion over it anyway I want!"

"Sell it and you're cursed till kingdom come!"

I started to tell those oafs to get off my property, when I noticed, in a corner atop the privacy wall, one odd fellow in a old, long, dark blue, oversize hooded cape. He lifted his hand at his waist as though to ask a question, discreet as a bidder at a society auction. I recognized him as nobody from Hmm, and saw a chance to change the subject. He was a slight chap, even gaunt from the looks of his hands and bits of his countenance hiding in the shadows of that cowl. Perhaps he hailed from the outskirts where transients and near-to-wells roamed. His peculiar clothing, however, was a bit debonair for a tramp.

I pointed at him. "Okay, we got us a outsider that wants to put his two cents in."

The mob quietened and turned to the stranger, who cleared his throat and muttered in such a soft-spoke voice that none of the words did I happen to catch.

"Spit it out, stranger!" I say.

The folks near him threw out snippets of what they thought they heard him mutter:

"Letters!"

"Deadline!"

"Lawyers!"

"Oh, yeah?" I say. "Whatever you got up your sleeve, Mr. X, we don't go for fancy paper law in these parts. Around here we settle our differences man oh e man oh."

Right then, for no known reason, the animal fell dead asleep, still standing up, and started snoring like a bad muffler on a monster truck.

I turned back to the stranger: he was gone.

Ez Penumbra, the candlestick-maker, says, "Is yer pet a him or a her?"

I boisterously shook my head, both in answer to the question and to shake the image and aura of the disturbing stranger.

Luther "Roof" Blissett, churlish village paperboy, asks, "Is it got a name?"

"If it does, I don't know it."

I grewn tired of the questions, so I gave the sleeping thingmajig a gentle poke with my big toe to bring it around, and the villagers went buzzerk:

"Don't you harm no hair on that poor animal!"

"He kicked that innocent baby like a empty pop can!"

"Innocent baby? It's a monster, and I barely nudged it."

"How'd you like us to clumb down and knock you around like a big goofball!"

I say, "No more free ride! It's a dollar a question from now on!"

Somebody threw a tennis ball that bounced off my head and then off the privacy wall and then off my head again. "Ow!" I says, and "Ow!" again, and the crowd roared like a drunken Roman mob. They started taking off their apparel and self-righteously hurling it at me: shoes, hats, bibs, toolbelts, horsehair leotards, dickeys, peds, and frilly underwhatnots, all accompanied by illiterate oaths and hexes. Suddenly, Lillian O'Leary's tartar bonnet landed on the still slumbering animal's head, it snapped awake, scurried up and over the wall, bonnet still on, and's gone. The villagers clumbed down and chased after it, whooping and hollering into the distance.

I wasn't about to ruin my day pursuing that rogue all over Hmm and back. If it ate somebody, so be it. If they fingered me, I'd insist on a jury trial. I could picture it, if you may. The animal would be sitting at the defendant's table with me, staring those jurors down with its doleful mafia eyes. If they convicted me, the beast would find them wherever they hid. That is, if we had a courthouse in Hmm besides the carport behind Dot's Billiards, or a judge besides that nudist Commissioner Ben Pan, or a sober policeman, or a constitution, etc. We did have a crossing guard, but one afternoon he went on a walkabout and never returned. We also had one regulation which proclaimed Daily Nap Hour from 11 a.m. to 1 p.m.

In fact, it happened to be 11 a.m., so I went in and lained down and had a dream about the animal. I was looking into its eyes, and I could see clear through them where a giant red goldfish swum tranquidly around inside its spacious empty head.

*

On my afternoon metal-detector trek to the beach at Lake Bleached Bones, I found a old canteen from Thrifty's with a bullethole clean through. I decided to put it on eBay as a relic from the Plopponesian War and make a killing from some city slicker. That is, if I could ever get on the village computer. I was 153rd on the waiting list.

When I got home, there seemed to be quite a sudden dust buildup on the fan light. But no, it was the animal up there, asleep again! That thing snoozed like unconsciousness was two for the price of one. I considered turning on the fan for the fun of it, but what if it freaked out and attacked the nearest thing around, namely me, since Shane was out campaigning.

It dozed on, snoring like somebody shaking a can of plums. While I had the chance, I clumb up on our chair and reached into that badlands of fur for a collar. I found it—a crumbling piece of red belt that Santa might of worn. I pulled it waryly around its sleeping neck: on a old piece of bandage tape, six big letters that looked like a child wrote them in faded magic marker: **YONDEЯ**.

# 7.

The next morning Yonder was nowhere to be found. If that was his name. Was he even a he? Could Yonder be a gal's name? You couldn't keep calling it it. Did Uncle Leonard scrawl that red "Yonder" on there? Any event, Yonder continued not being found, and we begun to wonder if we'd ever see him again.

"Good riddance to bad odor, Bro," says Shane. "That thing stank like seaweed air freshener."

I felt funny because, while my second thought was that if he was gone for good I might ridiculously miss him a little bit, my first thought was that my potential meal ticket had flewn the coop. I hadn't even come up with a good money-making scheme yet, except to rent him out for TV commercials. I thought he would be a natural-born silent spokesanimal, but the talent agent in Hmm, Ariel Bankhead, said I had to get him trained first. Si Long, the village animal trainer, lain his eyes on the sneering critter, crossed hisself, and ceremoniously slammed his trailer door in our face.

Miraculously, Yonder showed up just as Shane was slapping lunch together. She looked out the kitchen window and goes, "Cancel the Missing It Report. Look what's cleaning its unbelievables on top of our privacy wall."

There he sat, studiously slobbering his private selves for all the world to admire. After my legs did a little involuntary jig at the very sight of him, I tapped on the window, and with one leg still in the air (him, not me), he bent his neck back to see, lost his balance, tumbled off the wall, crashed into the compost, sprung out like a kangaroo, and stood there shimmying hunks of steaming compost every which way.

Then he was up the stairs banging his butt against the door before you could say lunch is served, please be seated.

Lunch itself was yam and mustard green preserve sandwiches from the garden. Yonder wolfed three of the five sandwiches that Shane had manufactured. You could do the math.

Shane worked a toothpick upside her molars. "Can't that thing get a job somewhere?"

"That thing's name is Yonder. Y-o-n-d-e-r."

"Who says?"

"His collar. It was written on it."

She made a suspicious face. "Why's it named that? What's it mean?"

I shrugged. "Someplace else? Ask Uncle Leonard."

"It's another one of his tricks. I don't like that name."

"I do." I wasn't sure I did, but if she didn't, I had to.

She peered at the animal as if to discover the secret of his name, and he peered back as if to hide the secret deeper. After about five seconds, she blinked. The animal had trounced her in the staring contest.

"So, *anyway*," she says, "can't *Yonder* get a job?"

"Animals don't get jobs." I knew because I had been trying to get him one.

"What about Rin Tin Tin?" Shane says.

"That's not a job," I say.

"What is it?"

"It's a documentary."

"A documentary." She plucked a bit of yam skin out of her front teeth and examined it like it was a UFO. "So, you think Rin

Tin Tin is a documentary. You think Rin Tin Tin actually catches criminals and puts them in jail?"

"I couldn't say, I wasn't there. Neither were you."

"Well," says Shane, "dumb TV show or documentary, Rin Tin Tin makes more money in one afternoon than you make fixing a thousand broken gizmos in a year."

She had a good point, so I ignored it. "Even if Rin Tin Tin *has* a job and gets paid, it don't *know* it has a job and gets paid, so it don't really *have* a job."

"What do I care if it knows it has a job, as long as it's contributing to the upkeep of the household, which that *Yonder* is *not*." The animal was moseying around under the kitchen table of our nauga-nook. He kept making the table buck up in the air and bang back down.

"Stop it!" Shane says. "Look at that thing. It inhaled three sandwiches and now it's hunting around for more. It's like a little buffalo roaming the prairie under there."

Which was a interesting comment, because a buffalo is what Low Stu was riding when he went out to the Chinese desert to die. But the gatekeeper at the Great Wall asked him to jot down a few notes on life, knots, veils, nothingness, heaven, death, rhinoceroses, wood, and other mysterious subjects. Those notes turned into the *Tao Te Ching*. If it had been a horse, Low Stu would had raced right by the gatekeeper, nobody would of heard of him, and I wouldn't have wrote this paragraph.

Shane says, "How big is that damn thing going to get anyway?"

"Good question. Let me see." I faked looking around. "Oh, I seem to have misplaced the *manual*."

"I'm none too thrilled with a stray animal prancing around my house like a big Hoover sucking up my hard-earned income."

"You mean your hard-*inherited* income."

That piped her down. She knew she didn't deserve that money any more than I did.

*

Ralphie Munch, the village vet, heard about Yonder and dropped in to give his expert analysis. Ralphie took one look and exclaims, "Oh, you got you a genuine *mix*."

I felt a rather unbecoming sting of pride.

Ralphie proceeded to examine Yonder. He asked me about the scar, that seemed to be healing up good. I lied. I thought what if somebody out in them woods was dealing illegal animal parts. I told him the animal had fell on a buzzsaw while saving a lumber-jack from a grizzly bear.

"Hmp," says Ralphie. "I heard tell on the vet grapevine of another mixed critter up north here not unrecent. Had to had passed on by now. Bad ticker. Heart strain, totin' all them species." I didn't much care to hear that. He poked, lifted, turned, dug, twisted, and studied Yonder like he was a new invention. The animal didn't seem to mind one bit. Ralphie sure had the animal touch.

"Is it a boy, by any chance?" I say. "You can't tell with a name like Yonder. I been leery to check the underbrush."

"Mmp," Ralphie says.

"What?"

He regarded me with a mystified visage on his face. "Got a odd odor, eh? Sweet and sour both, like a box of moldy strawberries."

"I beg your pardon?"

"The animal."

"Oh. Well." To tell the truth, it irked me that Yonder was letting a total stranger maul him willy-nilly without getting the least bit perturbed. Ralphie twisted him around like a Russian pretzel and he didn't even curl his lip. All I had to do was barely look at the big oaf and he gave me a warning growl, just for the fun of it.

"You gonna poke him and twist him all day?" I say. "You're upsetting him."

"It don't look it."

"Things is not always as they pretend."

"Why would it pretend it ain't upset?"

"To get my goat, why else. Let's wrap this up. What do we got here?"

Ralphie stroked his waist-length whiskers. "I'm guessing tundra monkey, ur-koala, a little ontelli, some margay and coati, Arctic wolf, ox, spotted sloth, maybe a touch of beaver, moonbird—"

"Moonbird!" I squeal.

"Yep, though I can't see how. They're extinct. See them big shoulders? Ain't shoulders entirely. Got you some mini-wingbones there. Them fur knots are actually pinfeather clusters."

"Pinfeather clusters!" Boy, what a quack. Well, you don't get what you pay for, because he was free. But only because I built him a nice all-pine x-ray machine for a hundred dollars, and he was still paying me back.

"You're fit as a fiddle, Yondy," says Ralphie.

Personally, I didn't care for Ralphie calling the animal by a nickname before I ever even did myself. "His name's *Yonder*," I said.

"Well, I'm off," Ralphie says. "Got my rounds." Which meant a day of rum and checkers with Ernie Anderson, the village *human* doctor. Two drunk quacks sitting around discussing philosophy and kinging themselves while the health of every human and animal in Hmm went to hell in a hambasket.

*

I returned from rigging up Lottie Engram's tea kettle so it sounded like her dead husband Rudolph whistling "You Give Me Fever," only to find that Yonder had wandered down to North Silence Holler and clumb up in the Conklins' walnut tree. From there he had been leisurely dropping walnuts upon all things great and small passing below, including a hounddog, the paperboy Luther Blissett, a wild pig and her family, two wandering troubadours, Mayor Shuffleboard, and a giant Indian squirrel. The latter stood up and threw the walnut back at Yonder, who caught it and fired it again at the squirrel, but it knocked the derby off the head of Mayor Shuffleboard, who had been lollygagging with one of the dancing gals in the alley behind Rosy's Cantina. The Mayor's bodyguards mistooked it for a assassination attempt. They quarantined the area, shot off flares, and started a general village maylay, during which Yonder fled the premises.

Eventually they pinned the commotion on the mixed animal. As the owner I was instructed by Hmmland Security to install discipline in my so-call pet. I was waiting up that night when he waltzed in like nothing in the world was wrong. A cube of butter wouldn't of melted on his rhomboid head.

"Yonder!" I say. "Sit down, Sir!" He kept standing. "Stand!" I say. He did. "Are you aware of the meelee you created today throwing walnuts at everybody? You threatened the civilization of the entire village." He stared at me as if he didn't understand a word I said and had no desire to. "I want your word that this is the last time I hear about such undistinguished aggression." I made some Old World gestures to illustrate my point, involving my thumb-knuckles, hipbones, and nostrils.

He looked deep in my face, gave up a timid walnut-scented fart, and blinked, which I took as a sign of dim understanding, or even better, shame. Oh, how the bridge of our communications was cluttered with obstacles and mysteries. Staring at him as he stared at me, each refusing to budge, I begun to notice what a troublingly picturesque mug he had, and it gave me a brainstorm.

Namely, I could make a few easy bucks by taking pictures of his mug and peddling them around the village. Then I thought—two birds with one stone—get Shane to hawk the pictures while she's campaigning. That way I could take a nap and wait for the dough to roll in.

I looked away first to let him think he'd won, and he settled into his bookcase and begun snoozing away triumphantly. I got the Polaroid and snapped a quick one but bam!—he woke up hysterical from the flash and took off like ball lightning who known where.

I set the picture to dry on the coffee table and began to calculate how much to charge per photo, when here Yonder raced back in, grabbed the picture and ate it whole, boom. There it is, then it ain't.

"Nice going," I say. "You ate my meal ticket."

He gave me a overcast look. I wondered about him ingesting that gunk, the magic developing glue. But he seemed as normal as ever. He had a stomach like a iron lung.

He sat about a inch away from the Polaroid camera on the table, gleering at it like a mortal enemy. At the time he was right in front of Shane's green and pink tulip wallpaper, and he begun to disappear before my eyes, as in become unseeable.

Frankly, his fur started turning into the same colors and layout as the tulip wallpaper. In other words, his fur begun camoflodging itself.

I wanted to call somebody to come see it, or not see it, but I was scared to move. I wondered if this was a way that Old God was guiding me to make cash off it. But if I snapped a picture of it, people would think it was only a picture of wallpaper. I could draw a black line around where he was, but it would look like something died, been outlined by a policeman and carted off. Who would want to hang that on the wall?

Then I was afraid he'd get stuck in that wallpaper pattern. It was bad enough as wallpaper, much less as him.

It struck me that this had to do with the camera and getting his picture tooken. He must have heard about Indian folklore where you lose a part of your spirit when your image is captured in that box. I got up slowly, placed the camera in the closet, shut the door, and pretended to lock the lock that's not on it.

Immediately he begun to relax, breathe normal, and change back into his regular colors and patterns. Then he contributed another walnut fart, and collapsed like a accordion into a six-hour nap. It had took a lot out of him, disappearing into tulip wallpaper to protect his soul from being took.

# 8.

Later one day, after reading the end of the *Reader's Digest Condensed World Literature* version of Jim Joyce's *Ulysses* ("He asked me. I said yes."), I looked around and couldn't find Yonder nowhere again. I had a bad feeling. I closed my eyes and had a vision of him hanging around with a crazy person. Right then Shane and him come bounding up the stairs like Bonnie and Clyde after a bank stickup, panting, sweaty, and delirious.

"Where were you!" I say.

"Jeepers, calm down," says Shane. "It was helping me scrounge votes. You should see this thing on the campaign trail. This here is a voter magnet. They can't get enough of it. I'm a shoo-in with it on my staff. And I don't even have to pay it. So I guess it does have a job after all."

"*Him.* It's a *him,* not a *it.* Yes, I guess *he* does have a job, if getting exploited by a miglomaniac is a job. Next time *ask* me before you steal him."

"I didn't steal him, he snuck up behind me. At first I thought everybody was glad to see me for once, then I turn around and there he is, hogging the limelight."

Yonder started slurping out of his drinking bowl. Water went splaying every which ways.

"What is that, a tongue or a oar?" I acted madder than I was because it surprised me how happy I felt knowing he was okay.

"He's a natural on the hustings. He stands there giving people rude enigmatic looks and they get confused and hand me a dollar and say they're going to vote for me. He's a spinmeister without even saying anything."

"I thought you were the one that said good riddance to bad seaweed."

"I changed my womanly mind. Politics makes strange bedanimals."

"You shouldn't have it out there mingling with these backward villagers. It could bite some goober and then where would we be?"

"*Him*," she says.

"Sued and in jail, that's where."

"Oh, can it. He's no more dangerous than any other political hack. Anyway, everybody's too in awe of him to come close enough to get bitten. They gawk at him like he was an ex-con or a king or something. I think he could get elected mayor himself if he was able to bloviate a little."

"Bloviate. What's that mean again? To be gaseous?"

"Not just to be it, to give it away, too, and generously."

"Well, he should be mayor by decree, then. Good thing he ain't dumb enough to run."

"Ooh, is somebody jealous?"

"Jealous! That's crazy talk! Jealous of what, a big smelly mutant? Hardly har har!"

"I meant jealous of me, but thanks for giving away how captivated you are by him *and* for hurting his feelings at the same time, as you can see."

Yonder regarded me with a expression that was both forsooken, bemused, and hungry. Then he stretched like a yoga fella, hopped on the table, and started eating a banana peel that was sitting there minding its own business.

"Get down off there where people eat," I say.

He bared his big front teeth and his many little other teeth in a alarming imitation of a smile. I grabbed the day's *Hmm Gazette* and rolled it up. He didn't even blink.

"Get down, mammal," I command. "Don't think I won't smack you with this."

He sniffled and commenced to gnaw a flea on his privvies as a means to defy my authority in my own blasted cottage. I started to bring that newspaper down on its behind—not hard, but enough to show him I meant business. He chomped on that paper and one second it's the latest village news and information, and the next it's confetti falling all over the kitchen.

I say, "Not dangerous, huh!"

"Looked like self-defense to me."

Yonder was glaring at me like a clerk at the DMV. I wasn't going to get anywhere with him. I aimed my vex at Shane. "You know what? It's time to pull the plug on this fool campaign of yours. You're a fortune-teller, not a mayor. Get back in the garage where you belong."

"OK, Alley Oop, if you get back in the cave where *you* belong."

I stood up and slammed my hand on the table. "You can run for mayor, queen, king, and wing-dang-doodle for all I care. But from hereby forward, *Yonder* is banned from all your campaign appearances. I forbid you to drag my pet into the dog-doo of politics. He's a simple stinking dumb beast."

"So's my base. That's his appeal. They see themselves in him. He's like the average voter who wants nothing more than to eat, sleep, goof off, avoid bathing, seek perverted pleasures, and get protected, taken care of, and babied. And they see he likes me, so they like me."

"He doesn't like you. He can't stand the sight of you."

"Oh, I don't know about that." Shane reached down and

scratched its goatee. "Look, he smiled at me."

"He curled his lip." I couldn't remember the last time I had been getting so trounced in a conversation. I tried a new tack: "Name one thing you want to do for this village as mayor."

"I want to promise everybody everything, which I'm already doing."

"Something concrete."

"I want to build a new concrete road that goes right next to our garage so after I'm out of office I can do drive-through fortune-telling."

"That's illegal, rotten, and corrupt!"

"It depends what the meaning of illegal, rotten, and corrupt is."

"Why are you even running? All you care about is yourself. Politics is suppose to be people helping people be happier."

"That's exactly what I'm doing. I'm helping people by expanding their opportunity for happiness by promising them everything. They feel good thinking of all their wishes that will come true when I get elected. Of course, the problem is, either I lose and feel bad, or I get elected and can't grant any of their wishes. Actually, the best job would be to run for mayor all the time and never have the election. That way nobody would be mad at me for not keeping my promises, and I could fund raise all day for a living. The only problem with democracy is the election."

"That's the most ridiculous piece of political pundintry I ever heard."

"Yes," Shane sighed, "it is pretty idealistic."

*

Yonder disappeared all day again and along about evening time showed up with a old bucket he had borrowed from somebody. He set it at the top of the stairs outside and slowly nosed it till it tipped over and fell and clanked and banged and rattled and ruckused all the way down into the yard.

Then he went and got it and brang it back up and set it there and observed me through the window with a long meaningful look, as though he wanted to make sure I appreciated what he was doing for me. Then he nosed it down the stairs again.

Then he kept doing it.

Shane was sitting there like she couldn't hear one note of the animal's obnoxious bucket symphony. Going through the village census counting likely votes on her fingers and toes, she was so self-absorbed she didn't hear a single clank. Then, when Yonder got tired of the game of driving me crazy and fell asleep sprawled in the middle of the stairs, Shane perked up and went, "Did you hear something?"

*

That night I got to thinking: maybe I should let Yonder help Shane get elected after all. With her as mayor we would finally get our share of the graft that runs through the political infrastructure of Hmm like diureeah through a golden goose. On the other hand, if Shane moved into the Mayor's Royal Cottage, I'd have to pick up her half of the mortgage. Unless she hired me as Secretary of Inventions, say, then I could move into the Mayor's Royal Cottage myself, live off the fat of democracy, rent our cottage out to tourists, and become a day trader in my pajamas in my spare time. There's only one bad thing about money: either it's crooked, there's not enough coming in, there's too much going out, or you got to work for it.

# 9.

If the tumult bubbling around Yonder was bad before, Shane parading him through town as campaign bait didn't help. Their curiosity peaked, the villagers got up on their ladders day and night, hurtling pinecones at our front door and yelling aimless insults in Pig Latin until Yonder deigned to go out and prance around the garden performing his growing array of egotistical tricks.

He liked to drag my hi-fi onto the porch and blast out *The Collected Hits of Korla Pandit*. Then he would rush downstairs to walk tightrope on the clothesline on his side legs; put a blindfold on and fake like he was trying to find himself; make his hair stand on end by crossing his eyes; turn his fur scarlet and form himself into a stop sign; tunnel under the wall and come up behind the villagers and roar and then catch them when they fell startled off their ladders; run backwards and pretend to bump into things that weren't there; expulse gas to the tune of "Cement mixer, putty, putty"; eat a brick while wiggling his ears; and act like he was having a intellectual conversation with his own tail. He would end the trick show by imitating how I walked with a little hitch in my giddyup due to my bum back from the railroad hand-car. Then he moseyed offstage just as the Korla Pandit album came to a blazing finish in torrents of exotic organ mystique.

The tricks were tawdry, mundane, and impractical in the real world, except for talking to your own tail, which could prove useful at parties. But the greenhorns on their numbskull ladders went nuts with ohs, awes, and general flapdoodle. By the Korla Pandit finale they was barely able to hold onto their ladders for swooning.

If he wasn't in the mood to entertain, I was forced to go out and field more questions from the balcony like his press secretary.

For example, "How many teeths is it has!" Irka Nelson says. She was the village amateur dentist.

"How do I know? I'm not reaching in that Venus fly-trap to count those chompers."

The mob took up a chant: "How many teeths! How many teeths! How many teeths is it has!"

I made up a number: "Fifty-five!"

Irka says, "What's it weigh!"

"A lot more'n it ought. Why don't you weigh him yourself the next time my sister exploits him out there as a prop to get your giggly, homespun votes."

"Stop ducking the questions!" somebody hollers.

"Who said that! I ain't ducking nothing! I've got a birdbrain answer for every birdbrain question you dream up! Who said that!"

Yonder, who had snuck out to eavesdrop on the questions about himself, now growled like he was protecting his breakfast. He gleered at somebody along the wall. I looked and who did I see but that shiftless outsider again, the one in the threadbare blue cape with the hood obscuring his head. He whispered in the ear of the man next to him, Fritz Lamboni, village pasta maker. Fritz nodded at him and shouts at me, "Do you have the papers for that animal?"

"I saw that guy tell you to ask that! That guy's a outsider! He's a buttinski! He's got no business asking nobody nothing. I got your papers right here, Stranger!" I made a obscene sign that included my crazybone, the back of my head, and my sacroiliac. By now

Yonder had took up a staunch position behind me, at once purring and snarling. He was a animal divided against itself, so he sat down. I holler, "Somebody pull the hood off that stranger's impermanent head!"

Underterred, the hooded one whispers again in Fritz's ear and Fritz shouts, "Stop ducking the questions!"

I say, "Don't listen to that wanderer, Fritz! The nerve of a newcomer like that! The only question a stranger should be asking is which way out of town!"

"Stop ducking the questions!" Fritz yells again, and the whole mindless lot, except for the hooded stranger that started it, who had already clumb down and disappeared, takes up the chant: "Stop ducking! Stop ducking! Stop ducking the questions!"

"I'm ashamed of you, people!" I say. "Crud, man. You side with a ironic newcomer over the master fix-it brother of a mayorial candidate!" I vowed the next time I laid eyes on that outsider I would shake some answers out of his shiftless hide.

Whyever Yonder had been upset, immediately upon the miscreant's exit the animal resumed his arrogant ways. Perhaps his own impudence was threatened by the foreigner's impudence. In any case, Yonder immediately struck a pose that resembled Napoleon crossing the Waterloo in his rowboat.

"So, how much *do* it weigh?" Irka re-asks.

"I'd say, oh, sixty, seventy-five pounds."

They wowed like a wave breaking, which inspired me to elaborate and further dismiss the dismal stranger from the windmills of my mind.

"The first time I picked him up he went limp as a eighty-pound noodle. He was mostly heavy in the middle, but in a changeable sense, like he'd swallowed several bowling balls that were rolling back in forth in there."

"How'd he done came for to be how he is all mixed in the first place?"

"That's classified, unexplicable, and there's childrens present."

"How's that whatchercallit take to getting hisself petted?"

"I don't believe Uncle Leonard was the petting type. Therefore, getting petted is a foreign substance to him. He purrs fitfully and watches your hand move over his fur with his eyeballs huge and his mouth a jar. To be frank, I wear Shane's old miner's gloves when I pet him."

"Its breath is interesting clear from there," says Little Jimmy Sammy of Little Jimmy Sammy's Snacks & Cakes. "It 'minds me of what I can't put my finger on."

"A combination of algae-covered tortillas and bus exhaust?" I say.

"That's them!" says Little.

"And not entirely unpleasant," I add.

"Is it got more tricks?" asks the windmill maker Dill Ring.

"He camoflodges hisself into tulip wallpaper." They stared like fish at me. "Oh, he can also read my mind."

"Who cain't, Lem!" Pearl Eh bellows, and the crowd giggled like a pack of drunk hamsters.

"You laugh, but when he watches me I can feel him brush aside my conscious mind like it was a stale breadstick, and zero in on the steaming pizza of my subconsciousness. When I tell him stop it, he moves his lips making fun of me saying stop it."

"It's doing it right now!" Pearl squeals.

"Hey, cut that out, Yonder," I joke, joining in.

"Is that the its name?" says Merle.

"Apparently. Or the name of its collar."

"Yonder! Yonder! Yonder!" the mob called. Then, "Yondy! Yondy! Yondy!" Then, "Yo! Yo! Yo!"

The animal made his fur swell up with self-regard and started patting the ground haughtily, as if counting his admirers. I reminded myself to call him by some dang nickname so I didn't feel so offended when other people did.

"Another trick," I say, "he hides his head under his front legs and tucks his tail in so you can't tell what direction he's pointing in. He becomes a hay bale with legs. By hiding his head and tail and not moving, he believes he's invisible."

"What's that thuck old hair feel like?" Jinx the pawnshop fella asks.

"One minute it's like a velvet pillow, the next it's like a thatch roof with a mind of its own. You might find your hand tangled in it like a velcro baby in a briar patch. His fur draws in innocent items as he goes by. Sometimes objects fly out while he's scratching, like a potato, a Slinky, a old argyle sock, or a wild hamster. He was up on the couch today and got in my lap. I guess he was lonesome, or thought I might be. I was trying to watch 'What Not to Wear' on The Learning Channel and he kept doing his ablutions, so I scooted him off. Then I couldn't find the remote. He started scratching his neck and the channels kept changing. The remote had secluded itself in his coat. One time I tried to brush him and the brush broke off and I couldn't even find it in there. His fur ingests items in what is known as reverse follicular overreaction."

I thought this was a very infotaining answer, with pathos and intrigue, but the mob ignored me, gawking over my head with their mouths open like barn doors.

I looked up and there was Yonder on the edge of the roof. He stood at the very tip of the eave with his bearcub nose pointing West, like the captain of a cottage ship, soaking up the spray of the adoring sea.

# 10.

Yonder, I, and Shane decided to take a little excursion out to the Unconscious Forest. I wanted to visit Chuck, the woodsman that had distributed Unc's inheritance to us, and see if he could fill us in on the nook and crannies of the mysteries of Uncle Leonard and the animal. Also, I wanted to give a long country ride to my Henry J jalopy. I'd recently modified it to run on sun panels and cow-doo gas, and wondered why it was only getting 142.8 miles to the gallon.

All the way there Yonder snoozed in the rumble seat as we toodled north by southwest along the immense redstone plateau that runs up the middle of the Hermengild Duchy and then down and around the Greater Pertelote Dominion. The regions got named for the Cornish and Tuath clans that five centuries before had warred over the area's natural bounty of tulips and wild goat-dung. The products together produced a beautiful glue that was used in the binding of the first book ever made in these parts, *Look Out Behind You*, by Erg Nth. Those old historic folks were one tough hombres. In fact, Hmm's one-footed founder, Lula Goetz Eu Seeque, was a 15th century outcast from a mixed union of two lovebirds from the rival clans. She lost her extremity escaping from the stocks, gnawing her own foot off and keeping it in her purse for sustenance while fleeing south to what would become Hmm when she got there. What doesn't kill you makes you plan a village in the shape of your missing foot. Nobody known much more about her but that all her four husbands met their Maker in ambiguous circumstances involving ancient household appliances. Her missing foot proved to be quite a shapely form for a hamlet, except for a extra big toe where the park juts out. She named the village after the first word she mythically spoke upon her birth: "Hmmmm," only with two less m's so as to fit on the plank of the village charter.

In any case, I and Shane drove clear down through Gnosis Canyon, beautifically desolate, and up and out into a Van Gogh realm of loomful sky and rolling lemon hills, interspreckled by a village now in then of haystacks, mudholes, cows, buckets, donkeys, chimneys, cropfields, shadows, huts, wells, lots of winsome country folk performing winsome country tasks, and silence.

It was the perfect setting for me and Shane to strike up a friendly sibling conversation as we drove. I thought up something I felt would be a rather absorbing topic that I might emerge triumphant from.

"'Unconscious Forest,'" I say, rolling the name around on my tongue. "I wonder what they mean by that."

"Who?" says Shane.

"Whoever that named it."

"What makes you think it's more than one person?"

"What makes you think I think it's more than one person?"

"You said, 'I wonder what *they* mean by that.'"

I was behind already. "Well, I don't think one person can go around naming a forest."

"You'd be surprised," Shane says. "Regardless, I have no idea what the gentleman or gentlemen meant by it, nor lady, nor ladies, as the case may be."

"It appears you're also picturing quite a large naming committee now."

"I'm not picturing anything. I'm simply rearranging your

misimpression."

"I'm just trying to wonder what they, him, or her meant."

"You could always *ask* them, him, or her. Of course, they're probably dead by now."

I had not thought of that. "Why would they be dead?"

"Because that's what people get around to being if enough time passes, which it probably has, since it's been named Unconscious Forest for nine hundred years or something."

That made me feel unexpectedly mystical and cozy. The people that named it "Unconscious Forest" were long dead and gone, but "Unconscious Forest" kept being named by them. "I wonder how you'd find out something like that. Who named a forest, and what they meant by it."

"It must be on a list in some drawer in an office somewhere."

"What office might that be?"

"I might have no idea."

"Maybe their offspring would know what they meant by it. But, of course, even if they knew, that don't mean they'd tell."

"Why wouldn't they tell?" asks Shane.

"They might tell, but that don't mean it would be the truth."

"Why would they lie?"

I shrugged. "Something to hide? Family secret?"

"What kind of a family secret would lead them to lie about what the name of a forest meant?"

"If I knew that, it wouldn't be a secret."

"You could know what *kind* of a family secret it was without knowing the actual secret."

"I suppose I could, but I wouldn't care to."

She made a eye-roll to hide the fact that she was falling behind. "Why don't you hook them up to a lie detector?"

"On what grounds?"

"On the grounds of detecting if they're lying about the family secret."

"You can't just hook people up to lie detectors to find out about a family secret. There's laws. There's decency."

"What's more important, finding something out, or laws and decency?"

"Depends how important it is what you're finding out."

"What if it's the family secret of terrorists intent on destroying our village?"

"The offspring of the people that named it the Unconscious Forest is terrorists intent on destroying our village?"

She sniffled sidewise in one nostril, meaning we both knew the entire conversation was slipping away from her. "I'll tell you something," she says. "We ought to hook you up right now and find out if you really want to know what their family secret is, or if you're merely trying to ruin a nice Sunday drive."

"People can fool lie detectors."

"Yes, psychopaths, *ahem*," she snorts. "I doubt the offspring of whoever named it are psychopaths who could fool a lie detector about a family secret."

"Why not?"

"Well, I would hope not."

"Why would you hope their offspring wasn't psychopaths that could fool a lie detector about a family secret any more than anybody else's offspring?"

She started to answer, saw that she had lost, let her melon head loll back, and pretended to start snoring. It was fake as cardboard pudding, but, win or lose, if somebody don't want to have a friendly conversation about the Unconscious Forest to pass the time, nobody can make you.

*

Yonder snapped awake in the rumble seat soon as we turned off North Ancient Dirt Road and entered the tousling trees. He put his big front feet on the top of the car and let the savory forest air blast his mug as we approached his old stomping grounds. A falling giant pinecone bonged off his golden noggin and exploded in a hundred spinning scales, which he chose to scarcely notice.

We pulled up to Chuck's cabin and before the jalopy could rattle to a stop, Yonder bounded out toward dead Uncle Leonard's place in the hidden distance. We called after him but he outran our voices and got swallowed up so quick by the deep and quiet forest it was like he was never there. In his wake, random flakes of snow begun making their lackadaisical ways down through the already darkening woods.

"What if he gets lost?" I say.

Shane shrugged. "He knows these woods like you know the couch. He'll come back. What do you think he prefers, foraging for acorns and sowbugs, or living the life of Riley with us in Hmm?"

*

Forest folks such as woodsman Chuck was no blabbermouths. Luckily, Shane brought along a big old family-size spaghetti sauce jar full of her home-stewed apricot brandy as a present for our host. He in turn brang out a box of dehydrated persimmons and frosty Nehi chocolate soda pop for me and Shane. He got to sipping and glugging on the apricot rotgut and it and the snuggly fireplace soon had his woodsman tongue oiled up mighty fine.

"Yep," Chuck comes right out and says, "Ol' Leonard got mixed up in your basic home-taught, test-tube, specie-cross-breeding, peetree-dish, rutting, backroom 'sperimentations."

I had dared to imagine the particulars of Unc's doings, but to hear it put into near English by Chuck, I was too disturbed to respond. Shane weren't: "Uncle Leonard *made* that creature?"

"From scratch. I don't know no specifics, but from hints and observations I believe there was wild, tame, and in-betweenxt critters involved, plus imported. He couldn't stop hisself, even after his mishmash yielt up a passel o' godless mutants, fifty-four hear tell, that he confessed to but never let me eyeball, not that I ast. The onliest one survived intact is that there Yonder a your'n. Oh, your poor ol' Unc. One minute he's proud as a mommy bee at the youngling he begot, the next he'd jabber that Yonder was a rotten sin on nature that he ought to e-o-radicate." Chuck made a slitting motion across his throat and my tummy sunk into my ankles. "Then the ol' coot got fond of the critter 'gainst his will. Bless his old crochety soul if the transplant didn't turn out to be too much for him to witness."

"Yes," I say. "Transplant. Now, what sort of transplant might that be?"

"Heart. Yonder had a bum ticker."

"You don't say. So, he got a heart from . . . where? What species?"

"Couldn't say. Weren't there. Some Doc come out, stuck it in. Leonard's old body itself give out a-watchin'. He told Doc his death-bed will and wishes. Doc brung the animal and belongings over, fire broke out, ball lightning maybe, the lab blew. I buried your Unc on the bluff where he loved sittin' and listenin' to the Rory at." One little silver tear worked its way out of Chuck's eye and meandered down a weather-beaten rivulet in his ruddy woodsman cheek. To hide his rickety emotional manhood, he got up and put "The Lawrence Welk Show" on the radio at a nice low background mummer.

I supposed animal transplants was okay if humans ones was. I looked at Shane to get her read on this whole new unexplicable information. She rolled her eyes, groaned, rose from her cracker barrel chair and begun straightening up Chuck's crap-strewn cabin. She got crazy-bored easy, and found a cure in tidying things. Scooping up a few bottles, tin cans, and oddments of clothing, she demurely placed them behind Chuck's faux-zebra davenport.

Chuck seen her clear as pie. He shrugged and went on drinking, like it happened every day. I resumed asking him everything I could think of concerning the origins of Yonder, and I wasn't shy. What animals Unc had mixed in? Where did he acquire the whatnot that went in the test tubes? What happened to the critters that didn't pan out? Why was Unc up to whatever he was up to in the first place? Did he have records of his shenanigans, formulas, and figurings jotted down somewheres? Had he ever got any permits for his sacreligious experiments? What was his plans for Yonder once he had slapped him together? Such as, namely, for good, or for evil?

Chuck had not one hard answer. Leonard never spilled the first bean, he said, but merely strolled over now in then after a hard day's Frankensteining, and him and him would pass a jug and watch New Wave videos that Chuck found in a sports car some French tourist drove into the swamp and abandoned. Chuck says, "Your Unc liked to relax with stuff that didn't make a lick o' sense." I told him I understood because after a hard day I liked to settle down with a little condensed Pynchon or "The Sid Caesar Show."

Shane continued her furtive activities. She begun gathering certain knickknacks that caught her eye. For a woodsman Chuck had lots of dainty figurine paraphernalia laying around everywhere. I guess you got so isolated out there you grabbed whatever companionship was handy. Memorybilias was probably good listeners and didn't sass you back like some people that lived with me. She fingered some enchanting thingyoumybob, a little colored glass sculpture of Hansel and Gretel and their candy cottage, for example, run her thumb over the little faces, then casually moved it toward the pocket of her double-breasted Casablanca overcoat and dropped it in. Chuck watched her as before, and didn't seem to mind, so why should I?

Every now in then I stuck my head out the cabin door and called, "Yonder! Yondo!" But he kept not coming back.

"By the way," I ask Chuck, "you mightn't known how ol' Yonder come by his name, would you?"

"Matter fact, I might. Leonard had his special spot, End of the World Bluff. Gives a specktackler view of the Rorybory Alice. He liked to hike out there and 'considerate on things.' 'Speriment things, I reckon. 'Loose my miz'ble self in yonder Lights.' That's how he put it. 'Sit ye here, while I go and pray yonder.' I buried him up there, per his last request." Chuck looked at the fire and I joined him.

After a while I said, "Hmm."

"Yip," said Chuck.

Shane continued pocketing Chuck's tsotchkes, brazen as a chipmunk stealing nuts. It was nice to not have her sarcasm hog the conversation for once.

Says Chuck, "One strange mystery I never did figger out— Leonard's Visitor."

"A visitor, you say?" He had gotten to rather slurring his words.

"*The Visitor*, I calt him. Seen him off in on through the years. Comin' and a-goin'. I ast your Unc about it. A glaze come over his face. All he says was, 'We goes way back.' But that last night—" Chuck stopped and polished off Shane's apricot mush. "Nice," he says. "Smoove." He smacked his lips like a big albacore. "Got more?"

"We'll send you a case. The Visitor, you were saying?"

"Yeah, the Visitor. He was there that last night. The night it all happened. Earlier. I seen him lurk up the path. You think your *Unc* was on the unfriendly side, this fella took the cake. Never give me the first hello. Looked like a ex-man-o'-God, booted out the monkery for who-knewn-what eviltry. Always wore that ratty blue cape with the hood a-hidin' his mug."

At this description, my knees gave like thin ice, my head rung like a gong. "Wait a minute," I say. "This hooded feller, he was there? At the transplant? And when Unc dropped dead?"

"Hmm," says Chuck. "Naw, that was later, I reckon." The apricot firewater had loosed both his tongue and his grip on the sequence of incidents. "Okay," Chuck says to himself, using his fingers. "The Visitor come, then the fracas and the hollerin'. Visitor left, Doc come, Leonard demised. Doc brang the transplanted beast bandanged up in the wheelberra, Leonard's cabin caught fire and the ditnation, then Doc come back with the bike, drums, last will in wishes. Then I planted Leonard, nursed Yonder, brang you him and the cash and junk."

"What was the fire again?"

"Couldn't say. Weren't present. Flash rain squilched it." He peered drunkly out the window at the obscured forest sky. "The woods has ways of its own."

"This Visitor," I say. "Soft-spoked fella?"

"Nary said a word."

"Skinny little chap?"

"Wiry, I'd say."

What was the chances of it being *two* bony, ghoulish, hooded chaps wandering around in a seedy blue cape everywhere that Yonder happened to be?

I glimpsed at Shane, wondering how she was taking Chuck's troubling yarn. She was just as self-ingrossed as ever. Her overcoat bulged from Chuck's doodads. She gazed at the fireplace longingly. The sun was lowing and it wasn't getting no warmer in that leaky shack. She unhooked a polished wood plaque with a big mouth fish from the wall, held it up toward Chuck and made a slight wrist flipping movement toward the fireplace. Chuck caught her gesture, frowned, shrugged, and nodded.

I never did figure out what eerie little business the two of them had going on between them that afternoon. She said she had got loony with boredom, and Chuck must of tooken pity. Maybe they were under a temporary depraved forest love spell together. In any case, Shane went ahead and tossed the fish plaque devil-may-care into the fireplace, and it flared up toasty like. Then she moseyed around breezily pitching others of Chuck's impedimentias into the flames, continuing in that vein till she started moaning and tenderly knocking her head against the log wall.

The shadows of the woods deepened; Yonder still had not returned. The conversation died and Chuck nodded off from the apricot pap. I threw a horse blanket over him, and Shane and me hiked off to Uncle Leonard's cabin half a mile or so away. We didn't say nothing but I knew we was thinking what would we do if Yonder wasn't there. Stray snowflakes whirled by like little drunkards. Through the dark forest a single crow went over like a hand, and the ground glowed with a veil of snow. As we neared Unc's charred cabin, you could see innumberable crows shuffling in the branches of the trees, almost blent into the gloom, watching us and whispering.

Yonder was there, thank Heavens to Betsy, safe in sound, conked out on Unc's old cot. Or rather on the pile of burnt black chunks of what was left of it. He was a sight for worried eyes, and when he came to he looked sort of happy to see us also, even though you could tell from his perplexed eyebrows that a part of him did not want to go. He was at those awful crossroads where the past and the future get holt of your heart and try to tear it right in two for you.

Luckily, the crows decided not to follow us as we made our brisk way back to the jalopy. I was about ready to start hurling pine cones at those smug hooligans. Yonder kept glancing over his shoulder at the burnt hulk of dead Uncle Leonard's place one last time until you couldn't see it no more.

I got down the rumble seat but the animal wanted to be inside. In fact, he jumped in the front like he owned it and curled up on Shane's lap.

"Oh, look at these ashes and scuz he's getting on my overcoat," says Shane. She tried to budge him but gave up. "Oh, who cares. Big goofy freak thing."

That was her way of getting around the fact that she had grown a fondness for the animal, but I pretended I didn't understand. "I think it's a *nice* coat."

"I meant *Yonder*."

I asked her what she thought of Chuck's story.

"Mad ravings of a pickled woodsman," she says, yawning. "Apricot brandy aside, he's been out there with the monkeys and deers too long, Bro."

I considered the possibility. "There ain't no monkeys in them woods, is it?"

But she was already conked out from the festivities and snoring like a loop-de-loop.

Meanwhile, Yonder kept studying me with a kind of pensive benevolent leer. It was hard to drive. "How about knocking that off?" I say. He continued eyeballing me. I had to pull over. "Okay, what's with the whammy, Buckaroo?"

He gave me a wide-eyed declarative look full of relaxed portent, unafraid but respectful, and clearly asking nothing. I took it to mean, "Lemuel, I just want to get it straight that you and I are formally stuck with each other now and for the foreseeable future, like it or not."

After which he yawned and fell asleep in my sister's lap, his fat head loitering behind hers out of my view. He was so big you could barely see her. It looked like Yonder propped up in the seat with my sister's head tacked on. I didn't see how he could be comfortable laying on all those memorybilias in Shane's overcoat. Nevertheless, before long they had got a duet of snoring going between them. You could of closed your eyes and swore a little motocross race was scooting up and down hills in the front seat there.

I put the radio on soft. All the way home I was thinking about things that were happy and lonesome at the same time. The snow fell light and the moon kept turning on and off in the El Greco clouds. My animal and my sister snored away beside me, with the heater clanking but working pretty good, and Sam Cooke crooning "You Send Me" on WNDR.

# 11.

The next morning I found myself all alone, which was fine with me, for I could be quite friendly in such a situation.

Yonder was busy snoozing on his back on a bulldozer inner tube in Shane's pond, opposite the garden. Three frogs sat on his silver, red, and golden belly, shamelessly sunning their fat green selfs. Shane was out having the first of 40 debates with Mayor Shuffleboard. I asked her what her debate strategy would be. She says, "Spreading rumors, innuendo, statistical outliers, subliminal neurolinguistics, and anything else I can make up."

I took the opportunity to squeeze in a little meditating, which I had slacked off of on ever since the animal first usurped my life.

I settled in on the living room floor upon my chakra-colored Sears & Roebuck meditation beach towel and got the OM rolling and the chi percolating. If you were me, you had to mix all day long with folks that wouldn't recognize a good spiritual motto if you put it in their pipe and smoked it. A fellow had better sneak in some serious meditating time if he wants to maintain his spiritual superiority over village riff-raft. Some country vulgarian burbling about his new piglets while you tried to reconfigure the angle of his toaster's spiral element axis was enough to drain your higher consciousness dry as a sandbox. That is, unless you meditated and donned a suit of spiritual armor to protect you from their tomfoolery.

One time I was fixing the springs on Dill Ring's barn door. I wanted to test out a motto from the *Tao Te Ching*. "You know,

Dill, profit comes from what is there, usefulness from what is not there."

Dill puzzled over it, sniffling and poking a stick at the back of his own hat so it come down over his face, then fixing his hat and doing it again. "Zatta riddle?" he says.

"No, it's a spiritual motto of higher consciousness, carefully designed to bring about a enlightenment extravaganza."

"Oh." He asked me to repeat the motto, which I did. Finally he says, "How you figger?"

"Well, for example, profit comes to me for fixing your barn door, but your barn door is useful to you only if you can open it, and when you open it it ain't there, so that things could usefully go in and out where it used to be."

"How you figger it ain't there? It's there, it's jist open."

"Yes, but it's not where it was when it was closed."

"It's near enough to be there when you need to close it again."

"Ahem, yes, but if you was a horse or a cow or wagon going through it, it's gone enough that you're going to think it's not there."

"What do I care if a horse or a cow or a wagon think the barn door ain't there, long as they go in or come out the barn when I want 'em to?"

See, Low Stu never met no Dill Ring. I should knew better than to try and spiritualize a bumpkin. They always had some way to slip out of the higher mindfulness you tried to trick them into. I believed in deep conversation, but you couldn't have it with just yourself, unless you pretended you didn't know what you was saying half the time.

Sometimes I suspected that Shane called the village together when I was asleep and planned deranged Kafkaest reparteé to tangle me up in just for fun. It reminded me of *The Castle* where K. the hero comes to survey a village for the peasants and falls asleep in the inn on the very first page, which is a good idea for any book hero. It relaxes the reader. The drunk peasants wake K. up and tell him he needs a permit from the Count of the Castle in order to sleep there. K. says, Okay, he'll go get one. A feller says, "A permit from the Count in the middle of the night!" and the drunk mob laughs in K.'s face. K. asks why did they wake him up if he can't get no permit anyway. "None of your guttersnipe manners!" says the feller. That was my life in Hmm—trying to help a bunch of notheads while they stood around turning me into the king of the notheads.

Therefore, you had to meditate. I was getting in a real groove, floating above the village, shaking my astral head with compassion at all the happy rustics below, when who jumped in the window but Yonder, funky and dripping algae from the pond. And what did he do but sit right next to me like a pile of wet alfalfa and assume a facsimile of a quarter-lotus.

I resumed meditating, but expected trouble. However, the animal begun making the OM noise right along with me. It wasn't *exactly* OM, more like the groaning of a heartbroke walrus, but after while we got our OMs harmonized as sweet as a couple otters playing in a barrel of rainwater.

You don't know how much I always wanted a meditation partner. Shane's philosophy was, "Higher consciousness is a fairy tale." She says, "It's bad enough being conscious at all in a village of cornballs, much less working to be *more* conscious."

Even just a minute of sitting there all quiet and still sent most folks running for the hills, but not Yonder. He meditated for five whole minutes, excellent for what I assumed was his first time. Then he sighed with the upmost repose, stood, stretched to in fro, looked me in the eye, issued a contemplative fart that itself sounded like a OM, and disappeared off elsewhere as usual again.

# 12.

The next day I had to go down and bail Shane out of the pokey for a riot that her and her esteemed mayorial opponent had incited during their first debate in the village gazebo.

The topic of the debate was, "Ought we to paint the church milk white, cloud white, sink white, or regular white?" Shuffleboard snuck in a irrelevant question about Shane's immigrant policy, and she says, "Let him come. Who'd want to move to this witless backwater anyway?" Slyly, he pressed her for more details. She got fed up and hollers, "A mayor named Shuffleboard who raids the village coffers for presents for foreign tarts from Ambo has got no business asking me about my immigrant policy!" He took that personal and pulled the plug on her mike, she beaned him with her tennis shoe, and everybody drunk or sober jumped in the gazebo for a brewhaha.

Shane come out of it nursing a kicked shin, a skull knot, a vengeful ego, and a fat bail bill. "Bro," she says, "I need help. I have to come up with more of a domestic policy than free basketballs."

Fortunately right then we heard a series of unorthodox noises from the attic. It sounded like all sorts of bulky objects bumping into itselves and getting scraped and shoved around.

"What the deuce is that?" Shane says.

"Earthquake?"

"Usually, in seismology," she says, "when you have an earthquake in the attic you have one in the living room as well."

"Science is built on exceptions," I observe. You kept hearing large items drugged around up there. "Maybe it's a new meter reader that got hisself lost."

"Yeah, or maybe it's an astronaut."

"How could it be a astronaut?"

"How could it be a meter reader!"

"Well, it's more likely to be a meter reader than a astronaut."

"It's not likely to be either one up in an attic that you can only enter through the bathroom by standing on something in the tub."

She was winning so I went for a low blow. "I wonder if it could be that immigrant you invited from the debate."

She had no rebuttal. However, she was correct that you can only clamb into the attic through the ceiling over the bathtub, so we looked and sure enough the trapdoor stood open like a cave, with the dragging noises continuing thereupin.

Shane grabbed my and hers bowling balls from the hallway, we put the balls in the bathtub, and I balanced on them while she steadied me. I stuck my head through the hole but whoever was up there—

"The animal!" Shane shrieks.

—not so gently dropped the trapdoor on my bean. I tumbled off the bowling balls and knocked Shane into the hallway like a ten pin hitting a seven pin.

After a respectful moment of us picking ourself up, the industrial din resumed overhead. I re-mounted the bowling balls and tried to push the trapdoor open, but it wouldn't budge. Yonder had shoved some heavy implement on top.

I decided to think positive: "I guess he probably won't do nothing very questionable or inappropriate up there."

"You guess a smug wild animal alone in the attic with no supervision won't do anything very questionable or inappropriate? And what do you base such a gorgeous conclusion on?"

"What's up there that he could hurt anyway?"

"Oh, just two hundred years worth of heirlooms that eight generations of our family have accumulated through wars, famines, bankruptcies, catastrophes, scandals, and loneliness."

"Well, as long as he's out of my hair, that's the main thing."

Shane says, "You know what, who cares about your egotistical animal anyway. I have to concentrate on that Shuffleboard Humphrey. I'm going to get him if it's the last thing I do."

I started thinking. "There's nothing in the attic that could be considered explosives, is it?"

"He had a skywriter plane today that wrote clear across the whole sky, 'SHANE WASHINGTON WILL RUN HMM INTO DITCH!'"

"Where'd Yonder get a skywriter airplane?"

"*Shuffleboard Humphrey* got a skywriter airplane. And where do you think he came up with the money for that? Well, I'm going to find out, and when I do, I'll take that old codger down like a sack of wooden legs."

"There's another campaign slogan."

Shane stomped off to scheme for power and prestige. I listened to the industrial beast in the attic. I wouldn't say it sounded like he was building something, but I wouldn't say it sounded like he was destroying anything, either. It was more like preparation for action that could go either way. For all I known, he was building a basement in the attic, which just might come in handy.

# 13.

Yonder loved the fog like a long lost brother. The first time he saw it moving in, he scampered to the top of the privacy wall and let himself vanish into its cool bright fleece. When it moved away he remained, but he had turned completely white in impathy.

His fur at times had the quality of shredded sponges and could retain oodles of dampidity. One night the village was socked in and his coat so bloated from the fog he got stuck climbing in the window. Early that morning he had took off over the wall and been gone all day, then shown up with someone's old naugahyde briefcase in his teeth. It was singed a little on one side, and bulged full of important paperwork or snacks or something. Holding the briefcase like that and his fur swole with fog, he looked like a giant silver-red puff fish coming home from the office through the window.

I tried getting that briefcase away from him. "Let it go! You better not gotten me in trouble. Whose is that? It's certainly not yours. Let go!" His jaws were like Fort Knox if he had something you wanted. Finally his fur dried enough to squeak in the window and he scooted with the briefcase up the bathtub wall and through the attic trapdoor and slam!

I stood there peeved and fumming. It reminded me of *The Castle* again. That hero-surveyor is trying to find out who hired him, what he was suppose to survey, and how to get up to the dang castle. All his information comes from village kooks and burrocrats that speak in obfuscatory and irresponsible grammar. In my case it was a attic instead of a castle, and instead of kooks and burrocrats, it was a mixed animal with no grammar whatsoever.

*

I thought I would take him for a walk through Downtown Hmm that evening after supper. I had a dual purpose, one of which was threefold.

First, I wanted everybody to dang well know that whatever Yonder was he was *mine*, not Shane's, in case they believed otherwise from him traipsing around with her on the campaign trail.

Second, I asked Shane, while I had Yonder out for a walk, could she try and find out what in tarnation he was building or destroying up in the attic.

Shane was not keen on the idea. She had other important plans—namely, soaking her lazy post-riot bones in a bubble bath and editing her mayorial acceptance speech down to three hours, even though she was still 40 points behind Shuffleboard in the latest *Hmm Gazette*/CNN Poll. She said she would do me the favor if she had time left over from her own selfish pursuits. She didn't say "my own selfish pursuits," but that's exactly what it was.

# 14.

It was one of those living picture-postcard Saturday downtown evenings that Hmm was world famous for. Up above, stars lain thick as batter, while below the populace strolled New Sawdust Boulevard in its peasant finery, admiring themselves in the reflections of one another's pompaded hair-dos.

All at once everybody spotted Yonder coming, bounding along like he owned the joint, plus me, who normally kept to the backroads. I had on my paisley Bermuda shorts, chapeau á la Art Carney, my tastefully see-through lime summer tank-top with "Bond, James Bond" written on it in homemade gold leaf, and some experimental coconut sandals I had recently invented and wanted to test out in the real world. It was the kind of outfit that if you saw a man wearing it, you had to think, There goes a fellow with enough self-confidence to choke a horse.

The village stopped in its tracks to admire the moving tableau of nonchalant originality that me and my animal presented. All of downtown tip-toed and rubbernecked as we sauntered along most devil-may-care. Let them eat their cake and eat it again was our motto of the moment.

It was exactly like I pictured it would be, though I acted like I couldn't be more blasé if I tried. We headed straight for the heart of Lula Park where the gazebo sat (that Shane and Shuffleboard had their debate riot in), with Yonder loping at my hip like the most loyal of sidekicks. Everything was humming along smooth as a silk ear. I was tooken aback at how happy I felt going for a public stroll with the little beast fella.

The adults hung back, trying to act grown up in the face of my irresistible pet, who mummered with amusement and humanitarianism as he pranced along. The children cried, "Yonder, Yondy, Yonda," and bounced around him like electrons in a big safe circle while their courage got built up. They skipped across the grass and tra-la-laud around the trees, benches, cow fountain, and statue of Founder Lula and her Four Dead Husbands, bug-eyed and stuffing their fingers in their mouths. The children, not the dead husbands.

Yonder and me plopped down on the warm evening grass near the gazebo, and the village and us took our leisurely nodding gazes of each other in the little lamp-lighted park.

I found a tasty twig of straw to chaw on to look casual. Then I realized it was a old piece of somebody's spaghetti picnic that had dried up, and I sput it out, "Ptui!" Everybody laughed, so I raised my eyebrows a number of times to show them it had been a planned trick.

One young heroine, Clare Cee, sidled lobster style from the pack of kids, her red hair wild as a campfire. She performed a pirouette and a summersalt to mislead everyone, pointed at the moon, for no earthly reason, and, right in front of Yonder by then, pulled a rose from her sleeve, stuck it behind his ear, and darted abaft Founder Lula's statue as if he would chase her, which he didn't.

The crowd rewarded Clare with a rumpus of applause, during which she reappeared with a curtsy and several bellicose sneezes, perhaps from the pollen from her rose.

Yonder appeared to be a good sport about it, until he whipped his tail around and knocked that rose off his ear, caught it mid-air, and ate it—Chaw, Chaw, Chaw, Gulp!—and then sput out the stem, thorns and all.

"Whaw?" says the village.

Yonder got distracted by a plump June bug flying around his head like a bi-plane around King Kong. He didn't move a inch, but his eyeballs made crazy 8s and went the color of emeralds as they followed the aerial path of the woozy bug.

Suddenly, Yonder opened his mouth, the June bug zigzagged in, and the animal snapped his trapdoor jaws shut on the unmindful bug—Slam!

Yonder swallowed dramatically, scratched one flappy ear, sniffled, opened his mouth wide in a glorious yawn and out flew . . . the rose! And continued to flew!

You could of waved a doily and knocked over the whole village.

The bizarre aeronautics of the rose resembled the flight of the June bug itself, and for good reason. After a spell of zagging and zigging, the rose's petals fell like little silent fireworks, leaving nothing but the June bug itself, in living flight, like Jonah from the whale, nor the worse for wear, and flying with more dexter and jaunt than ever, and off into the Hmm night.

Well, that did it, that broke the ice. All the caution and doubt of the village crumbled in a country cheer for Yonder's Rose and June Bug Trick, and for the mixed trickster who pulled it off. I rolled out of the way to avoid the high tide of children who scrambled forth to clamber on Yonder like gnomes on a Shetland pony. Even the grown-ups gathered their innocence and drew nearer the mixed one and his confounding allure.

The animal stood at upmost peace, as if he wasn't even there, motionless as a woolly mammoth in a storm of children joy. He allowed the small fries to crawl, trundle, climb, roil and coil around his back, neck, legs, and vast platinum yellow-orange head, that I could see now had a lion-like quality to it, while across his face played countenances both steadfast, futuristic, wry, and carefree.

"Lemuel," says Farouza McDonald, daughter of the village dictionary keeper. "Where did that guy's name come from?"

"Came from yonder," I say. "Named after the Rorybory Alice. Them yonder Lights my Unc used to meditate at under while praying the animal up."

Farouza turned to the village and announces: "Yonder! Y-o-n-d-e-r! Derivation: Rorybory Alice prayer lights! Used in a sentence: Well, there's Yonder yonder. Y-o-n-d-e-r! Yonder!"

"What games does Yonder play, Lemuel?" asks Catalina Hill, Hmm anti-litter czar.

"He eats a lot," says I.

Says Catalina, "Eating's not a game."

"You must had seen him eating," I say.

"'You must *have* seen him eating,'" she says.

"I certainly had. I barely seen him doing anything but."

Catalina giggled for some childish reason. "Does he know how to play 'Go Fetch'?"

"He may know how," I say, "but I suspect it's beneath him."

"Not if I throw it high enough," says Catalina. She grabbed a handy stick and hurled it with all her might. "Go fetch, Yondery!"

As suspected, the animal preferred not to fetch, although he did observe the item with concern as it sailed end over end into the growing distance.

"Catalina! Child!" cries old Marge "Grammo" Vigil. Grammo was holding onto a gingko tree for dear life. "You done threwn my cane across the park, girl."

"Ooops, sorry, Grammo!" Catalina lit out to retrieve it, which ignited Yonder to gallop off around the park and burn off some mixed energy. The only problem was that a half dozen of the innocents still hung on his fur and one by one they flewned off into the grass like passengers from a runaway stagecoach. As they scrambled up and after him he formed himself into a dark golden ball and rolled around wobbly with them giving chase, all the while odd objects sailing out of his coat, from a magnifying glass to a blackboard eraser to a copy of *Don Quixote* I'd been looking for.

Yonder slammed on the brakes, the kids piled-up all over him, bedlam ebbed, and Id Madrid, son of the village rainmaker, inquires, "Yonny, can you play hide and seek?"

The animal proceeded to weave a mixed oral sound vine that included traces of lamb, seal, moose, and parrot.

"What do you call that?" says Id.

"Lamb, seal, moose, and parrot," I says.

"Are those in Yonda?" asks Id.

"Well, they came out of him."

Id addressed the beast: "Yondmo, can you count to a hundred backwards and then go ollie ollie oxen three three three?"

Yonder gave the lad a empty mirror look such as Low Stu might give a young monk that asked him the meaning of life.

I say, "Just go hide and see, Id."

And that's not only what Id did, but every adult and kid, too, went and hid.

I didn't feel like hiding. I didn't go for games. I was a thinker, a serious fellow, the unofficial philosopher of the village, if I may. I didn't care to lose at silly things. If I was going to lose, it would be at something important, like a conversation, a silence contest, or a stare-down.

By then, the last of the giggling villagers had concealed themselves in hill and dale around the park. Yonder pretended to keep his eyes closed as he commenced a eerie purring yodel that could fairly be interpreted as counting.

However, when the animal's eyes popped open, they were filled not with the playful radiance I anticipated, but rather unabridged alarm. Perhaps his fourth helping of radish pudding at dinner had caught up with him. I say, "What's wrong, Yond?"

His ears rotated like radar dishes, sweat broke out on his fur-head, and he issued a dull growl of fear. His eyes focused over my shoulder. I turned to see the source of his anguish, perhaps the statue of Founder Lula and her Four Dead Husbands? With a gasp I realized it was a certain familiar miserable entity lurking in the shadows of the gazebo.

"You," I say, meaning none other than the hooded Stranger from my press conferences, who was also the skulking Visitor that Chuck told us about. "I know who you are," I say, although I didn't.

In response, the Stranger/Visitor didn't respond.

"I'm gonna get that guy right now," I announce to whoever wanted to join in, which was nobody, because they were all hiding waiting for Yonder to seek them. I straightened my tank top and shorts rather aggressively, but the adversary made no run for it, nor moved a muscle. Though he appeared scrawny as a rooster, I hadn't no idea how off his rocker he could be, nor what weaponry he had sequestered in that cape.

"Is this dope annoying you?" I ask Yonder, as if I wanted to make sure before initiating mortal action. The animal's eyes dialated, nostrils puckered, and whiskers quivered in the affirmative.

Once again that cynical phantom had ol' Yonder in a knot. I didn't get it. The beast was a veritable factory of destructive options. From stem to stern he boasted bio-weapons and strategic tricks galore—teeth, fangs, claws, jaws, breath, camoflodge, mind-read-ing, impenetrable vaccum-like fur, bug-swallowing magic, toxic gaseous expulsions, super leaping skills, so forth. Yet in the pres-ence of this brooding skinnybones, Yonder melted like a candy bar in the glovebox. I knelted; he leant his shoulder against my ribs. A trembling like a little train passed from his heart to mine.

I'd had it up to here with this Stranger/Visitor hanging around everywhere butting into my business and flapping the unflappable Yonder. I pointed at him in no uncertain terms. "Hey, you. You're the Stranger/Visitor from my Uncle's Unconscious Forest, aren't you?"

He mummered something iniligible in a rather wispy voice for so malevolent a figure.

"Aha," I say. I decided that Stranger/Visitor was too bulky a name. I would call him Strangitor. "What did you do to my Uncle, *Strangitor*? That's right, *Strangitor*. You don't like your new name? Tough. Chuck said you were up to your topknot in those dark activities out there that night. Oh, so you thought I didn't knew about that. Well, well." He might of twitched at my words, but I was squinting to look scary and couldn't see too good. "What's eating you, anyway, huh? Have you ever thought about minding your own business for a change? In fact, empty out your pockets and flaps and maybe I'll trust you enough to give your ears a good boxing for old times' sake."

The ominous one made a smirking noise, while Yonder's teeth chattered like maracas. Now I *had* to take a run at Strangitor, since I kept implying I would. I hadn't took two terrified steps toward him when Yonder emitted a squeal like bad brakes at a red light.

I turned to look and Lordy! Yonder was not there.

"Yonder!" I say to the absence where he had been.

I turned back to Strangitor and there he was, likewise *gone*.

I rushed to the nearest tree, figuring my poor pet had hid behind it, but I tripped over a pile of nothing and went sprawling like a goose.

Truly, it was nothing there but a rather prominent lump of grass. I reached out and patted it—it was *Yonder*. The mere presence of Strangitor had led the beast to transform into the grass, or the precise color, shape, arrangement, and texture of the grass. I couldn't see him but I could feel him under my hands like a grassy, furry, little washing machine, rattling with dread.

Having no idea what direction Strangitor could be waiting to pounce from, I had to get my dear animal out of there. I picked him up: it was like lifting a 100-pound invisible limp barrel of wet grass. My bad back took it and barely kept on ticking.

Once we reached a safe distance from Lula Park I tried to put him down, but he wasn't having it. He clang to me like the last twig on the cliff. I had to lug him all the way home, with my backbones grinding and tendons clanking like old trolley cables. I wondered how suave I might have looked, toting a big monkey-size armful of wiggling grass.

As payment for my back, I begun to feel like something of a hero. My bravery was the only thing that kept me from dropping him, except that he clong to me like a straightjacket.

As we neared the familiarity of our privacy wall, he calmed down and begun returning to his normal colors, patterns, and textures. Finally, inside the cottage and the door locked, he ceased shaking and sweating. Furthermore, he gave a yawn right in my face in which both dinner, lunch, and breakfast was represented, but he continued cleaving to me.

I was trying to pry him out of my arms with the crowbar Shane keeps around to threaten talking heads on the TV, when guess who came stumbling forth in her inside-out bumblebee pajamas scratching herself. "What the hell's the racket," she says. "I need my campaign beauty sleep, Bro."

I finally pried Yonder free from me and he hopped up and crammed himself into his favorite book shelf. He regarded me with a flicker of gratitude for having saved his mixed skin. His eyes fell shut and he started up a snoring meditation.

I collapsed on the couch and recounted for Shane the adventures in the park, from my and Yonder's triumphal entry to our ignoramus retreat from Strangitor.

Shane flopped herself onto the couch beside me. "What are you endangering my campaign manager like that for?" I should of knewn better than to try to squeeze pity out of a mayorial candidate. She tapped her rosy cheek and and furrowed her vast forehead as she machinated. "I don't like the sound of this Strangitor one bit."

I decided not to inform her that the Strangitor in the gazebo was the same person as the Visitor that Chuck talked about as well as the heckling agitator at my press conferences. It was too complicated, plus I liked knowing things she didn't.

"When I'm mayor," she says, "I'll pass a law that only people who are already *in* Hmm can *be* in Hmm."

A inane sociopolitical discussion with my addled sister would take my mind off both Strangitor and my aching back. I say, "What about people who get born here after you pass the law?"

"Have them submit a citizenship petition. I'll decide it on a case-by-case basis."

"How can a baby submit a citizenship petition?"

"If he can fill one out, he can submit it."

"He *can't* fill one out, that's my *point.*"

"If somebody can't fill out a citizenship petition, that's grounds for exile right there." Shane was getting herself in a knot in her inside-out bumblebee pajamas trying to explain the purity of her political philosophy.

"You can't exile a baby," I say. "What's he suppose to do, crawl out of town?"

"How did he get into town?" One of her legs was bent up under her and the other arm was trying to wrap itself around her head backwards. "Would you say a terrorist isn't supposed to crawl out of town? There will be no discrimination in a Mayor Shane administration. Everybody illegal will have to crawl out of town, terrorist or baby alike."

"Campaign slogan."

"So, you're sticking up for a potential terrorist, this enemy of the state, this Strangitor?"

"How dare you! I hate Strangitor a hundred times worse than you. You never even heard of Strangitor till ten seconds ago."

"I heard of him now, and before the word gets out, you better stop harboring an undocumented alien who's harassing my campaign manager and undermining the common welfare."

I know when a conversation is done all the distracting it is going to do. "Speaking of changing the forgotten subject," I say, "did you get up in the a-t-t-i-c and find the nature of you-know-whose p-r-o-j-e-c-t?"

"Huh?" She spelled it out on her fingers. "Oh, that. No, I was busy with various urgent official campaign activities."

"Like what, naps? Tell me once in for all, how self-centered can you possibly get?"

"There's always room for improvement. Go do it yourself if it's so important."

"I would, but somebody's sitting in the bookcase waiting to wake up at the first creak of the trapdoor."

"How interesting," Shane yawns. Immediately she fell asleep in her inside-out pajamas. I thought of taking a picture of her like that for a campaign poster. I poked her foot with the crowbar and she got up and started sleepwalking back to bed. "Make way for Her Lady Mayorship," she mummered. "Friends, babies, terrorists—ask not what Mayor Shane can do for you, ask what Mayor Shane can do for herself."

*

I made my favorite bedtime beverage—a cup of hot cherry cinnamon cocoa with a pound of stale mini-marshmallows crammed in—and sat down to read the condensed *World of Silence* by Max Picard. It's a book about people and animals and other things, and how they get along with silence. Max says animals are much better friends with silence than people are, because they don't have to keep talking all the time to prove they're still there. It's one of those books where you like to stop and look into outer space to marvel in baffledom at life and who you are.

Later I remembered that me and Yonder had left the whole village hiding in the park, and I hoped somebody had got around to calling ollie ollie oxen three three three.

# 15.

By the carefree way Yonder acted the next morning, you'd thought the previous evening was a walk in the park. He come to, sprung from the bookcase, inhaled his flapjacks and soysages, and strutted around like a majorette at half-time. It's a good thing that *people* don't get over terrible experiences that quick, or the world would be in a big mess.

"Hey, short stuff," I say. "Don't you remember what happened last night?"

"Don't talk to me," says Shane in the corner of the nauga-nook behind her *Hmm Gazette*.

"I *wasn't* talking to you," I say. "I was talking to Yonder."

"Yonder doesn't talk. He's an animal. Don't be a dunce, it reflects badly on me."

"He might not talk, but he knows how to listen. He's a *polite* animal, at least."

"Polite? He's polite as a kick in the pants. That animal wouldn't know polite if it picked him up and knocked him into next month."

"Who would?"

"Me, that's who."

"I'd love to see that."

"Thank you," she says, shaking her newspaper. "By the way, you were right about that mutant being a sad excuse for a campaign manager."

"I never said that."

"You should have."

Yonder took a book out of the case, lain on his stomach, opened it and peered into it for some personal reason. I started to grab it from him but saw it was one of them flamboyant mysteries of Shane's. It was very uncivilized writing—a plot that meandered all over the lot, half-formed themes that didn't make no sense, lots of cornball metaphors, forced and unfunny jokes, a bunch of sloppy self-centered characters, smart aleck dialogue, run on sentences, and too many adverbs and adjectives—but it wouldn't likely do him no long term damage.

Right then I got a load of the headline in the *Hmm Gazette* that Shane was sulking behind:

"SHANE PLOMMETS IN POLL, 84-10, 9% Undecided."

"Now I see why you're so grouchy, getting plommeled in that poll."

"What poll?" She pretended to see the headline for the first time. "Oh, look, a poll. Peachy keen. For your information, Brutus, that poll is crooked as a barrel of clothespins."

"Clothespins ain't crooked. It's two pieces of wood fastened together by a integrally molded wire clasp structure. Something crooked has got to be one continuous thing that's bent at a sharp angle. You could use, er, um, how about, 'crooked as a barrel of hockey sticks.'"

"How about, er, um, 'dumb as a barrel of brothers'?" She smacked the paper with the back of her small but meaty hand and proclaims, "That high-and-mighty Marvin Wopper." As publisher of the *Hmm Gazette* Marvin controlled village polls. "He's had it in for me ever since I made his lamebrain paperboy Luther Blissett tie my paper up with a string instead of a rubber band. Did you know that a rubber band is one of the dirtiest things in the world, because it's impenetrable to germs, so they have to sit on top of it waiting to jump off on the first person who touches it?"

"I'm aware that's part of your belief system, yes." Then I noticed a anomaly with regards to the poll. "Hey, that paper ought to check their arithmetic facts. Eighty-four plus ten plus nine adds up to ... bzz, bzz, carry your three, bzz, bzz, bzz ... *a hundred-and-five percent.*"

"Hmm?" Shane studied the headline. You could hear the rusty gears of addition and subtraction grinding away inside her puzzled forehead. "Oh! So, maybe I'm not half as bad off as I look!" Or she could be twice as worse off. "Zounds, man," she says. "If I got those pinhead undecideds, I could be in striking distance."

She was in striking distance of third place in a two-place race. I was sorry she was getting trounced, but it was for her own good. If she turned out to be as rude to the village as mayor as she was to me as sister, she would get herself run out of town on a drunken haybarge.

"With my unruly charisma," says Shane, "I ought to be so far ahead you couldn't even see me from here. Running against a guy who's got one leg in the grave and one arm in the long-johns of graft and debauchery. If it was a fair race, I'd have all hundred-and-five percent to myself. But it's as crooked as ... four left turns. I'd like to know where Shuffleboard gets the cash to parade floozies in and out of the Mayor's Royal Cottage. And he calls them 'consultants', shameless as a goat. He's spending dough like he plucks it off a hundred-dollar-bill tree. He even stole my idea and gave everybody in the village a brand new basketball!"

"Oh, *that's* what all that dang bouncing was out there this morning."

"It's plagiarism!"

"Wait a minute, I didn't get no basketball from Shuffleboard."

"It would be a waste of a basketball since he knows you're voting for your own sister."

"How's he know that?"

"I'm in no mood for jokes."

"I don't get it."

"You're about to."

I noticed that Yonder had devoured half of Shane's bad mystery. I don't mean he read it, I mean he ate it. As he chewed, he would look up now in then to catch a few snippets of our conversation, which he regarded with a look of both nonplusment, charity, and indigestion. Shane hadn't no idea he was supping on her literary delight, and she felt bad enough already without me informing her.

"Maybe you're plommeting in the poll because you forgot to address the issues," I suggest.

"Oh, I hate issues. Issues are stubborn and annoying." Then they ought to be your best friends, I thought. "The only issue worth addressing is the corruption of Shuffleboard Humphrey."

"But you got no proof. Just wild in new window."

"Wild *innuendo* is better than proof, because you can never pin it down enough to disprove it."

"You need more than unfound rumors if you want to stop the corruption."

"*Stop* the corruption? That's treason talk, Bro. Corruption is patriotic as a slap on the back, a big wet stinking cigar, bombs bursting in air, a free chicken dinner, and a suitcase bulging with greenbacks. Corruption is the pus that heals the political organism by oozing out and greasing the wheels of the machinery that drives our glorious land. I don't want to stop it, I just want a slurp."

She was mixing metaphors in a rather distasteful fashion, but that wasn't the worst of it. "How was I deceived to think you wanted to clean things up here in Hmm?"

"Easily. However, once I win by any means necessary, I'll clean up all right."

"Boy, oh boy. Ain't there one lousy thing you want to improve in the village?"

Shane threw back her slightly clock-shaped head and giggled like a magpie. "The village is perfect just how it is. If you improve one lousy thing, they'll only expect you to improve other lousy things. It'll throw off the whole perfectly lousy balance. Well, there is *one* thing I want to improve—who the mayor is. Then I'll have the money, power, and savoir faire to improve two other things—me and my standard of living."

"Well, I never. Don't you want to use your mayorial power to do good deeds for your neighbor, like the Bible says?"

"I certainly do. When I'm mayor, I'll be happy, and my happiness will be a good deed that rubs off on my neighbor by osmosis. I'll lounge around the Royal Cottage and everybody will call me Her Mayor and feed me gum drops and jump off the sidewalk when they see me coming. They'll be happy just thinking about how happy I am. Enjoying my power will be a constant good deed for my neighbor, like the Bible says."

"I'm too speechless to talk," I say. "Where's your *ideals*?"

"Right here," Shane says, and she made a blasphemous village gesture involving a foot, a ear, and a gizzard. At that moment she spotted Yonder polishing off the last page of that mystery of hers. "Stop! Cease!" she hollers. "He ate *The Riddle of the Traveling Skull*! You blasted animal!" She yanked the page out of his mouth. He growled but let her, then gave me what looked like a wink, though it might of been a crumb of the book in his eye. "He ate Harry Keeler," she says. She held up the shreds of the last page. "Look at this!"

"He must not be getting enough Vitamin Bad Mystery Writing in his diet. You ought to at least let him finish it."

She crumpled the page and threw it back to Yonder; it stuck to his forehead like velcro. "As if being behind by seventy-four points isn't bad enough." Yonder sent his tongue up to grab the page from his forehead, then sput it out. He rolled his head with a air of glum accomplishment and belched long like a calf full of cud.

Shane sunk around herself into the nauga-nook. "I don't know what those huckleberries want from me," she sobs. "Hey, wait." She sat up. "Maybe they'd vote for me if I promised to keep Shuffleboard around as, say, Secretary of Issues. Then I could do softball interviews and photo-ops and royal banquets with visiting dignitaries. Oh, crud, who am I kidding?" She flang herself like a medicine ball back into the nauga-nook. "I ought to take the two dollars left in my campaign coffer and drown my sorrows in a root beer float." She moaned and began banging the back of her head against the nauga-nook.

I felt so sorry for her that I wished there was some way I could help if it wasn't too strainuous and didn't take too long.

Yonder went over and rested his red-golden snout on the lime formica nook-table and regarded Shane in all her shallow and self-centered anguish. His oblong face registered a expression of ineffable tenderness toward the suffering candidate: his lips parted slightly and then stopped as if he was going to put his care for her into words, but remembered he hadn't no words to put it into; his eyelids come down and went back up in a blink of fond mournfulness, slow and sweet as honey blinds; his head tilted sidewise as if too many feelings had filled it up; and finally he give a nod that passeth understanding, but likely meant, "There is so much more to what you poor dear human dupes know than meets the eye." He glanced outside with purpose, suggesting, "I must part for now, but my concern for your helplessness remains strong." And a wobble of trepidation in his eyebrows hinted, "Upon my return, all will be much better or much worse." At which point his big clear gray eyes shoned moist, and he trotted out the window and's gone.

"Huh?" Shane says to Yonder's prophecies. "Whatever." She began reading the comics, tears of gloom traipsing down her plump village cheeks. "The only thing I can think of that might save my campaign," she mummers, "is to sell that animal. All he does is eat, sleep, undermine my campaign, and give me long pious glances." At that, she brightened up remarkedly. "Hey, I could raffle him off. Those misfits would line up for a mile to buy tickets on our little monster. I'd make enough dough to plaster Hmm from one end to the other with pro-me propaganda."

"That's a wonderful idea," I say, "except for two minor glitches. One: some might see raffling off your campaign manager as a sign of desperation. Two: he's not 'ours,' he's 'mine.' And three, he's not for sale in any form, never was, and never won't be."

"I could rent him to somebody for a couple of weeks."

"This is a most disgusting line of remarks. Why don't you just get a job to pay for your propaganda?"

"I have a job—running for mayor."

"Go back to fortune-telling for a while."

"I hocked all my equipment at Jinx's."

"Too bad. You could of predicted you're going to win."

"I did predict it, only I'm not, so I wouldn't be able to go back to fortune-telling after I lose anyway."

"Have you ever predicted *anything* correct?"

"Once I predicted I would get up off this nauga-nook, pick it up over my head and hurl it at my ill-bred brother."

Instead of throwing the nook at me, she started flopping around and shrieking and bawling. Finally, she curled up in a ball, and I left her to her own devices. You can't cheer somebody up that's already happy wallowing in their own luxurious misery.

# 16.

I had a dream.

Now, nobody likes to hear other people's dreams. When Shane starts telling me one of hers I writhe around like a cockroach in a spiderweb. Other people's dreams are too looooong and too full of obvious Freduan symbols. They act like it's a hit movie instead of a direct look into their tawdry subconscious. Why are you even telling me this? Don't you have any shamelessness?

Therefore, I'll try to keep this short, and if you figure it out symbols-wise, keep it to yourself, I got enough problems as it is. It don't have anything to do with me anyway, it's about the animal.

I dreamed Yonder got famous in all the villages of the region simply by hanging around and making people feel funny and go, "Wow!" "I never!" "I'll be!" "Unpossible!" "What are it!" "If that don't take the cake!" "Hmm!" and "I don't believe what I'm seeing!"

Sure enough, somebody got jealous of Yonder and made a anonymous call to the Mystery Police. The Mystery Police come to the cottage and confiscated him while Shane and me were hypnotized by a infomercial for time machines. The Mystery Police stuffed him in a potato sack and took him to a basement in their secret headquarters in the boondocks.

(This is still the dream.)

Yonder sent a picture to my intuition showing the exact building he was in, with a arrow pointing to the basement. I rode my bicycle there and found that Chinese weightlifter ex-scientist couple, the Ehs, Merle and Pearl, marching around outside guarding the place. I told them I'd been sent to relieve them for lunch. I had on a Mystery Police uniform myself. They took off for a snack wagon that appeared fortutously in the distance. The Ehs turned out to be a lot more agreeable in a dream than in real life.

I knelted down to peek through a little porthole into the basement. In a room that looked like our kitchen, there Yonder lain, strapped down and blindfolded on our nauga-nook in a tuxedo. Then somebody powerful snabbed me by the back of my neck (still the dream) and lifted me in the air. I thought it was one of the Ehs but he turned me around and it was *Strangitor*!

He wore long ornate red-black hair and a Mystery Police uniform instead of his hooded cape. Even though his face was blurred by his dancing hair, I knew it was him by his sinister conceitedness. Strangitor spoke, gruff as death, though his breath smelt like cinnamon: "Say, isn't that your mixed animal in there?"

"Where? In there? No, I don't believe I know that fellow."

I heard a cow moo sadly somewhere in the dream.

"I think you do know him," Strangitor says. He pointed a finger at me as slim and pale as a flame. "I think that's *your* mixed animal."

"No, no, as a matter of fact, I never heard of him before."

The dream cow mooed once more.

"Yes, I'm certain," says Strangitor, "you are the best friend of that mixed animal."

"No, I am not! I never seen him before! And I'm offended you continue making these outlandish charges, Sirrah."

Strangitor chuckled under his breath. "If you say so, *Lemuel*."

He let me go and right then, Caesar, a actual cow in Hmm, went, "Moooooo!" in real life outside the cottage, and I woke up like I got shot out of a cannon.

I was sweating like a bottle of cold soda pop, my sheet was wrapped around me like a gooseberry vine, and I had a tear in one eye from fear of Strangitor and the Mystery Police, and a tear in another eye from pretending thrice to not know Yonder.

I would of gave anything to get back in that dream and tell Strangitor that Yonder and me *was* best friends in the world and what was he going to do about it. But I couldn't go back, and I couldn't undo how my subconscious kept pretending to not known him. I did go out in real life to find him, searching his favorite haunts inside and out, hoping to tell him how much I like him, and hold him some, if he will, but I couldn't find him at all nowhere.

# 17.

Remember the recent fog-sequestered night when Yonder crawled in the window holding that old naugahyde briefcase in his teeth that he tore up into the attic with? Well, the morning after the Mystery Police dream, I was imbibing a bowl of jicama porridge, when I see the animal skitter over our privacy wall for to carry out untold mischiefs in the village. Shane was busy sleeping off more campaign antics, so I took the opportunity to discover for myself the truth of the attic project once in for all.

I begun snooping around the perimeter of the cottage to see how the critter might be ingressing and exgressing up there. Hello and behold, I come upon that selfsame old briefcase, lying upside-down on the ground against the rear of the cottage. It was singed, battered, and chewed open, with telltale mixed animal toothmarks and slobber all over the lock. Inside it was empty as a little naugahyde cave, except for the stinks of feet, rotten pipe tobacco, and blue mimeograph ink, not necessarily in that order. I didn't like the looks of those stinks one bit.

On the outside of the briefcase, carved in its ancient naugahyde, half worn away by wear in tear, three initials lay, namely: L.V.M.

"Hmm," I say. I knelted there ruminating on those old engraved initials, running my fingers over them like a blind detective. I about swallowed my Black Jack gum when it hit me what they stood for.

My Uncle's whole full name was none other than . . . *L*eonard

*V*ictor *M*iddleton.

I leant against the cottage, seasick on the unexplicable. My brain went weak kneed pondering how Yonder got holt of Uncle Leonard's briefcase. He had to had walked to the Unconscious Forest, a perilous 365-mile round trip, or hitchhiked—even scarier to contemplate—or, worse, rode a bus or train with all those shady characters, or, worst of all, took a taxi with some unscrupulous driver that goes the long way to jack up the fare. Although how many taxi drivers would pick up a animal like him going to the very heart of the Unconscious Forest to start with?

I remembered Yonder had spent the day in Unc's burnt cabin when Shane and me visited Chuck. I could see it all now: the animal found the briefcase, stashed it in the rumble seat, then retrieved it at his leisure when we got home. But what and the world had been inside it to the bulging point that was no longer in it that was worth so much that he would go to all that trouble for—and where was whatever was in it now?

I got so exhausted thinking up the questions I hadn't no energy left for the answers. I looked up to Heaven for guidance and comfort and I see a open air-vent in one of the cottage gables, a vent that a certain very flexible animal might had managed to sqwuck himself in and out of.

I fetched the ladder and clumb right up. I quickly realized that while Yonder might of been slipping in and out of that little passageway, I wasn't going to. I had got myself stuck in the middle of the vent like a pig in a polka.

I howled for Shane and banged on the attic wall with my forehead until she finally bumbled forth to investigate. First, she had herself a big helping of horse laughter at the sight of me sticking out the gable vent like the butt part of a gargoyle. Then she went and got her lucky hatchet and clumb up and gingerly chopped me out of it. Lucky indeed, for I plommeted inward to the attic floor instead of outside to the plankstones far below.

In the process Shane knocked over the ladder and had to hang onto the vent and somehow stuff her stout self through it after me. I darn near caught her as she crashed to the floorboards. She had a big helping of moans and groans, then we stood there silent, surrounded by the swirling attic darkness, sister and brother agog in a cloud of unknowing.

"Have you got a light?" I say.

"I don't smoke." Her voice was peeking into the darkness, frightened of itself.

I checked my old barncoat pockets and found a box of matches, the very ones I'd confiscated when we kept lighting up Uncle Leonard's rotten corncob pipe two years previous. I received a little electric shock when I pulled the matchbox out of my pocket, that I attributed to static in the attic dust.

I struck a match. Our jaws swung loose as incense burners.

First, Yonder had the gall to haphazardly shove all our Washington family heirlooms up against one wall, namely, the Revolutionary War couch, the Ming toaster, the Tiffany lava lamp, the turn-of-the-century combo icebox/radio, and the like. Not to mention my old projects, including the self-cleaning bathtub made of dehydrated vinegar cement, the pollen perch for lightning bugs that would of replaced electric bulbs, and the Thereamen Electromagnetic Oscillator Box that I built for Shane's boy friend that never heard of her.

We turned around and where the heirlooms had been, in the whole middle of the attic, there stood half a dozen ceiling-high mounds of the most baffling objects, natural and man-made, that the animal must had been secretly appropriating from the village and environs since the moment he arrived in Hmm. Both of us could not mouth a word, so full was our eyeballs of the bewildering array of items that we were attempting to behold.

There was a driftwood table, half a bongo, a pile of old bird nests and cocoons, wheels of all sizes arranged in bizarre misorder, a antique sink full of caterpillars, Middle European lawn ornaments, pulleys and ropes and chains, a stained-glass tableau of the Garden of Eden, a cache of doilies, moth-eaten comic books, a rusty windmill planter, a curtain of seaweed (the match went out and I lit another), a brand-new scarecrow, a bolt of purple damask, mildewed calendars and album covers, a jewelry box full of gingko leaves, bottles of strange colored liquids and marbles and tiny bones, a necklace of tin cans, a pine box of black sand and pink feathers and red gumballs, a pyramid of colored wigs, a instructional tango video, three pogo sticks, a stack of Easter bonnets—and that's barely a third of only one of the half dozen hillocks, I'm telling you.

We stood there gawking in awedom at this eerie cornucopia, this stolen harvest of the near world's more disgusting, ridiculous, ragtag, and marvelous jotsam and fletsam ever gathered in a cottage attic by matchlight.

Shane whispers, "You got yourself one true madman mixed animal on your hands."

But my fix-it/inventor mind had already began intuiting a method to his mixed madness. I perceived ambiguous coherence in certain impossible combos, like the half a bongo and the caterpillars, or the red gumballs and the Easter bonnets.

The match went out and with hands atremble I lit another.

"Oh oh," says Shane. "Take a gander at this."

She was referring to a flimsy card table in the midst of these perplexful mounds of hoard. Upon the table lain what appeared to be a immense blueprint of sorts, a fascinatingly crude schemata with hundreds of multi-colored diagrams, arrows, weird emblems,

100

child-like symbols and formulas, mathematical insignia, stick fig-ures and higherglyphics, and undecipherable notes upon notes going all over the place and around and back again. The blueprint lapped over both sides of the card table like sheet water and flowed to the floor and beyond.

"Well, I never," whispers Shane.

As new-fangled and full of surprises as Yonder was, it was no way in hell he could write, because if he could, all bets was off.

"Uncle Leonard had to have written this," Shane says.

I took a whiff of the blueprint: rotten pipe tobacco, mimeo-graph ink, and feet. So this was what that big bulge in the old brief-case had been, folded up. "This is the master plan, Sis."

"Master plan for what?"

"For whatever all this is."

The match flickered. Shane spied our emergency kerosene lan-tern, grabbed it, and I lit it up. The whole attic and all of Yonder's eccentric gleanings sprung forth in illumination and hobgoblin shadows, more dumbfounding the brighter they got.

"Can you make hide nor hair out of any of this?" I ask.

"Nuh-uh," mummers Shane.

"What could it be? Let's brainstorm. Could it be the parts and plans of a rocket ship?"

She looked at me funny in the lantern light. "A rocket ship? How about an atomic bomb?"

"I doubt Yonder would know the secrets of a atomic bomb."

"I doubt he would know the secrets of a rocket ship."

"He's more likely to build a rocket ship than a atomic bomb."

"Why?"

"Because you have to have a electron splitter to build a atomic bomb. Where would he get a electron splitter? With a rocket ship, it's only a engine, a tube, fins, a couple chairs, and a window."

"Do you see a single one of those items here?"

Well, there was the stained glass window depicting the Garden of Eden, but that didn't seem appropriate for the windshield of a rocket ship. "Oh, yeah, well, why would he want a atomic bomb?"

"Why would he want a rocket ship?"

"To explore outer space."

She began to riposté, then sighed in defeat. "Look," she says, pointing at the top of the blueprint. Printed there in large slow painstook childish handwriting, exactly as on the animal's fleabit collar, was one big word:

"YONDEЯ."

And who did we hear outside right then but Yonder hisself and all his personal sound effects ascending the side of the house with mucho gusto.

Shane and me took one look at each other and voted to panic. Putting the lantern out, we ran around in the darkness bumping into ourselfs, knocking over a bunch of Yonder's stuff, and then sprawling all over that. We dove behind the sleeper with our hearts booming like the first thunder of a bad storm.

I was so scared I got mad. "Why are *we* hiding? *He* should be hiding from *us.* He's the one that stole all that crap and dragged it up here. It's *our* dad-dang attic."

"Shh," Shane says. "Who cares whose attic it is? What good is a stupid attic if we're busy getting digested inside of a smug animal?"

"Oh, he wouldn't eat us."

"Why *not?*"

"Because he *loves* me."

"What about *me?*"

"You should of thought of that before."

She busted out crying. "If he tries to eat me, you better stop him!"

"I'll try, but there's no sense in both us getting aten and nobody left to tell the story."

"The hell with the story, just don't let him eat me!"

Right then we heard him leap from the air vent and land in the attic, "Thwomp!"

Shane gave a petrified gasp and my heart dropped like a watermelon off a bouncing buckboard.

The animal scurried around, groaning like a punched kangaroo at his disrupted office. He apparently could see in the dark, and he wasn't nowhere near stupid: you had your ladder, your hatcheted air vent, objects we'd knocked over in our panic, nervous smells, drool, DNA, echoes, Shane's breath—evidence of our presence strewned ubiquitously about.

He whimpered like a heartbroke marmoset while rustling the blueprint on the card table, trying to determine how bad we had mucked up his plans of mixed animals and men.

At first I thought Shane was praying, but it was her teeth clattering. She got so scared she dozed off and started snoring like a drunken muskox. I poked her in the ribs but it was too late—Yonder had heard. The floorboards creaked in our direction, and when he put a paw-hand on my shoulder I about rocketed out of my own flesh and blood.

"Oh, hello," I say to the darkness, although I noted that Yonder's eyebrows and whiskers was somewhat phlosphlorescent. He must have had some deepsea fish in him, seahorse perhaps. I lit the lantern and me and my mixed animal regarded each other. His eyes were as sad as a pair of San Francisco sunsets.

I could of blamed the whole intrusion on Shane, who continued to snore defenselessly, but I didn't think he'd buy it. "I'm sorry, Yonder, man. We let our curiosity be our guide. I don't think we hurt anything too bad. I'll help you restore everything to its previous luster. We shouldn't have invaded your private space, even if it's not legally yours. Plus, there's the issue of stolen goods that could put me behind bars as your executor. I'm responsible for any wrongdoing that my pet carries out, however remarkable." I didn't expect him to understand every word, but I trusted my tone of voice would convey a self-serving regret. "Although we feed you and clothe you, and you produce no known income, nor fulfill a single practical household purpose, I apologize if you can't help from being unjustifiably offended by our good-intended curiosity."

He sighed and returned slump-shouldered to the card table amidst the mounds of magnificent assemblage. I followed him over. "Could I help you with whatever you're doing?"

He threw me a backhand look of amused trepidation. This is composed of a scrunching of one side of his mouth, a looking up in the air to the other side with his eyes wide, and a full-hearted half-snort through the left nostril. I took it to mean that he cared for me against his will and deeply wondered why.

I took another scrutiny of that blueprint. It looked like something a gang of 9-year-old Einsteins drewn while hopped up on cartoons and candy bars. I asked him about that "YONDEЯ" scrawled at the top of the plans. He tapped his chest with one paw. "I know you're Yonder, for goodness sake, but what's your relationship with this blueprint?"

He rolled his eyes and hung his tongue out to one side, which I interpreted as him pretending to be mystified by my foolishness, or else that it was impossible to get across what he wanted to. To get the upper hand back, I went for the translation that was most insulting to me.

"I believe it's a legitimate question. If you want all due difference and respect, try giving some first."

He gave me a disappointed snerl and ran his eyes over the

stupefying atticscape he had created for Old God knewn what purpose. His lower lip quivered and he moaned like a jammed garbage disposal. He looked at me urgently, tapped his chest again, then tapped the blueprint, then tapped the air next to him, then gave the empty space in the air a shy and adoring smile, as if he was carrying a torch for whatever he was imagining there.

I took a wild stab in the dark: "You love me?"

He rolled his eyes, groaned, and a great forsakenness crossed his big, silver, red, golden face like a cloud of locusts crossing the sun.

I couldn't have wanted worse to understand what he was trying to say. I believe we shared a terrific sorrow for how our communication was like through a glass, darling.

Looking back, it was at that moment of duo heartbreak that I felt the first fire of longing to invent what would become the so-call Yond-O-Lator.

"Dan Blam it," I say. A teardrop popped out of my eye and toppled down my cheek before I could wipe it off with a manly thumb swipe. It was not a good example to set for a young animal fella trying to make his way in a village without pity.

But all the sudden, slowly, Yonder got a big idea (eyebrows rose), he cheered right up (mouth parted expectingly), but then he got scared (face fur grew dark), then he cheered back up, then got re-scared, then a sultry concoction of both. It was fascinating, but finally just more of the same incomprehensible miscorresponding.

That's when I caught a tender, indeterminate, foreign serenade coming from somewhere nearby. I thought it was Shane on the sleeper taking her snoring to a whole other musical level, but saw it issued from Yonder himself, staring at me in the lantern light. His mouth barely moved as he voiced a bevy of remarkable, barely audible uulations.

Ralphie Munch claimed Yonder had moonbird in him, but bird song was only the beginning of whatever he was daring to try to express. The general leitmotiv was at once otherwordly, amateur, melodious, cozy, and troubling.

As he produced his soundments, he pointed at certain objects. While indicating the windmill planter and the seaweed curtain, for example, he made a burbling refrain that resembled the hum of bumblebees mixed with baby talk, yodeling, soft exotic scat chanting, and a hint of little shifting balsa wood gears. My ears and brains struggled to translate his obscure lilting narrative into something plumbable.

As he tapped the blueprint where a stick figure of a porky-pine sat next to a formula of higherglyphics, his flummery became more insistent. I detected in it flashes of everything from a muffled be-bop recitation of low guff cooing, to rumors of drawled flapdoodle, to the syncopated gabble of something almost like a medieval Russian bear cub accountant inventing shorthand musical calculus symbols to hisself.

As he continued his grabbag of trillings through barely parted lips, Yonder watched my face the way a bird would watch a sleeping cat to see if his song was entering the cat's dream for some delicate and mysterious persuasion. His uneffable ballad produced in me thrills of loss and yearning. The cantata was clearly a effort to break the language ice from the mixed animal side, but it served to perplex me even more than simple misunderstanding. "I hear you, Yond," I whisper. My voice sounded flummoxed, as if my words were made of big wooden kindergarten letters tumbling out of my mouth.

I kept hearing a actual letter or syllable almost emerge from his brook of reverberations, but when my memory reached for it, another mystifying undercurrent of hums, guggles, susses, blurbs, churrs, ripples, croons, hushes, umlauts, pings, tootles, warbles, and half-inkled mumberings had arrived in its place.

I thought I known my animal by then, but what a unexplored continent he remained. How ardently he studied my face while transmitting his incomprehensibles. He watched me like a card shark, a mother, a sentry, and a lion tamer. I didn't want to hurt his feelings by not understanding, for fear he would stop trying to communicate and never try again, but it was one of those rare situations where you had to be totally honest no matter the consequences.

"I don't know what you're saying, Yondy. I'm sorry. I know it's beautiful, and true, my tantalizing animalito, but I don't understand, though I want to more than anything in the world."

He stopped, lowered his head, then dropped to the attic floor like somebody hit him with a haymaker. I shrieked and started to attend to him, but he jumped right back up and gave a head-bob toward the trapdoor. I followed him as if he knew what he was doing.

I had forgot Shane behind the sleeper, happy as a goose snoring her life away. Yonder gestured toward her feet like he'd done this sort of thing before, and I grabbed them while he got her arms. We lifted her onto the sleeper; she giggled in her dream. I wondered what Shuffleboard would pay for a snapshot of her getting toted around like a sack of drunk fish.

We rolled both sleeper and Shane off the trapdoor, Yonder opened it, and we jumped down into the bathtub. He led me outside where it was nighttime already. He appeared to be indicating I should clamb a ladder and join him atop the privacy wall, which I deigned to do.

Yonder stood against the stars in a poise of self-grandiloquence, although a tremble ran through his shoulders, which I blamed on the chill night air. He looked at me like he wanted to tell me something, but weren't sure how I'd take it.

"Go ahead and try," I say. "We're all friends here, or at least I am."

He pointed Napoleonly at faraway February Mountain, which oversees Hmm to the north like a dark craggy queen sleeping on her side.

Peering where he was pointing, I couldn't make out nothing but the black sky and the blacker mountain. I pulled out my keychain-spyglass that I invented from a lipstick tube, pieces of the rearview mirror off Shane's old Edsel, and a false eyeball that washed up on the beach. Using the spyglass I made out a small pin point of flickering light on the mountain. It had to be somebody's campfire, high on the west face of the forbidding peak. It made me sad to think of somebody up on that lonesome mountainside in the mist of such a cold grave night.

Continuing to point at the microscopic illumination on the mountain, his arm-leg a-tremble, Yonder looked in my eyes and with his other equally shaky front arm-leg made a solemn gesture, as if slowly pulling the hood of a blue threadbare cape over his big head and somber face.

# 18.

I spent a sleepless night ruminating over Yonder's ominous gestures, which could only mean one thing—the person tending the campfire on top of that mountain was none other than the dreaded Strangitor hisself. I had no idea how the animal come by such info, nor what it meant to him, nor what I was suppose to do with it.

At the crack of 3 a.m., I felt a presence and opened my eyes to the sight of the mixed critter. He stood there staring at me with moonlight smeared all over his face. I shrieked. He pulled me outside by the cuff of my astronaut pajamas and before I knew it we were headed clean out of the village.

"Hold on," I say. "Where are you taking me?" I thought maybe Shane was trapped somewhere, like on The Lassie Show. "Did Shane fall in a mine?"

Yonder frowned, gestured toward February Mountain with the back corner of his head, then employed his forehead and chin to indicate me and hisself.

"Huh? I hope I'm misunderstanding, because I ain't going up on no February Mountain, especially not to see no Strangitor. Why in blazes would *you* want to visit that sneaky weasel? You been petrified of him at every opportunity."

He begun to growl and weep at the same time. The weeping had a little hiccups in it. I calmed him down and convinced him to go back home momentarily. Over breakfast, we resumed our adventures in miscommunication.

By the velocity, overlap, and contradictions of his cavalcade of signs, nonverbal noises, omens, and facial panoplies, I understood there was urgency to the matter, and that the mystery involved not only us, February Mountain, and Strangitor, but also my camping equipment, his attic project, and something about the moon and stars.

I asked him as many questions about the proposed trip as I had asked Chuck about Yonder's origins, and got about as many answers. But he kept up his bewildering, distraught, rapid-fire pantomimes till he wore me down. He was going up the mountain whether I accompanied him or not. The thought of that poor animal alone with Strangitor on that dark slope sealed the deal.

I figured I would be able to sidetrack him on the way, or maybe Strangitor would split the scene by the time we arrived. Packing my camping gear, I remembered that Shane was still conked out on Gramps' sleeper in the attic.

I hurried up to rescue her, only to find she'd snoozed peacefully through the night. At first she couldn't remember where she was or how she got there. I helped her down, she gulped coffee, then lit out on the campaign trail with a bucket of paste and a wheelbarrow full of posters. The posters depicted herself in the sky with angel-shaped thunderclouds on each shoulder, the sun breaking behind her big grinning head, and on a red banner across her bosom the golden words, "OBEY THE BIBLE AND DO A GOOD DEED OR BE SORRY FOREVER! VOTE SHANE!"

*

Before I and Yonder embarked to the mountain, he got across to me, using more confounding charades, and then a pretty decent mudball drawing on the side of the garage, that he would like a bath before we set off.

110

He wanted a *bath* before climbing a grimy mountain to confront his mortal enemy? Perhaps it was a cross-species warrior ritual. I say, "Why don't you jump in Shane's pond and scrub yourself down with a pawful of algae?" He looked at me as if I'd insulted his mother, if he had one. "Okay, okay. I don't know what this is, a confrontation or a date."

I poured a gallon jug of Fuzz 'n' Fur into a barrel of pickle water, dumped him in, dunked him, swooshed him around, and scoured him down.

By the time I finished he was sound asleep. I had to tip the barrel over to get him out because he weighs 100 pounds when he's dry, 150 when he's wet, and 200 when he's wet and asleep. I hosed the suds off and stuffed him in the village dryer on "wrinkle-release" for a couple minutes, tossing in a sheet of Shane's organic soysage-scented fabric softener. He came out a little woozy, but clean as a fluffy platinum whistle.

*

It was still dark as the motley duo of him and me walked, rode a railroad hand-car, and hitchhiked to the base of February Mountain. We got a ride from a milkman that was slower than walking, and another from a traveling haberdasher that tried to sell us a hat. I already had my traveling butterscotch tam o' shanter on. Yonder didn't have no money to his name, but the haberdasher played on his vanity and tried one chapeau after another on him. He settled on a purple porkpie that guess who ended up paying for.

By sunrise I was being guided by the beast up the wild west side of the mountain. Hiking behind him, I reluctantly admired the tilt of his overpriced porkpie. I still had no precise idea what the outing was for. Yonder had been terrified of Strangitor only yesterday at the park again, and now he was dragging me up there to encounter the villainous chap? Of course, it could of all been some dark endeavor I was too innocent to recognize, some monstrous joint enterprise Yonder and Strangitor was in cahoots on from the git-go.

As we hiked higher and the oxygen molecules thinned out, I begun to go queasy pondering our appointment with that taciturn skulker. Who knew what furious rumble would transpire on that grim mountainside, worlds away from my warm, clean, well-lighted little cottage.

But you know what? In life, every once and a while, you might find yourself wanting, for some mysterious reason, to go ahead and trust somebody you don't know all that well, somebody even half-wild and irresponsible, in a situation that's perilous, irritating, unfathomable, and involves travel. If so, trust your heart, but leave bread crumbs along the way.

*

It took the whole day to trek up there, but it only seemed like a month.

Tough guy world author Ernest Hemingway said it about his buddy, crybaby hypochondriac world author F. Scott Fitzgerald, when they were bumming around Europe together: "Never go on a trip with anyone you do not love." I'd change Ernest's saying to "Never go on a trip with anyone whether you love them or not."

Yonder was the most self-centered travel guide you ever heard of. All the way up the mountain he did whatever he wanted whenever he wanted, and acted as if you wasn't even there, except for when he got hungry.

He stopped hiking and took a nap when he wanted; he ate the snacks you packed (including wrappers) without leaving you any; he wandered off to explore every distraction, byway or burrow he fancied; he hacked through mountain brush and let branches fly back and smack you in the kisser; he clumbed trees so fast you had no idea where he went, then dropped acorns on your head; he pointed one direction and went in the opposite; he suddenly camoflodged into the current terrain so you tripped over him; he circled around behind you and made ambivalent noises to spook you; he acted like he didn't understand questions you asked him about the natural ecology that were so simple a idiot could of asked them; he rudely communed with owl, bobcat, squirrel, monkey, trout, hummingbird, and salamander right in front of you in animal vernacular, unconcerned that you felt left out; he emitted dizzying hind vapors from the soysage fabric softener sheet he must of aten in the dryer; and he got up from that nap and started hiking again with no warning while you snoozed away and woke up alone, scared, and witless.

I got lost 15 times trying to follow his serpentine zigzag reverse corkscrew egotistical style of guiding. Once I had to yell, "Please, Yond, for Old God's sakes, come and find your poor lost guardian, man!"

Finally I started dropping pieces of my garbanzo bean sandwich so that I could at least get back to where I started dropping them. Yonder was in front of me and I noticed him picking things up. I thought it was little natural mountain souvenirs he was collecting for Shane, little rocks or twigs. Finally I figured out he was leading us in a big circle and eating the pieces of sandwich that I dropped!

"Is this a big joke to you or something?" I say. "Could you stop gallivanting around and lead us in a straight line to wherever the hell we're going!"

He gave me a look consisting of a half closing of the eyes, a bringing together of the front paw-hands, a half smile full of subtextual paradox, and a artificially differential head dip, that I took to mean, Your wish is my command, Sahib.

Then he proceeded to demonstrate why he was part monkey, goat, moonbird, and mule. He shot up the face of the cliff in a straight line through the trees and over jags, juts, boulders, and chasms, covering 100 yards of treacherous vertical territory in five seconds.

I did not try to follow him. I stood there with my arms crossed and waited until he stopped and turned around. He pretended to be surprised that I wasn't right behind him instead of so far below he could barely see me tapping my foot. He descended just as swiftly back down and regarded me with a expression of perfectly fake puzzlement and concern.

"I don't know what I should expect from a critter that has the morals of a bon bon," I say. "Go ahead and guide however you like. But remember—let your conscience be *your* guide."

He gave me a sad nod, turned slowly enough for me to catch the beginning of a ambiguous smile, and recommenced the trek with a measure of restraint, humility, and sober purpose that lasted about a minute and a half.

# 19.

My philosophy of life is: Don't have a confrontation at night with a prowler, arsonist, and possible uncle-killer named Strangitor on February Mountain with nobody on your side but a miglomaniac animal created by a madman. However, by the time we got where we were going, I was too exhausted to be scared, much less philosophical. In fact, I didn't even know we'd arrived. I thought the light was the glow of the Rorybory coming over the ridge, and that Yonder had simply decided to rest his mixed bones by a big old mulberry bush.

I plopped down beside him. "I have blisters on my aches and splinters in my hunger pangs. Is it any chance there's a February Mountain Motel around here?" I caught my breath and heard something. "Listen. That's that sound the Rory makes—that *buzz*. Like a billion bees inside the Lights, the yellers and greens and purples. Some folks say it's only in your head, that buzz, from the ions in your innard ear. Others say it's electric-magnetic winds blowing from the sun through the colored clouds, pouring through the trees, trillions o' pine needles just a-buzzin' and a-poppin' and a-cracklin', like a universe-size radio stuck betweenxt stations. Some folks even say it's the dead communicating from outer space."

The animal placed one suction-cupped paw-tip on my lips and tipped his head to indicate something through the bush required my attention. I took a look and my heart caught in my throat like a gopher in a safe-trap.

There in a small clearing, who sat in all their menacing glory but Strangitor hisself. Even more incredible, he appeared to be *meditating*, in a three-quarter lotus upon a giant flat red rock, next to a campfire and a actual honest-to-Pete Indian-size wigwam. As always, the bloke had on that tumbledown cape, maintaining his face as a mystery of fluttering shadows in the cave of his cowl.

It was a life-threatening crisis, but I was so weary, plus had a touch of mountain high, that I beheld the encampment as a fetching vision: the great red rock, the yellow wigwam, the towering black forest in a surrounding circle, even the ominous Strangitor. All you had to see by was the dappling campfire that cast its shy light over the glade. I wished I'd been a painter and had a moment to slap together a landscape of the enchanting little life-threatening scene.

Watching Strangitor meditate, I begun oddly calming down. After all, he was working on his conscious contact with the universe. His nirvana must have entered the mountain atmosphere and sifted down upon me. Of course, I knew from the Tao that good things like meditation could be twisted around to wicked purpose by a rogue like Strangitor.

I tried to think of a saying from Low Stu to girdle my loins for the showdown at hand. What come to me was: "Fish cannot leave deep waters. Heaven's net casts wide. This is called rolling up your sleeves without showing your arm." I felt stronger simply wondering what it meant. I looked up to Heaven in aimless hope and saw the sky as a big, black, upside-down cup with stars sprayed inside. That made me hanker for a hot cup of java, a apricot cruller, and a fresh copy of the *Hmm Gazette*. I begun to get homesick. I even wondered what Shane might be up to.

I listened through the natural hum of the mountain and realized that Strangitor was chanting some slow, melodical, idealistic, and non-English refrain in a pleasing but once again rather treb-ular pitch for so sullen a hombre. It sounded like "Der one, der one, der one." So, he was German, I thought. I remembered a few German words. "Der one" meant "The one," I believed, which may have meant Old God. If Strangitor believed in Old God, maybe he would only hurt me and Yonder a little and not completely kill us.

Yonder bobbed his head in rhythm with Strangitor's chant. Not only wasn't the animal scared, he was getting hypnotized. "Hey, snap out of it!" He blinked and looked around. "This is nothing but a big ambush," I say. "You should of planned this bet-ter. We're in the middle of nowhere with a merciless demon that could—"

Suddenly Strangitor emitted a harrowful groan and begun to wobble topsy to one side and waver turvy to the other. Then he tipped all the way off the rock backwards, rolled longwise like a hooded log, and lain there, nary moving a muscle.

A cry like a squeezed dove leaped from Yonder. He started forth to give aid and comfort to the enemy. I grabbed him by the tail and he farted and a electric shock wave shot through me. "Ouch! Don't go out there. Can't you see, this is a *trap*."

Yonder paused to consider the possibility, but when Strangitor kept not moving, the animal couldn't stand his own impathy and rushed out to aid our surely malingering foe.

I remained behind the bush and planned my escape. I expected Strangitor to spring up, grab Yonder, and they would brawl them-self limb from limb before I could pretend to try to join in. I'd have to find my way home alone, after burying them up there in the dark, or else haul their bodies down the mountain with tigers and gorillas catching the scent, then eating me first because I'm freshest and most interesting. Dead, I would never discover the meaning of the adventure, would never transmit the story of the battle of good versus evil, or at least mixed versus evil. I had to guarantee my own survival so to tell the tale to generations to come, though I would have to come up with a bittersweet and obscure moral.

I peeked out. Yonder was dragging the cloaked one back to the meditation rock. He propped him up against it and commenced to tenderly smack him around under his hood to bring him to, in vain.

I gathered myself and went around the mulberry bush, keeping one eye on the thrilling forest darkness that had us and the timid campfire surrounded. In the foliage you could hear mummerings and footflops of assorted who known whatnots. I stood behind Yonder as he gave Strangitor a good brave sniffing. Then without no further ado the critter proceeded to lift that old hood clean off the evil madman's whole head and face.

# 20.

Sirrah, as Yonder unhooded that terrifying mystery face, you could of knocked me over with a dandelion puffball.

For it was not Strangitor sitting there in Strangitor's cape at all, but instead a pasty, undernourished, cockeyed-looking, redheaded *gal*!

"Where'd Strangitor go?" I spunned around. "Where's Strangitor?"

The gal remained catatonic, though her toosled scarlet hair seemed to fly and swoop in the suddenly wild campfire light.

Yonder gave me a sidewise glance full of exotic calmness. His eyes were gentle, his head tilted, his chin relaxed, and his mouth a modified parabola, all which I took to mean, "Lem, why are you surprised to find this young woman sitting here in Strangitor's cape?"

"Huh? Are you saying you knewn it was her under there? Then why'd you get so scared every time you seen her?"

In answer, Yonder pointed at the gal, made a big circle in the air, then a scared face, shook his head at me, hit his own heart with his back foot, then made some kind of a tricky complicated rigyoumyroll with his front paws that reminded me of that children's hand story: Here's the church, here's the steeple, open the doors and see all the people.

"I got no idea what you're talking about. What's the sound of two hands doing childhood higherglyphics? Look it—your mystical senses failed us, man. Couldn't you even *smell* it wasn't Strangitor? You never had the first inkling. At some point, *Strangitor switched hisself with a gal.*" Yonder tenderly condescended his eyes at me. I gasped at his gall. "Face it, pal. You got tooken."

I glared at the senseless redhead. The tip of her tongue stuck out like a drunk or a baby. In one Sherlock Holmes flash I figured the whole thing out: "You know what, Yondo? Let me explain things for you. This redhair ragamuffin is Strangitor's *moll*. Which means Strangitor himself is fixing to bust from that treeline and ambush us any second."

I looked around for a weapon. I thought about grabbing the gal by her feet and swinging her around, figuring she was unconscious anyway and wouldn't feel much if I happened to connect with the charging Strangitor.

In response to my disturbing insights, Yonder completely ignored me. He continued his ministrations to the fainted gal. He held her frail pink wrist like he was taking the pulse of a rose. Could he even count, much less know what a pulse was? She twitched like a horse at a fly bite. Was he trying to shock her awake with jolts like he gave me? He sniffed her head, pinched her cheeks, fluffed her hair, and other oddments that I considered forward but may of been a legit way to bring her to.

I took a moment to decide that the gal was not completely unattractive, though askewn, flour-faced, and unexplicable. She belched once—something from the cabbage family—but failed to regain enough consciousness to write home about. Her head lolled around like a pale, red-headed bowling ball.

Then, beyond belief, Yonder began licking her entire face with his oversize flapjack tongue.

"Stop that!" I say. To my amazement, he did. "That's revolting.

She's not well to start with. Look out, let me in here." I elbowed him out of the way. "Go boil some water. I mean *fetch*. Don't even try to boil it. Just go fetch some water." I made some apt charades. "Find that stream we crossed over back there and get some kind of container and fill it with water. And make it snappy."

Amazingly once more, Yonder the Disobedient bounded off to do what I said, leaving me alone with this still slumberous Strangitor-impersonator.

I tactfully dragged her near the fire and propped her against a big log, figuring the heat would sweat out whatever affliction she had. You hoped it wasn't catching. I sat next to her with my hand over my mouth and studied her face. Her expression looked like she was trying to untie a knot with her feet. Even unconscious, she looked like she had all the troubles in the world stored up in that fair, high-plains forehead of hers. I looked around and made sure nobody but hidden mountain critters was watching and gave her earlobe a good solid flick, and I'll be—she come to just like that. Her eyes popped open all big and buzzerk. She grabbed her ear and flailed her limbs around like a whirly dervish, catching me in the stomach with one muddy moccasin and knocking my wind out. She was not making a very good first impression.

Her alarming green eyes raked me over with a conceited wariness, from my tam 'o shanter to my eye black to my vest to my camoflodge socks to my homemade, pressed hemp hiking sandals. I hoped she didn't think my *leiderhosen* meant that I spoke German, too. *Leiderhosen* means "regrettable breeches," which are snug mountain shorts, and would be odd for a modern man to wear unless he known himself quite well. Shane made them out of itchy wool that distracted you from how cold your knees was, sticking out like brass doorknobs in the mountain air.

I noticed that the campfire made Strangitor's moll's pleasantly suspicious face look like a trembling milky pink rose against that downtrodden dark blue cape. Her first words was not so picturesque: "What are *you* doing here?"

"Oh, suddenly you speak English, eh? And quite good, too."

"Did you bring him?" she says.

"If you mean Strangitor, that's your job, not mine. In any case, I'm the one asking the questions." I smirked to give myself confidence, because she had come to a lot peppier than I expected. "I'm in charge here on this mountain," I say, "and that's all the information you're entitled to until we determine your precise identity and purpose."

She impertinently smacked her lips like something tasted funny, then struggled to get to her feet.

"Stay right where you are," I say. "Don't try nothing funny."

She curled her lip at me but wisely stayed put. "What *happened*?" she says.

"Well, I'm not a medical professional, but, in my opinion, you fainted and fell off that rock."

She winced, I assumed from my astute diagnosis, but then she pulled a pinecone out from under her that she'd been sitting on. She begun feeling around on her toosled head.

"What are you doing now?" I say.

"Looking for bumps, do you mind?"

"Why would you have bumps?" I thought it might be from whatever unattractive ailment she had.

"I fell off a *rock*, Detective, why do you think?"

"I think it didn't knock no manners into you." I scanned the shadowy treeline and underbrush, deciding it could be to my advantage not to tell her I wasn't a detective. "So where's your beau Strangitor?"

"My boo what?"

"Oh, play dumb, okay." I felt rather carefree compared to how I ought to, with Strangitor romping around out there. I likely had the mountain high. The gal's cape flopped open and for a moment I lost track of my gentlemanlyness to glimpse her rather skinny figure in the colorful ensemble she had on under there.

She yanked the cape shut. "Hey, what do you think you're looking at, Buster?"

"I can't help it if your cape flopped open. Nothing personal, but you could slap some more meat on those bones of yours."

"I've been fasting," she says, accompanied by the first sign of proper lady-like shyness since we met.

"What for, if I may inquire?" I accentuated my politeness, hoping it would rub off.

"Atonement," she mummers. "For the bad I've done."

Well, well, a hint of humility to go with the shyness. "Like what bad you done, Madame?"

"Like ten years of—" She caught herself. "That's none of your business, is it?"

"I don't know what it is, how would I know if it's none of my business?"

"Trust me."

"I don't know why I should, considering the rather unfavorable first impression you keep making on me. Frankly, in my view, you have the etiquettes of a cavegirl."

She squinted at me like a interesting bug was crawling across my face. "As a matter of fact," she says, in quite a taunting little tone of voice, "I'm fasting for *world peace*."

"Oh. Good. How's that coming along?"

She looked at me like I was being rude as well, but I really wanted to know. I didn't follow the news that much. "Let's get down to business," she says. "Where's my animal?"

I assumed that was her pet name for her beau. "Strangitor? How would I know? Watching us from the bushes, I imagine."

"What? I'm talking about *Yonder*."

"Yonder? *Your* animal? *My* animal is busy fetching. On your behalf, much less. But you know what? I'm here to see Strangitor, not his *spleenific* moll." Oops. I knew right away spleenific was not quite correct, so I upped the ante to distract her. "You know what, let's get him out here right now." I stood and called bravadoly into the darkness: "Yoo hoo, Strangitor! Ollie oxen three three three, tough guy! You disgust me! You make my stomach turn over like bad potato salad! Come on out and I'll knock your block off for you! Sending a gal to do your *dirty work*!"

"*Dirty work*! *Dirty work*! *Dirty work*!" echoed terrifyingly from the mountain. I set on the log and fumbled with my shoelaces to calm myself down.

"What in the devil are you babbling about?" the gal says. "Who's *Strangertorn*?"

I had forgotten that "Strangitor" was my private moniker for the phantom. "Strangitor," I say, "the fiend that normally dons that shackledown frockment you got on."

"Dons *what*? My cape? Nobody wears this *frockment* but *me*."

"Well, you better check the DNA. Somebody else *has* been wearing it, as if you didn't know. And for your information, that high-horse tone you're riding is not the best bet for a gal in your circumstances."

Her face went red as if I'd made a forward suggestion instead of friendly advice. "Look, Bucko," she starts, when the mixed animal come barreling out of the treeline at full gambol. "Yonder!" the gal cries.

He skidded to a halt and spote a great mouthload of mountain stream water right in her face.

"Oughk!" she says.

"Cease, Yond, cease!" He swang my way and caught me with the last of his spotement. "Gluwrd! Ptui!" It had the flavor of moss, troutdung, and garbanzo beans.

The gal wiped her face with a corner of the cape, then begun to squeeze and kiss Yonder like she knew him in a past life. He responded with far too much glee for his first encounter with the gal friend of Strangitor. I needed to teach him to discriminate better when it came to squeezes and kisses, if we lived through this.

Nevertheless, I say, "On behalf of my pet, Ma'am, I apologize for the spotement." Yes, she was on the wrong side of the fray, had a shady background, a missing gear or two, and not hardly the prettiest lass on the block, but a gentleman is a gentleman.

"Thank you, Sir," she demurely returns.

Yonder sat panting. He looked back in forth between us mathematically with forehead furrowed, as though he was trying to fit a ten-pound idea into a one-pound container.

I noticed that a mountain fog had come loitering in from both above and below, leisurely surrounding the three of us and the campfire in a sandwich of bright gloom and mystery.

# 21.

Yonder lay between us, quite pleased with himself under the gal's petting. I started petting him myself in exasperation at how him and her had took to each other. I made sure our hands stayed in different territories of his fur, and I believe she did, too.

As for Strangitor, had he conked out in the forest? Got drug off and ate by bears, alligators, etc.? If so, oh, revoar. You'd think a tough guy like him getting aten would put up a fuss that we would have heard. "Okay," I say, "for the fourth time, where's that feller I call Strangitor and you call what, Dreamboat?"

She peered at me in the campfire light, "Would you like some health tea?" says her.

"Oh, change the subject, eh?" Tea was rather a casual activity for the crisis at hand. "I guess health tea can't be no worse than Yonder's spewment."

She set a kettle on a grill over the fire and gathered cups and makings from the wigwam. It was a nice change, her hospitality. "I'm glad you're here," she coos.

"Thank you, although I don't why."

"Of course, it would have been easier to take care of this while I was in the village."

"It sure would of, whatever it is. The animal drewn up the itinerary, not me. And anyway, I never even knew you was *in* the village."

She paused with the tea making. "Do I not assume correctly

that you've come to your senses?"

"What senses might that be?"

"You're here to talk turkey about Yonder," she says, half a question.

Yonder says approximately "Em?" at his mention.

"I don't believe there's any turkey in him to talk about," I say, "not that you would know."

"You'd be surprised what I would know about that animal and plenty other matters."

I wondered if she knew what Strangitor was suppose to knew. "Do you know what Yonder's project is in our attic?"

"Of that I have no idea."

"But you acknowledge that he does got a project going up there."

"Why wouldn't I, since you just implied it."

"Well, Yonder implied that coming up here could shed light on his project."

"How did he imply that?"

"Sort of a mixed charades."

She regarded the animal, assessing the possibility. "I see," she says, but how could she?

"His and my mutual communications skills are rather limited." I almost started telling her about how I believed he had tried to talk to me in the attic, but caught myself, in case it was all a plot to make me look stupid or crazy. Again the Yonder-O-Later sprung to mind. I had a flirting vision of somehow alchemizing the nature of language atoms themself, so they could transmit meanings from one species to another. That's how genius hit you—sudden and quiet as a 2by4. "Actually," I say, "it's that *Strangitor* fellow whose cape you led us on a wild goose chase in that's suppose to know what the animal's doing in the attic. But since you're his honeybunch, I thought he might of told you."

"Listen, Hoss," she says, narrowing her eyes like slices of lime. She poked a long bony fingernail-gnawed finger against my nose, bending it to one side. "I'll say this once and once only, for the second time." She raised a pinch of the shoulder of her cape and shook it. "This *cape* is *mine*, and I don't know any *Strangitor*." She was a most convincing liar. "Please get that through your big, thick, village head."

I knew how to take a joke, since I was winning the conversation. "Okay, but please don't talk about my big, thick, village head like it wasn't even here." I winked at ol' Yond.

She frowned to keep from smiling, then returned to making tea. "It's a precious remnant of a life gone by."

"My village head?"

"The cape."

I recalled Chuck's shrood comment, and decided to steal it. "Not to get personal, but it looks like a garb some bum monk might wander the outback in."

"Maybe you're not half as half-witted as you appear."

"Thank you," I say, although her compliment actually applied to Chuck. "I prefer not to hide my wits unless I can't help it."

She sent a thoughtful half-smile into the woods. "It was a going away gift—the cape—from the abbess at a convent."

"Oh, so, it's a *nun* cape."

"Yes." She blushed against her will, which become her. "Well, I don't know if it's an official nun cape from *Rome*."

"May I see the tag, if you will?"

She lifted the collar to show me, then caught herself. "The *point* is, it's an *emblem*—my cape—a reminder of the bad years I left behind. Lest I forget. But I'm in the good years now, with the help of a certain creature who, when I met him, I was wearing it."

I enjoyed her roundabout way of appreciating my help, but not her calling me a certain creature. I eyed her over, trying to picture the varieties of sacreligious experience she had reveled in in days gone bye. I was proud of her for the new years of goodness, but I had a certain natural curiosity about the old years of badness. I wondered if Strangitor had lured her off the garden path. I could see it all now. What a wave of pillage and plunder they must have waged across the countryside. Well, these two gangstas was about to meet their Waterloo right here on February Mountain. When push come to shove, I would slap a citizen's arrest on the gal while Yonder took care of the wily Strangitor. Maybe there was a reward out for these banditoes. I could already see me and Yonder on the front page of the *Hmm Gazette*. I would have to make sure he didn't hog the glamor and limelight. I mentally picked out a good expression, probably somewhat shy yet philosophical in my *leider-hosen*, as if I was took aback by all the fame and money, and wished only to return to my anonymous life of service to the community and its appliances.

On the other hand, since he was increasingly a no-show, I begun to conclude that Strangitor had abandoned his lanky moll and slunk down the mountain to pursue other interests in the out-law singles scene.

The tea kettle went off. "Would you like some honey?" she says sweetly.

"I could use a dab. By the way, Yondo the Bottomless Pet ate all our hiking foodstuffs on the way up, not to mention his own porkpie hat. You wouldn't happen to have any cookies or macaroni salad to go with that health tea, would you?"

"How about some fresh cabbage?"

Cabbage seemed far-fetched for a camping trip snack, but I was too hungry to make fun of it. "I certainly would."

She ducked into the wigwam and I heard a clunk like a ax chopping something head-size in two. She emerged with half of a big raw red cabbage. I wasn't thrilled to have somebody as unpredictable as her slinging a ax around, but Yonder certainly perked up at the presence of edibles.

"Roughage!" she says. "It scrapes out your toxins."

I broke off a chunk for Yonder, who inhaled it and looked for more, which he wasn't getting from me.

"It's kind of rubbery," I say. "Do you have any salt? Mustard? Relish? Plum sauce?"

She made a funny face. "It's better for you plain."

"Better for me, not my appetite. Could we bar-be-que it a little, bring out the juices?"

"Eat," she says.

Chawing away on that flubbery foliage and watching the gal dally about, I took a moment to notice that there was something about her daffy hot-strung emotional procedure that entertained me against my better judgment. Not that I didn't hold a constant eye on the fogbound treeline for sign of her lovebird, the tardy mastermind, Strangitor.

She come over and set down beside me rather forcefully. She flicked my shoulder with the back of her fingers. "Now, you honestly believe it was this guy *Strangitor* who was up on your garden wall as you pompously answered the villagers' pointed questions about Yonder?"

"Huh?"

"You actually think it was *Strangitor* in the park in the gazebo?"

I about choked on my health tea with honey. "How do you know about them events?"

She grabbed the front of my hiking vest, stuck her face right in mine, and whispers, "Because, Professor Plum Sauce—it was *me*, that's how."

She let me go and I straightened my vest. I was double bungled, from her preposterous claim, and from getting too close to her fiery green x-ray eyes. "Yeah," I say, "except but only then, you'd be Strangitor, wouldn't you?"

"Then, psst, I *am* Strangitor."

"Except Strangitor ain't a gal. Checkmate."

I didn't play chess, but everybody knew what I meant. I had her dead to rights. For collaboration I turned to Yonder, who regarded me with one eyebrow raised, his head tilted at a 90-degree angle, chin away, and a sympathetic if wry smerch on the downside of his mouth. This expression could mean only one thing: "I tried to tell you, Boss, but you wouldn't listen."

I looked back at the gal. "*You're* Strangitor?"

"I'm the person you dementedly *believed* to be this Strangitor, yes."

This news hit me like a busting dam, a dam that had held back tons of fake facts about Strangitor. Did I have even one single bit of proof that Strangitor was a terrifying invincible *man,* instead of a bemusing wreck of a *gal,* with her commotion of red hair, meditation, raw cabbage, and becomingly clumsy face?

Answer: no.

I looked at Yonder for a third opinion. All he did was start to disappear, namely, camoflodge hisself into the colors and patterns of the dirt, leaves, twigs, bugs, and pine needles on which he lain. He was trying to flee the shame of deceiving his owner about Strangitor's identity. Or maybe he *had* tried to tell me, felt the backwash of my ignorance, and was now disappearing in sorrow.

At Yonder's chameleonization, the gal begun lavishing compassion upon him, as if she'd seen it before and knew exactly what to do. She petted and babied the big lump of mulch his appearance was turning into. In response to her soothings, he cut short the camoflodging and begun to reappear as his own self, just like flicking a light switch. I suspected this camoflodge had no purpose but emotional manipulation, which amounted to a blatant abuse of his superpowers.

However, first thing's first, because, in case you missed it:

*Strangitor . . . was . . . a gal.*

This bulletin bewildered the pants off me, but it also meant me and Yonder was not about to be attacked by a butchering madman out of the fog. I still felt like I ought to be outraged at getting deceived, especially since I had played a major role in the deception. Accordingly, I gave her a big glare of fake chagrin.

"Why are you mad at *me*?" she says. "Because I am who I am, or because I'm not who you thought I was?"

"Nice try," I say, "but no sale." She wasn't going to trick me out of my indignity before I was ready. She smiled incongruously, as if I had held a door open for her and she was too good to go through it. Reaching behind her for a couple thigh-size chunks of wood, she set them on the dwindling fire and tended it up to a toasty blaze.

The set of old facts about Strangitor sunk in my mind like old comfy furniture in a lake, and a set of strange fresh facts bubbled up like new furniture that was still wrapped in plastic and would be uncozy to sit on for a while.

"Now, look here," I say. "Did Yonder knew you was Strangitor all along?"

"I don't doubt he did."

I scratched my head to emphasize my contemplation. "If he knew, then how come he was so scared of you as Strangitor, whenas now he's your buddy—bringing you to, fetching spotement, grooming his South Forty in your presence."

"Yondy is a fluid and changeable soul. Why don't you ask *him*?"

"That would be silly except I already did. He gave me a bunch of facial paradoxes and that 'here's the church, here's the people' hand saying."

She mussed his ears while I rubbed his belly. He purred so loud it threatened to drowned out our conversation. "Perhaps he was afraid of my association with Leonard," she said, "or with you, with how you might respond to me, unpredictable as you are."

"Oh, in that case, thank you." Most gals like their men sensitive, but also erratic and moody now in then.

"Mainly," she says, "I think he was scared of *himself*."

"Ha. I never met nobody happier with themself. If you made him write down a top ten list of his favorite people, his name would be on it eight or nine times."

She mystically stirred the embers. "But everybody has a little rattler inside they haven't made peace with. Some shadow that stops them in their tracks. Sure, he knows who he is, what he is. It gives him that charming confidence. But what makes him most different from other animals—he knows something of his future, and has a touch of unease about it, about something in particular that might happen. If he'll be capable of doing what he may be called to do, to undergo, being the special individual that he is, so far from the herd."

"Yes, he's a herd of one." The conversation was slipping away from me, but I wasn't sure because I had no idea what it was even about. "How do you figure he sees into his future?"

"It's in his blood, his heart, his eyes. Can't you see it? Something profound, something anticipatory."

"He's profoundly anticipating dinner," I say.

Yonder looked suddenly up into the night and we followed

suit: Five feet over our heads, with a rustle and a whoosh, a immense white owl stole through the clearing, ogled us below, hoots, "Yon-dr!" and's gone. Yonder put his head back and yodeled like the offspring of a coyote and a clarinet. In the space where the owl had flewn, the fog swirdled tolerantly back in upon itself.

"Did you hear what that owl said?" I say.

"'Yon-dr,'" she says, matter of fact.

"Boy, you seem pretty composed for just witnessing the unpossible. How could a owl say Yonder? Especially the letter d, for instance?"

"A bee can say the letter z."

"A bee's only supposed to say z and a owl's only suppose to say who."

"Only Yonder isn't about what's only supposed to be."

"Maybe it was a giant white parrot."

Then I remembered something. "Hold on a minute. If you're Strangitor, then you were the one Chuck saw going and coming from my Uncle's cabin."

"True," she confessed.

"And that means you were involved in torching Unc's cabin and him meeting his Maker."

"*What*? Who told you such nonsense?"

"Don't you never mind who told me such nonsense. Chuck the woodsman told me such nonsense."

"Chuck the woodsman is full of baloney and a yard wide."

And at that she proceeded to give me her version of the events surrounding both the end of Uncle Leonard and the beginning of Yonder the mysterious animal, starting where she wanted, and progressing in the exact order that she felt like, which, if you ask me, is no way to tell a story.

# 22.

Strangitor the Gal poked at the fire as if at her own memories. "Leonard and I," she began, "we had a stark difference of opinion regarding Yonder's raison d'être."

"His raisans what?"

"His reason for being. His true purpose in the world."

"Whoa. True purpose in the world? This here's just a animal, a plain old pet."

Yonder raised his ears and frowned in appreciation of my straightforward assessment.

"I should have known," the gal mummers. "Like uncle, like nephew."

"Yonder can *seem* complicated," I admit, "but a complicated pet is still a simple animal. He's here to freeload and hog the attention and do a few fancy-dan tricks for the riff-raft. You and Unc sound like Plato and Aristotle bloviating on the Ideal Form of Government."

I expected her to be flabberblasted that I would be familiar with the Ancient Greeks. But she never missed a beat: "Yondy is a *million* times more important than any damn Ideal Form of Government, my smug little Philosophia."

Before I could decide if that was a insult or a presumptuous endearment, she jabbed the fire and resumed her yarn:

"Poor Leonard had so little joy in his miserable life, he wanted to bring some into mine. He insisted I have *fun* with Yonder as my pet, and nothing *but* fun. Whereas I envisioned a greater good than just my fun pet. I believe a treasure like Yonder belongs not to one person, but to the world, the universe, and beyond."

All I heard in that jumbo was her calling Yonder *her* pet again. "By 'your pet' you mean how he temporarily 'belongs' to anybody that happens to stumble upon him, like a patch of wild strawberries? Like, *everybody's* pet, in general, for a couple seconds?"

She tilted her head and squinted at me exactly like the animal did when I missed some point he was trying to make. "Well, you know," she says, "Pop did make Yonder for *me*."

A twinge of foreboding stang my heart. "Pop who what?"

"Your Uncle Leonard. He was my father."

The mountain gave under me. I grabbed Yonder for ballast. "Come again?"

"Well, stepfather. I'm the previous offspring of Leonard's wife Constance."

"Huh? I never known he was married, much less had a wife. Did you say *offspring*?"

"Yes," she says, matter of fact. "Constance, my mother, she was a mountain gal up in Greater Pertelote. Tough as they come." She leaned back on the log, stretching her feet out, getting down to business. "I never knew my real father. She said he was a drunk and a philanderer. Like father, like daughter. He disappeared under hushed circumstances, as troublemaking folks are apt to do up there. His clan blamed her and wanted blood. She fled with little me down into the Unconscious Forest. Shortly, she and Leonard bumped into each other while washing up in a pond. They hit it off. Both naturally irascible, both Cubs' fans, both had a scientific cross-breeding bent. She was a gardener and amateur botanist, experimenting with new vegetable varieties. They got along as long as they could, experimenting away. Then he grew more ornery, hermetic and penny-pinching, and she grew restless. She sent off and landed a scholarship at Flora U., up in Pale Province. He laid down the law—it was education or him. She grabbed me up, took off, and became quite a vegetable-fusing sensation in those parts. You may have heard of the turniloupe?"

I gave a ambivalent nod because that's all I could move in the quicksand of all these breaking news.

"Now and then through the years," she says, "I went back to stay with him when Mom was traveling. On one of those visits, Pop and I together hatched the idea of Yonder. More tea?" she said, pouring.

Breathtook by her whole auto-bio-jive, I wondered what this uncle-stepfather arrangement made me and her as far as blood went. I'm not too hot at family trees. My brains get tangled like a kite in the branches. "So, that makes us... ex-step-niece-in-law-nephews?"

She laughed. It was the first time I heard her do that. Her laugh trilled like a little waterfall of light. It might of been a tad loud for my taste, and slightly too high of a pitch, but otherwise it was perfect. You can never make a gal laugh too much, even if you did it accidentally. "Step-cousins," she says finally. Her laughter hung in the silence like a jiggled chandelier.

"But not blood," I say.

She smiled and her face came on like a porch light on a lonely lane. "Not blood," she sighs.

We looked right at each other and she coyly fingered her turbulent hair. Her hand got stuck in it and my eyes started to cross on me. Somebody less worldlier than myself might of gotten carried away, but I cleared my throat in a manly fashion and took charge by saying: "Well, well."

She politely became so bashful that she had to turn away. "Look at Yonder," she whispers.

The animal was inspecting in his paw a fat tick he must of just plucked from his classified territory, judging by the undaintliness of his corresponding position.

"That's nice," I say. He had certainly recovered fast from his guilt at deceiving me about the identity of this skinny chatterbox inchantress.

"May I resume?" the redhead announces.

"Resume away," I say, with a air of beatnik phlegmatism. Strangitor the Gal was one cool customer, and I wasn't about to be left behind.

"Pop had no other kids, step or not," she says, "so he doted on me, when he was in the mood. As a father he didn't really know what he was doing, but he did what he could with what he had. One day he gave me a funny little drawing book he had made, a book of different animals. I found I liked parts of a lot of them, so later I cut the parts out and put them together the way I wanted. I showed him the motley creature. He was angry I'd cut up the book, but I cried and he softened. As he smoked his stinky old pipe, he pondered the mosaic image, this way and that, as if something in it was speaking to him. He went out walking, came back a couple hours later, and declared, grumpy as ever, 'I'll built you that mix animal,' and he shuffled off to the back room right then and there, twenty years ago."

"Great day in the morning," I say. Yonder rolled on his back and luxuriously displayed hisselfs to the toasty campfire. "I guess that's where Unc first come to be a amateur scientist."

"We used to watch Mr. Wizard together, and he had a postcard from Einstein that he must have showed me a hundred times. I memorized it: 'Dear Leonard, My intellectual development was retarded, as a result of which I began to wonder about space and time only after I had already grown up. Stay inspired, Al.'"

She paused to wipe a tear for Einstein, or Leonard, or somebody. "Maybe Pop had an inborn gift for tinkering with nature, or he caught the bug along the way. After I put the idea of the mixed animal in his bonnet, he went down to the Salvation Army and bought a nice secondhand microscope, an old computer, textbooks on animals and chemistry and biology and DNA, and an armload of miscellaneous science charts, and found a box of test tubes and petri dishes in a dumpster, etcetera, and just went to town. In no time, twenty years later, voilá: Yondy."

"It took him twenty years to slap Yonder together?"

"Twenty years of trying, one night of doing."

Without warning, Yonder flipped to his feet and tore off into the fog like a arrow and's gone.

"Yonder!" I say, then remembered that Strangitor wasn't out there stalking us anymore. All it was was his fellow animal kinshipmen. "Did you ever get inside Unc's secret room where his experiments was going on?"

"Nobody but him ever set foot in there, not even my mom. But sometimes, when I stayed there, late at night, half asleep, there would be faint sounds and eerie smells and I'd imagine bewildering scenes in that room that might not have belonged to this world. Whatever was going on in there, he took all his secrets with him when he died, burned it all, or had it burned."

"Oh, *he* burned it."

"I'd left by then. I heard tales, but who can you really believe out in those woods?" She gazed off into the fog like the past was lurking in it. I bet she was missing Leonard some, thinking of the night he went on to his Maker. He was a dirty crazy mean old bastard, but still her step-Pop, and he had gave her the animal, even though now he was mine.

Right on time Yonder come bounding from the fog, all swollen up with it, and plopped down between us to soak up some fire heat again, self-satisfied. I figured he must of took hisself a good mountain forest dump out there.

Then I thought of something. "Why did you pull all that rigyoumyroll on my privacy wall and at the park?"

"Oh, that." She leered into the fire. Secrecy played over her lips like shadows on a plum. "I was shy," she says. "I wanted to get to know you, but I didn't know how."

"Hmm." I didn't believe a word of this sweet nothings, but my heart ignored me and skipped a beat on its own. "Asking cryptic questions at a person's press conference and spooking them in a gazebo is a funny way to get to know them."

"Oh, thank you."

I hadn't meant it as a compliment, but I could see how I might of. Amidst all the other amazements, I'd began to consider if I liked her or not, a dangerous occupation for a man with my history of bad luck in the gal department. Once again I was drinking in one of their life stories like it was a glass of lemonade instead of a load of caviar impter with flashing red lights, warning bells, and a runaway freight train a-steaming my way.

A big part of being a gentleman was knowing when to take some pressure off a personal conversation by changing the subject: "In fact, how old is Yonder anyway?"

She studied him and he studied back. "He can't be too old."

"I agree. I think he's full grown, although he looks to be growning still. When did you first meet him, by the way?"

"It was," she thought about it, "last solstice."

"*Last solstice*? That was just before *I* first met him."

"A week before, to be exact."

The timeline of this story seemed to have a life of its own. "With your and his lovey-dovey behavior, I thought you had knewn each other a long time."

"Well, you can't always believe what you think."

"Hmm. But, so, before that, you graduated from the convent, eh? How does a cute gal like you get herself involved in the nun field, if I may?"

Her funny face got sad as a face could get and not bust out weeping. She looked sidewise into the fog and the fog took a tactful step back. "She hurts herself and everybody around her for ten years, that's how. I was bad, I was vicious, I was cruel."

"Naw, naw, naw," I protest. "Only if you got a evil twin."

She picked at her fingernails in the face of my compliment. "You wouldn't like me if you knew me. I get hurt, I'm proud and scared, I hurt back. Hurt worst those who loved me best. My life was one long tawdry downward flush. A dark tossing swamp of booze, drugs, bad companions, angry men, lost years, living wild." She looked up at me, the campfire in her eyes. "I hated, I stole, I locked my heart. I crossed the territories looking for myself, looking for a man, looking for God, found the devil. Sold everything, spread my pain far and wide, woke up in thousands of nowheres. I was too gone to care. But Lemuel?" I blinked from the green fire that jumped from her eyes and blinked again from her saying my name for the first time. "Always this little flame inside kept burning, burning away. Wouldn't go out, no matter how hard I tried to snuff it. Kept whispering to me, Seize your life, *do* something. But *what*? It was too late. The pain, the lostness filled my soul like boiling tar. I wanted to throw myself overboard in a stormy sea. It was either end it, or join a convent."

"Whew. I'm one fella that's glad you joined that convent. Now that you're out, I mean. It wasn't Sister Waymaker's by any chance, was it, down Spotless Coulee?"

"Why, yes, it was. Do you know it?"

"I do. I went there one time for a little meditation getaway from fixing things, and I ended up putting a new toilet in. Nice gals. Polite, quiet, clean. Most of 'em. Although you shoulda seen the what-all that was cloggin' that pipe. Course, that had to been long before you got there. So, you graduated as a nun?"

"Not quite. Problem was, I asked too many questions about God."

"Like what?"

"If he was there?"

"At the convent?"

"Anywhere."

"Where else would he be?"

"Nowhere."

"Ain't nowhere a part of everywhere?"

She give me a look of exasperated appreciation. "It was more than that. I expressed too many nasty opinions about people, too. Sister gave me every chance. I couldn't help myself. I got worse, cruel, hopeless. A mad beast. I hated myself too much to let anybody help me. I was worse in there than I was on the street. I even got some old boy to sneak in pharmaceuticals. Sister had no choice. She let me keep that old cape. She wanted to wait till it got warmer, but I was afraid I would hurt somebody. I left in the middle of the night. It was black and cold and the rain felt like fire. It was the end. I'd gone in to be a redeemed woman of God, I came out a faithless zombie ready to die. I hadn't talked to my mother for three years. I called her to say goodbye. But she was going out the door to some big scientific conference somewhere—Anathusia? I lied, said I was fine, working in a library. She made me promise to call back. She had to go. Then, 'Oh, Leonard's been trying to reach you.' I hadn't talked to him longer than I hadn't talked to her. He was never a sympathetic man, as you know, and in my condition, who knows why I went to see him. You're ready to end it, why go to the biggest misanthrope you know? For the final straw? I thought about turning back every step of the way, or wandering off into the wilderness and never coming out."

I wouldn't want to feel any more yearnful and burning a pity for a person as I did right then for her. Also I couldn't wait for her story to start getting better, as it seemed like it had to, since she was still here, telling it.

"Somehow I made it there, to the Unconscious Forest, to Pop's little cabin, my erstwhile childhood home. I'd long forgotten the promise he made to me when I was a child, about creating the animal. I wrote him off as an old misanthropic quack who tried to love me the best he could. I expected nothing, which was exactly what I had to give. Pop moseyed out to meet me like he knew I was coming, like he saw me every day. He said, "I got ya sump'm," and he called 'Yonder!' into the woods. An answer came, a cross between a lion and a seal. Then the animal himself charged from the trees and skidded through the leaves to a halt at my feet. I took one look and fainted like a cut sapling."

I regarded the animal, who was hanging on her every word tighter even than me. His eyes gazed like polished eight-balls and his fur moved like a field of grain in the firelight. "He *is* a bit scary on first sight."

"Oh, I wasn't scared of *him*. He was nothing but pure simple burning wonder. He glowed like coals, like a mighty animal angel. No, I was overcome by the *vision* of the *future* that rocketed through me at the sight of him. Destiny had prepared me. I was hungry, exhausted from the trip, anguished by failure and exile. My wasted life delivered me to that animal, and my father delivered that animal to me. In an instant I saw he was the way I would save myself," she says, "and the world."

Now, I felt sorrier than ever for her. The very worst and nuttiest thing you could do in this world is to go and try and save it. It is the exact opposite of the best and most sensible thing you could do, namely, mind your own business.

She says, "The entire vision burst in my mind, like a palace built in a blink. I would make Yonder an ambassador of peace to the whole planet. When I came to, I told Leonard exactly that. 'No, not never!' he thundered. 'It's yer *pet*. Have fun with the damn thing! Play like hell! Just fergit about doin' no damn do-goodin' with it.'"

I assured myself again that Unc had left him to me *after* all this business she was raving about, and that she had to knewn it.

"I told the old goat," she rushes on, "'Either Yonder is mine or he's not. If he is, I'll do what I want with him. If he's not, then you lied your heart out when you said you made him for me.' I said, 'Pop, I'm taking this animal on a world peace bus tour, and if you want to stop me, be my guest, but I'll never forget and I'll never forgive.'"

World peace bus tour!

"The old misanthrope laughed in my face. 'World peace bus tour!' he sneered. He unleashed a mean, cruel, hateful, rotten lecture on the mean, cruel, hateful, rotten ways of 'so-call in-un-humanity.' Then he proceeds to rub my nose in my degenerate past. 'How could somebody who done all the dope and drank a ocean and screwn whatever breathed git the gall to try and brang peace to a whorehouse, much less the world.' Unquote."

I gasped. I was tored in two. No way was Yonder hers, and I'd straighten that out. But first I wanted to go yank Unc from his grave and slap him silly.

She had worked her own self up to a lather. "I told that nasty coot I had as much right to bring world peace as any other degenerate. If he didn't like it he could go straight to hell. Oh, he got madder than a piñata full of yellow jackets. He said, 'Onliest way you git that animal is you swear you keep him chained in your yard. You haul that unholy furball on a damn world peace tour, they'll steal it and stick it in the circus. Or cut him up in scientific bits and sauce. And then they'll come lookin' for me, your poor old helpless Pa that spun that beast out of nothing through plain God-gave genius, that they'll call it witchcraft. They'll hang me at the stake! Mark my words and don't say you sorry when it come to pass.' He said he never should have constructed that animal in the first place, and that nobody would ever get their hands on his formula to make the same mistake again, or worse. Then I left."

"With Yonder?"

"No. He was running around, keening in anguish from Pop's and my fracas. I wanted to just knock the old bastard down and grab the poor animal, but Pop had told me Yonder was ailing and needed an operation. Something about his heart. Keeping all his different genetics together took a toll on his little mixed ticker. I didn't know if he was lying, but I feared if Pop and I kept fighting, Yondy's heart would crash right then and there. So I left, I ran out. Without him."

I shook my head speechless and allowed a teardrop to traipse shamelessly down my face right in front of this gal that I absolutely had to ask on a date now with what she been through.

Yonder placed a paw on her hand and a playful gaze of forgiveness across his big face, consisting of one raised eyebrow, a chin dip, lower lip out, and nodding ears. The gal put her other hand on his paw and he put another paw on top of her hand. "I'm grateful you didn't come into my life before I was ready, Yondy," says her, "before I had reached the end of my profligate ways."

I thought, "profligate?" I believed that had to do with teaching in the legal profession. How did she fit being a law professor into such a busy schedule? I barely had time to unplug somebody's sink and invent a doodad and the day was done.

The gal tossled the animal's head and cast a lopsided mysterious leer my way. She says, "Pop had the brain of an untrained backwoods genius, but a heart as hard as a big city sidewalk. I hope he learned the lesson of love that he was put here to learn."

I nodded as slow as sap, because that's what I was, as far as catching on to the message behind her meaning. I say, "I'm awful sorry you gone through such a rumpus, even if you did bring it on yourself mostly." She nodded with a surprised self-understanding. I decided to change the subject by showing interest in her. "So, you were a law professor somewhere in there?"

"Huh? What?"

It struck me that I might not know what "profligate" meant after all. Her and him begun regarding one another with audacious goo-goo eyes. I felt left out. I decided to slip into flirt mode myself. If they wasn't that troubled by their own shameless story, why should I be?

"How come I never even heard of you before now, gal?" I begin.

She answers playfully: "A combination of Pop playing it close to the vest, and you not paying attention." For punctuation, she bent and kissed Yonder's forehead, but came up sniffing with a scrunched face.

I thought of something. "By the way, since your name ain't Strangitor, exactly what is it, if I may?"

"I thought you'd never ask," bashfully says she. "Mabel."

"Nice to meet you, Mabel. I'm Lemuel, which you already known."

"Enchanté, all the same," she says, curtsying where she sat, and

I curtsied back.

We giggled clumsily and wiggled ourselves around. We got up and stretched and batted at the fog and sat back down and fell quiet. The fire responded with a snap, pop, and a crumble, casting its flames higher in elemental harmony. Yonder snuggled Mabel on her cape like she belonged to him.

I says, "Boy, he sure likes you a lot more now than he did when you was Strangitor."

"Yes. He sees I'm no threat to your love for each other. He's not sophisticated enough to see the difference between big love and little love, if you know what I mean."

I didn't, but I was too smart to ask. "Yes," I say. "Interesting."

"Are *you*?" she says.

"Interesting? I believe I am, to me, anyway."

She giggled like a chipmunk. "No, do *you* know the difference between big love and little love?"

"I certainly do. One's bigger."

She reached out and touched my face with the back of her warm, soft, knowing, and lanky-fingered hand. I heard a woodpecker somewhere. "Are you cold, Lemuel? I think you might be getting cold."

I realized that the woodpecker was my knees, chattering like coconuts.

Mabel stood and removed her cape with a bullfighter flourish, revealing a fetching mustard-colored pedal pusher ensemble that agreed with her moccasins. Before I knew it she had draped that precious dilapidated cape of hers—that she never let nobody else wear—right over my shoulders as sweet as you could be.

"Oh, no, no, wait, no, no," I say, "you couldn't, I shouldn't," but surprisingly I made no move to take it off. It bore a cozy wool lining and was sultry with her slightly funky mountain Mabelosity.

She ducked inside the wigwam and emerged with a orange blanket that she drooped over Yonder, who purred so loud you thought someone was emptying a ten-gallon water bottle into a horse trough. For herself she brought out a bright green parka that clashed pretty as Christmas with her snarled-up scarlet hair. She scrunched against the log a little closer to me and I felt happy as a natural born moron. It was good there on February Mountain with the campfire and my animal and this Mabel, and everything as explained as it needed to be for the nonce. Sometimes you didn't need to find out everything about somebody in order to find out everything you needed to find out. Or so I thought.

# 23.

Mabel stirred the fire and it popped and muttered in rebuttal. "So, Lemuel?" she says with a odd modesty. "It would have been gentlemanly of you to answer my letters."

So suddenly had she went sheepish, I assumed she meant *love* letters. Wowee. She must of been in love with me from afar and sending me mash notes, even though I never known she existed before today, except as Strangitor. I liked her some already, why not, we were conceited adults, and had a little mountain high going as well. But love letters before we even met? That was worse than Shane with her guy from Ambo. And speaking of the devil, had said love letters gotten shanghaied by a certain envy-ridden mayorial candidate/sister perhaps?

"What letters, Mabel?" Which was both coquettish and true, for I had never actually received them.

She looked at me funny. "Now that I think of it, can you even read?"

"*What?*"

"English."

"I mean, what *nerve*. Madame, I read more books backwards than you read forwards. I got a bookcase you couldn't sqwuck another book in with a shoehorn and a can of Crisco. I know more words than there *is* words. I have a framed requisition from Kafka to his boss asking for a new pencil sharpener." I don't know where that last one come from, I made it up.

She ignored my résumé. "Did you or did you not receive my letters about the deadline?"

Yonder had ceased purring under the orange blanket. His head fur begun to tense and darken. I eyed him with suspicion. Could *he* be the cause of the missing love letters? Had he ate them to keep her from coming between us?

"What deadline?" I wasn't only playing dumb now. "What would a deadline be doing in a love letter, whether I received it or not?"

"*Love* letter?" Mabel says. "Wait a minute. Remember that first ridiculous 'press conference' of yours in the backyard? You said, 'Yeah, sure!' when I asked you if you were going to meet the deadline."

I scoffed. "I couldn't make hide nor hair out of a word you said. I thought you were a wandering kook from the toolies. Anyway, you can't expect somebody to tell the truth at a press conference, whether they understand the question or not."

She closed her eyes and lowered her forehead to meet her hand. "He has no clue why I even came to Hmm," she says. I didn't particularly care for her talking about me to herself, or perhaps to the animal, not when I was sitting right there. "You have no idea what's happening, do you?" Yonder withdrewn like a turtle under his orange blanket.

I say, "If you're referring to me, I have a lot of ideas."

"Lemuel, did you hear *a single word* of the story I told you?" She brought her face over close and oogled me. "I've come to claim Yonder. He belongs to me. He and I are going on that bus trip around the world."

I backed away and stood up. "What? No, no, no. That yarn was about you and Uncle Leonard, not you and me."

She stood up and we faced off. "It's about you, it's about me, it's about Pop, it's about every person dead or alive on an old sad lost planet trembling and cracking with fear and fury. It's about every individual who needs Yonder like a hungry soul needs manna." She regarded me with a desperate pity. "Bless you, my dear Mr. Love Letter, but this animal is *mine*, and I'm taking him for a higher purpose."

"My eye!"

"All right. We can do this easy, as I've been trying to do, or, if you insist, we can do it rough. Please don't make the same dumb, fatal mistake my poor, dear, stubborn, raging stepfather made."

"Or what? I'll make any poor, dear, fatal mistake I want to. Your dumb stepfather was right about one thing—if you ain't got the brains to see Yonder was made to be a simple pet and not no world gadget, well, I do. That animal ain't going on no high-fa-luting bus tour. He'll blumber around Hmm getting in trouble with me for the rest of his unnatural life and that's that. He's *mine*. Leonard left me him fair and square."

"Not fair, not square, and most important—not *legal*." Mabel whipped out a singed paper from the rear pocket of her pedal pushers, unfolded it, and slapped it against my chest. The paper, not her pedal pushers. "This document supersedes whatever non-sense Pop might have babbled to some daft woodsman." I took the paper and read the goldang thing with growing flabberbastardness:

I, Leonard Victor Middleton, of sound mined and body, hearby leave all I got to my oonly child, knewn as Mabel, includeing stocks and bondes, equitys, the Unconsciouns Forreste, and everything in my home and hoseholt, includ-ing my experaments and their outcome, namely the one knowed as Yonder, such as he may be, so help me, Olde God. Yours' truely,

Unc had signed and dated it two weeks before he croaked, three weeks before Chuck delivered me the animal. "Oh, no," I whisper. I didn't know nothing about the stocks and equitys business, but I knew my stewardship of Yonder stood in grave jeopardy. I read the will again, my spirit fluttering like a motherless baby bird in a nest teetering over the abyss. The prospect of losing Yonder to Mabel and the world slain me. I was amazed how radical my cherishment for his darling mixed soul had come to be. "Oh, no."

"Oh, yes," Mabel whispers back, as if she cared what a war she had started inside me in the name of world peace.

Well, I awaked from my idiot's dream. This gal, this *Mabelitor*, had pulled one cruel romantic hoax, had waylayed my heart under false pretenses. Her and her nun cape, her breathtaking saga, her mustard pedal pushers, her rambunctious ruby hair, her bugfree porch light face, her chandelier laugh—all a big vulgar sham from topknot to moccasin.

"Pop illegally bequeathed Yonder to you," says Mabel, "to try to stop me from taking him on the tour. But it defied this his only legal will and testament. I hate to do it, Lemuel, because we were beginning to hit it off, and still may, depending how this goes, but I warn you: if you refuse to turn Yonder over to me, my attorneys will be on you like ketchup on French fries. That deadline was today. Right now."

"Never. Not today, last week, not never." I wrapped my arms around the blanket Yonder was hud under and slud him close to me. "Your attorneys can dip themself in batter and jump in the devil's frying pan. Was a word of that whole story true, or just bunkum to steal my heart and my animal?"

"All true, Lemuel, every word. Yes, I hoped it would persuade you to turn him over peacefully, but I did enjoy our lovely conversation, and I'd be offended if you thought otherwise. You're a unique fellow with helplessly captivating ways. I want Yonder not for me but for the world, and I'm also glad I'm getting to know you. My hope is that our tender beginnings could blossom into who knows what."

I fought the urge to believe her. "You're glad I'm getting to know you, but you have your ketchup lawyers waiting to jump on me like a French fry? Where are they, in the bushes with Strangitor? Oh, wait a minute, *you're* Strangitor, aren't you? Yes, yes. How does your mirror even look at you at night? You're nothing but a lowdown dirty rotten skunk of a miserable redhead scorpion of a backstabber pedal pushing rattlesnake of a—"

"All right, all right, please," she interrupts. "I'm sorry. Forget the lawyers. How about a million dollars instead?"

"—cabbage-gnawing Jezebel of a— How about a *what*?"

"One million dollars." She looked serious as a cop. "Let's make this simple and quick."

"Tsk, Madame. You should be ashamed to even joke about buying a priceless critter like this."

"I'm not joking. I am ashamed to drag money into it, but you forced my hand. And isn't world peace worth a little shame?"

"You should have started at, oh, ten thousand. I might of took you serious."

"Why pussyfoot around? You deserve every penny. You've had a tough peasant life. And now, my friend, your ship has come in."

I could feel Yonder under the blanket flopping and writhing at Mabel's brazen ploy.

"As if you really got a million dollars."

"Lemuel, you read the will. I inherited vast wealth from my stepfather."

"Vast wealth, my foot. You saw Unc."

"I saw Howard Hughes, too. It happens all the time, old coot in a hovel has secret fortune stashed. Way way back, according to his executor, Pop concocted a multi-use oil/polish out of treebark, tobacco, and termites. He sold the patent to Jackson & Jackson for a tidy sum and invested wisely."

"Unc had millions and left me toys and a pet?"

"Some pet. Even if he *didn't* leave it to you."

Under the blanket Yonder shuddered and rumbled like a rocket ship about to blast off. "Look, how do you figure some poor little oddball animal could bring anybody world peace?"

"He brought me world peace the second I laid eyes on him. He brought world peace to everybody at the park, didn't he? He brought you world peace but you're too stubborn to see it. His mere existence makes nothing impossible. Look, he's made you an instant millionaire." The temptress whipped out two more pieces of paper and handed them to me.

One was for me to permanently sign away all claims on Yonder. Good luck, Delilah. The other was a cashier's check for a million fat ones. It looked legit—a watermark, that big One followed by all those fat little zeros. I brang it to my nose to see if it had a stink of brimstone to it. Wooziness come over me. I say, "If this wasn't dirty money before . . . "

"What money isn't?"

I looked her straight in her spinach green eyes and we commenced a staredown by firelight, measuring one another's immortal souls.

I hiss, "What kind of a person *are* you?"

"What kind of a person are *you*?"

For all I knew, she was full of humbug without a dime to her name. She must of known I'd run this million-dollar scrap of hogwash past my financial advisers at Hmm First Bank & Mattress Shop. Of course, under no circumstances would I ever turn over any mixed animal of mine for money of any amount. On the other hand, what was the harm in rolling such a tantalizement around in your mind a while, as long as you had no serious intention of taking her up on it.

Before long, the staredown started getting to both of us. We sweated and twitched like warthogs in a sauna. I went queasy thinking about the million, and her tough gal smirk took on the quavers. I hid my miserable temptedness best that I could, while spiritual regret at her own sinister proposal squeezed a tear out of her evergreen eyes that now I noticed had a trace of crocodile in them.

Finally she blinked. I gave a snort of victory and we both sat down to rest. I returned my gaze to the check, running a fingertip over the stamped numbers casual like. I would give her some time to consider how much lower she could sink.

"Just think about it for a minute," Mabelitor says.

"I'm not thinking about anything for a minute," I say defiantly.

Well, well, well, I thought. Here was that famous windfall I'd been hankering for from the start, dropped in my lap like a big green bomb. All I had to do to be the richest person in Hmm was sell my dear Yondy down the river, into a life of homesickness, bus fumes, global potholes, public appearances and interviews, foreign take-out, and countless strangers in strange places gawking and grinning and poking at him and stealing his soul in the name of world peace.

Of course, with a million dollars I could hire a team of scientists to help me perfect the Yond-O-Lator. Then I would have the Yond-O-Lator without no Yonder, but I'd get rich again from the Yond-O-Lator and buy him back. Unless Mabel didn't want to sell, or worse, unless he didn't want to come back to the farm after being in gay Paree.

Under the blanket you could feel groaning tremblors pass through him from the intolerable uncertainty of the moment. His fate hung by the thread of my ramshackle ethics.

I remembered Mabel saying Yonder had been terrified of some ordeal he had to underwent in the future. Could that ordeal be this right here, getting bought and sold? But if he known this temptation would happen, why would he brang us up here? Had he knew I would turn her down? How could he, since I wasn't sure myself? Maybe he had a unnatural urge to march into the yawning mug of destiny, just to test and forge his individual soul. If so, what right did I have to stop him, simply because of my flimsy scruples? And as far as him missing me or me him if I did happened to sell him, we hadn't even knewn we existed till Chuck stuck him in the Helms truck and rushed him to Hmm, and we seemed to been doing more or less all right up to then, didn't we?

On one hand sat the mixed animal and economic insecurity. On the other sat world peace and a million dollars. Tick tock, tock tick . . .

"This is even lowdowner than your lawyers gambit," I diffidently declare.

"Is that so," says Mabel, regaining her hold on the situation as mine faltered.

"You actually think I'd sell Yonder for a lousy million dollars?"

"Hmp." She watched my qualms wobbling. She blatantly looked me over now, like a detective staring at a shifty sweaty stinking suspect about to crack.

There had to be a way I could come out of this with the animal and a bit of loot both. "Not that I'd ever do it," I say, "but what if I was to *lease* him to you for a week? For, say, oh, six hundred thou?" She eyeballed me with a expression like a shovel. I haggled: "Five hundred thou? A week of Yonder bringing peace to a country or two is better than no Yonder bringing nothing nowhere."

Mabel's face curdled with pity. "You don't get it, you poor sweet country muffin. I'm not leasing him. I'm not even buying him. He's mine already. I could get an injunction and grab him, but I'd like to avoid the court system for my own private reasons. And I'd like to ease your burden if possible, for any fool can see you've developed a fondness for the creature."

"He's not a creature! Don't call him a creature!" If I was going to contemplate renting out both my integrity and Yonder like a pair of used sleds, the least I could do was insist on better semantics.

"Decide," she says. "Choose."

"I choose to decide that you're a bad gal. You are a very, very, very bad, bad, bad gal."

"I *was*, yes. You'll never know how bad. Yes, I wasted half my life on fear, meanness and self-will run riot. But if God allows me to live the second half, I'll redeem myself by bringing peace to the world. In the meantime, I notice that you keep not rejecting my offer." She smiled and tapped the contract, like a gal Mephistopheles.

"I'll sign right there soon as dinosaurs ride down Main Street on bicycles built for two. You known not what you're doing, Mabel. Nobody good would use cash nor insult nor lawyers to acquire a dear soul like Yonder, not even to bring peace to earth, much less the universe."

She raised her hand as if to catch a bug and brought it down smack on the mountain floor. "Damn it, Lemuel. Your simpleness is otherworldly!" My stubbornly wavering morals was getting to her. "If you still have the measly brains your village God stuffed in your thick skull, you'll grab the million and liberate Yonder to fulfill his divine purpose. You'll be working for world peace just by sitting around the garden watering your rutabagas and collecting interest. You know, you could buy a whole lot of mustard seeds for a million dollars."

Boy, could you ever. My morals was crumbling like crackers over a bowl of Shameless Soup. "Now, let's see, one more time—just *exactly* how is a weird little fella like Yonder going to bring world peace to the world again?"

"You're stalling."

"Specifically, if you may."

She sighed. "Simply by being himself."

"I don't believe it. World peace by being himself? Unpossible."

"You have to believe something impossible every now and then, Lemuel, just to wake your sleeping soul. The impossible part of everything is the very part that makes faith in it worthwhile. Try it, see what happens. Yonder makes you believe it—the impossible—just by being, just by being himself."

Under the blanket Yonder quaked at the existential crossroads of minding his own business versus saving the world. He didn't have nobody but me to protect him from her crusade.

"*Anybody* could be their *self*," I sneer. "It's the easiest thing in the world to do."

"You might be surprised. Anyway, there's no self like his self. People will be transformed by his stubbornly unambitious charisma, by the baffling wonderful things he does and doesn't do. They'll want to get near him so much that they'll completely forget about their fear and their greed and their going to war with each other."

"What if they fear and they greed and they go to war with each other precisely in order to be the ones that get near him the closest and quickest?"

From her nervous blink you could see she had never considered that possibility. She wasn't half as smart as I thought she was, but she kept trying to act like I did. "Stop stalling," she says. "Sign.

Don't think about it, just sign. You know you're going to eventually, so get it over with"

"Don't we need to book motels and convention centers years in advance for a world tour?"

"*We*? Look, I've had it with you. Take the million or leave it. He's mine already. I'm doing this out of the goodness of my heart."

"No, you're not." I'd had it with me, too. "You're doing it because you're lousy with guilt about bad things you done in the past, but this evil Machiamillion scheme is worse than the worst thing you done before *ever*."

She jumped to her feet. "If you really loved Yonder, you'd beg me to take him for his own sake and the sake of the world!"

I jumped to mine. "If you really loved world peace, you'd start right here and leave me and him the hell alone!"

"Love means stop thinking of your damn self for one second."

"World peace means minding your own business."

At that moment, the orange blanket twitched terribly. The animal popped his paws out and again made that same moving, silly, enigmatic "Here's the church, here's the steeple, open the doors and see all the people" tableau that little children make to amuse themself.

"Not now, Yonder," I counsel. "I'm trying to save your fate from this ruthless Mabel."

"Yonder's fate is set in stone," says her. "What we're deciding is *your* fate. You go down this mountain broke as a wishbone, or else rolling in remuneration."

What finally did it was not her satanic offer to buy the animal (which, after all, was only capitalism at its finest), but her plain old-fashion pushiness. I got my fill of pushy people at home with Shane and Yonder. I didn't need any more of it on my vacation.

"If you're going to tempt somebody," I say, "don't push them around at the same time."

But Mabel just pushed on: "I'm two seconds from snatching my rightful animal and leaving you in the poor house where I found you."

"Try it. You'll find out pronto what world peace is all about."

By then we were in the other's nose, set to start knocking ourself around the clearing. I wouldn't never hit a gal in any situation, but what if she ripped her Mabel mask off and underneath was the real Strangitor all along, and there I'd be getting torn asundered simply because I was a gentleman.

"Bottom line," I say. "Yonder's mine."

"No, he's not, he's mine."

"Oh, man, if you wasn't a gal."

"If you weren't a thick recalcitrant rube."

That wasn't a very good insult. I believed "recalcitrant" meant second-hand vitamin pills. "Then you're a phony ex-nun with a screw loose in a flea-bit cape that would stoop to any length." Except for one thing—I had on her flea-bit cape.

"You're a savage hayseed who doesn't deserve to own a genius animal that was made to serve the highest human principles!"

"You got morals lower'n a polecat for trying to buy him!"

"You got morals lower than a wolverine for denying world peace!"

"You don't care about world peace, you just want to win this encounter!"

"What? Your so-called 'love' for Yonder is nothing but obstinate self-centeredness!"

I gasped. "You wouldn't know world peace if it kicked you in the pants!"

We went on till we were screaming and spewling like gargoyles come to life. We was nothing but a cavecouple drooling and howling, not one decent intention between us. Our veins stuck out like gopher tunnels in our foreheads and necks. Our words raged like war and rumors of war in that little fogbound campfire mountainside clearing. Wild animals for miles around were shaking in their boots, wondering what the battle was about and when it would end and what would be left of us afterwards for them to pick through for a late-night snack.

# 24.

We would have commenced raining blows upon ourselves, but Yonder, in order to escape our hateful caterwailing, begun to crawl toward the dark treeline, the orange blanket covering him still.

"Look what you made him do!"

"Me?" says Mabel. "You're scaring the devil out of him!"

The edge of Yonder's blanket snagged on a stake of the wigwam and began to pull off him as he slithered away, and as it did, it revealed inch by inch some grisly type of transformation that had been transpiring over him and which now our eyeballs strove in vain to fathom.

"What *is* that?" Mabel wails. "That's not Yonder!"

"No," I say, "that can't be Yonder."

But it was. On his belly Yonder writhed across the clearing floor, too impaired to stand and walk. What we beheld was the pity-ridden, horrorful, and heart-wretching spectacle of a fellow being that had his whole biology literally wrested inside-out by a suffering that you prayed was not caused by you, though you damn well known it was, and shrieks of guiltful anguish issued from my and Mabel's souls.

Somehow Yonder had been atomically degenerated by our screaming match. So sensitive was he to rancor between his beloveds, his very fundament had underwent a ravaging reversal. In other words, his body no longer included any external substance covering his physical insides.

Steam rose off the animal in sheets from the cold mountain air meeting his exposed warm-blooded innards.

That is, you could see his entire interior exactly as if he hadn't no fur nor skin nor blubber to protect him from anything in the world, because that's precisely it—he didn't have none. Yondy's muscles, arteries, brains, nerves, and all his other private inner organs and gizmos had surfaced in appalling response to me and Mabel battling over him in the name of our highest concepts and principles.

The critter crawled laboriously toward the safety of the freezing darkness, away from us and the campfire and our ideals. His bare heart hammered at his ribs like a little steaming red sun pounding at a white cage.

The vision was so horrodious you felt like you weighed ten thousand pounds with the knowledge that you caused it, and couldn't do nothing to uncause it. It was too late. We had spake what we had spoke, hated and shrieked what we had hated and shrieked, and now our eyes and minds were breaking upon the rocks of the consequence.

Worse, in that half a moment we stood there paralyzed, my horror told me if I touched him, I would get it myself—my skin and fur and blubber would disappear, too. O, mad, selfish, loathsome, cowardly terror that for even a moment overcame my concern for Yonder.

I grabbed the discarded blanket, dreading that his coverings was stuck to it, but no—only blanket. Mabel and I rushed and grabbed our desperate darling Yondy before he vanished into the cold foggy February Mountain wilderness night forever.

We swooped up our repulsive sweetheart from the clearing floor and embraced him like a raw slab of misery in a sandwich of repugnant love. All our bygones about who owned who vanished.

We hugged the helpless fellow like a 75-pound boiled potato. His whole body hissed as the icy night stang his helpless nude internals. Like a newborn baby alien he twisted and mewled in our arms.

"Did things stick to him?" Mabel blubbers. She meant from crawling over the clearing floor. We turned him over and he was clean as a whistle, just gleamy wet innards. The dirt, pine needles, bugs, and mountain guck had impossibly refused to add to his woe.

A flurry of fireflies swept out of the fog and surrounded the poor animal and us, criss-crossing in formation like a fretful net of protective blinking lights. Cries and groans of mountain beasts came at us from every angle of the feral darkness, and the foliage crackled with their stricken prancing. Owls and other night birds swerved over the clearing on watch. You could feel the whole mountain spinning and reeling in protest of Yonder's agony.

We held him and cooed his name, for what else could we do? His whimpering, contortions, and dimming eyes told you to tell him it would be all right, though so much was the horror, the horror, that you could barely speak to lie, but we lied for all we were worth.

I hate to confess I had a terrible case of the willies holding his naked pokey white ribs and wriggling purple liver and so on against me, as if he was butchered, and I made little grunts and squeals and gags of involuntary abhorrence and trying to not throw up, which I hoped Mabel would take as cries of compassion.

I hoped our germs weren't invading him. His sweet frightened heart we watched a-pound and his speeding lungs a-going up in down trying to get air and all the other pulsating what-have-yous. It astounded me what kept his myriad parts from falling out in our hands or thumping onto the mountain floor.

"How could this happen?" Mabel asks, then answers, "We did this! We made this happen to him! Yondy, oh, Yondy! How are we going to get him all the way down off the mountain to a doctor in time?"

The only doctors in 200 miles, Transplant Anderson and the vet Ralphie Munch, was likely passed out drunk somewhere, or off playing checkers. "What could a doctor do anyway, if we don't even have the skin and fur and blubber to sew back on?"

"Yeah, where'd it go? And if they did have other skin, it would never mix with his DNA. Although how did his heart transplant work?"

I hadn't thought of that. "Maybe we're just having a hideous nightmare. Maybe you got holt of a bad cabbage and we're seeing things. Or that trout water! Maybe this ain't even happening."

"Oh, it is." Mabel took my finger, slipped it right between Yonder's ribs and poked his thrombulating heart. I shrieked. "Oh, Lemuel, if only we could reverse time and take back what we did and said!"

"If he would only come back to normal, you could take him around the world on that awful bus tour if you want."

"No, you keep him right here in poor little Hmm where you think he belongs."

"Do you hear that, Old God? We give up what we want. Just give Yondy his regular body self back again!"

But nothing happened, and in fact Yonder took a turn for the worst, gasping and shuddering like his little mixed motor was on its last leg.

"Oh, please, please, please, Old God!" I holler.

"Oh, please, please, please, anybody!" cries Mabel.

You could feel your darling shaking like the last leaf on the tree. Plus, he was getting so heavy you thought your arms was going to pull out of your shoulder sockets.

"Somebody tell us what to do!" I pray. "Old God, animals,

trees, mountain top, fog!"

Wild fauna poked their heads in and out of the clearing, a choir of animal caterwailing at Yonder's affliction. I hoped they didn't turn on us for our part in it.

Our beloved critter made sounds that could only be interpreted as a soul and a body groaning at the crossroads of a life that ain't ready to pass on and a life that can't stand no more the pain that it was in.

"Hold him," Mabel says. I did and she begun CPR, cupping his hairless skinless snout to breathe air in and gently pressing his ribcage over his lungs to ease it out. She tried it till Yonder shook his head and howled.

I say, "We got to wrap him in something, he's losing his life heat."

"Here," Mabel says. We opened our coats and hugged him to our body warmth, then wrapped the blanket around us all and drew to the fire close as we could. You still felt life fleeing from him, with wailing accompaniment.

"I can't stand it!" Mabel says.

I got so crazy desperate I looked around for a rock. "Maybe we're suppose to start thinking if whether to put him out of his misery."

"No!" says Mabel, then softer, "No."

Yonder screeched with tribulation, piercing the night with his wild compadres in a desolate harmony. We had to shout over their lamentations.

"He's so suffering so!" says Mabel.

"We have to do *something*."

"It'll be too horrible!"

"It's too horrible now."

Mabel held him on her lap while I found a likely rock, the size of a heart, and came back and raised it over him before I could think.

"No!" says Mabel.

I lowered the rock and held it to my chest.

Yonder groaned and tossed like a ship getting ripped in two on a reef. His pangs lashed you like whips.

"Do it," Mabel says. "Quick! Quick!"

I raised the rock again. "Yondy, little pal, forgive us for what we done."

"And are about to do."

"Don't look, close your eyes."

She closed hers but his reached for me like dying flames.

"Old God," I say, "if you don't want us to do this, please send a sign. We can't let your poor little mixed animal named Yonder suffer no more. Right or wrong, we can't. So, speak now, please, or forever hold your peace."

I was looking for a lightning bolt to rise out of the east and knock the rock out of my hand, or a band of angels to waft over the foggy treetops tooting on bugles.

But nothing happened.

Except for one thing.

Namely, the appearance of a very certain stink. That is, a unique and unmistakable aroma that was about as far from the majesty of lighting bolts and angels tooting bugles as you could get. In fact, a odor that once you smelt it, you never forgot it.

In other words, it was *rotten pipe smoke*, and not just any rotten pipe smoke.

Mabel and I took one whiff and looked at each other with the undeniable knowledge of exactly what that infernal stink was.

Specifically, we smelt the putrid tobacco of dead Uncle Leonard's pipe. Don't ask me how, why, or wherefore.

And not only did she and me smell it, Yonder did, too.

He ceased howling. He stopped shaking, trembling, and tossing about. He sat up in our arms, sniffed the night air, listened and surveyed, alive and alert as a sentry to something that was bigger than the torment of having nor skin nor fur nor blubber. Something more important and powerful than death itself had entered the mountain clearing.

# 25.

Hello and behold, so transfixed were we three by the stupefying pipe reek that, before we realized it, Yonder's outer belongings had begun coming back on. We were eyeing the treeline for the source of the stench when, like the sparrows returning to Capistrano, the animal's personal coverings slowly but surely commenced growing back somehow. We felt him stirring in our arms and looked down.

"What's *that*?" I shriek.

"Fat!" Mabel cries. "Hallelujah!"

Yonder, near death a minute before, chittered as his blubber re-materialized like white pudding around his palpitating inscape. You wouldn't believe such a naushating event could bring you such ecstasy. It was a miracle—a revolting, disgusting miracle.

"Look, his pink skin," says Mabel. "His coat!" His beloved fur sprouted from his skin like red and yellow grass from pink turf, sparkling and fluffy as if straight from the laundry.

"Here he comes, come on, Yonder!" I say. "Look at you, boy! You're coming back!"

The critter experienced this transformation with shifting expressions of infant wonder and death-defying exhaustion. Mabel sobbed to beat the band, and we both jibbered apologies to each other and to Yonder for the hatefest that had turned him inside-out.

The fireflies peeled away one by one, while the multitude of yowling mountain beasts calmed and rustled away into the underbrush. We sniffed the air for the pipe stank, in vain, for it had dissipated as quick as it come.

Yonder further responded to these tempestuous events by falling asleep in our laps like a sack of cement. Nobody never earned a nap better than him right then.

Me and Mabel knelted on the mountain floor, our Yondy in our arms snoring like a muffled jackhammer. We sobbed and slobbered our thanks to Old God that watches over all inside-out mixed animals everywhere, at the very least.

\*

We spent the night in the wigwam, the three of us. It was cozy, somewhat giddy in the aroma department, and bewildered with weariness. I maneuvered the dormant Yonder in between me and Mabel in case she got any big ideas. Not that I was too big to have a few myself, for I was, but I planned to be too gentlemanly to act on it, with mountain thunder rumbling and the foliage rustling all night with Yonder's pals making sure he was okay.

Mabel and me dodged the topic of who would be in charge of him once we got off the mountain. Yes, I had declared in a panic that she could take him on her bus tour, but she'd promised the same about me keeping him in Hmm. I didn't say it, but he wasn't getting on no bus. He hadn't survived the disaster only to be swept away on her wacky peace scheme.

"You know that smell?" Mabel says. "That tobacco? It was Pop's."

"Yep. Except it couldn't of been."

"It couldn't, but it was."

"He's dead, buried, and don't smoke no more," I remind her.

"It sure seemed like the sign you asked for."

"What if we'd had colds and couldn't of smelled it?"

Mabel put on her imagination cap: "Perhaps some forest vagabond stole a chunk of Pop's stash from the burned cabin and was hiking around here puffing on it and we got a whiff."

"That would be some coincidence. The vagabond swipes Unc's tobacco, then hikes hundreds of miles away where his step-daughter and nephew was camping to puff on it."

"How do we explain the effect it seemed to have had on Yonder? The stink snatched him from death's door and restored him like turning a spigot. Of course, that could be a coincidence, too."

"That's a lot of coincidences," I say.

We lain on our backs in our sleeping bags and thought about coincidences and mysteries, or at least I did, while Yonder snoozed in between. Everything was calm and collegial. The animal even turned down his snoring, like the bubble machine in a fish tank.

"I hope he taught us quite a lesson," Mabel says.

"Even if he didn't know what he was doing."

By then all the fog had wandered off, and a yonder of stars huddled at the smoke hole in the top of the wigwam.

"Look," says the gal. "They're snooping on us."

"We don't mind," I say. "Or least I don't."

She laughed like a little fire burbling. It was a most pleasant atmosphere to ponder impossibles in, as you drifted into a well-earned slumber with no resistance nor reservation. Adventure, a new gal, tragedy diverted, a revived Yonder, world peace, and love is one thing; a good night's sleep is something else.

*

We slept like three buckets of coal and rose with the sun for a so-call breakfast of more raw cabbage, plus fresh-squeezed mulberry juice. It was a feast compared to how hungry I was, as long as I didn't picture a plate of steaming buttered hotcakes drenched with melted candy bars.

Yonder seemed none the worse for wear, running about and monkeying in the foliage with who known what other fauna gals and pals, just like nothing happened.

We packed up and broke camp. The wigwam turned out to be inflatable and squeezed down to the size of a lampshade, which we strapped to Yonder's head. Him and her started down the mountain, while I took a moment to drink in the enchanting vision of my home village far below in the glow of sunrise. There sat little Hmm, in the disconcerting shape of Founder Lula's missing foot, a tiny herd of cottages and farms in the green teacup of the ancient valley. Puffy pink clouds floated above it like bunny slippers, only new and fresh, not worn and smelly. You missed your village, looking at it like that, with people too small to even see, much less bug you. You couldn't wait to hike down and get home. You was thankful you could dwell there your whole life, and not have to venture into the great unknown of the non-Hmm world beyond, where unfamiliar, unbeseen, and untowards things could happen at any moment.

Lickety-split we hiked down February Mountain. Going home was always quicker than going someplace you'd never been. Plucking mulberry seeds out of our teeth while Yonder scouted ahead for the most difficult path down, me and Mabel decided that she ought to accompany us to the cottage and climb in the attic to see if she had any insights on what Yonder was up to there. Of course, that was one of the mysteries I'd been led to believe we had clumb the mountain to find out. It just goes to show—never follow a mixed animal anywhere unless you're sure what for, and even then don't count on it.

# 26.

We traipsed through downtown Hmm like three grimy banditos of happiness. The village stopped to give us the once over. I felt manly, mysterious and hep, until somebody shouts, "Your fly's open, Lem!" I looked before I could stop myself and everybody laughed, then they roared greetings and love at Yonder and ignored Mabel and I.

Even though he just been knocking on Heaven's door, the animal found enough energy to walk behind me on his back legs, imitating my distinctive amble, and swinging his arms around like I do when I'm making a important point—plus he still wore the wigwam lampshade tied to his head. The village went delirious. I was so relieved he was still around to make fun of me that I chuckled a little myself just to be a good sport.

*

When we walked in the cottage, Shane was snoring away on the couch like a helicopter ready for take off. Pieces of scrap paper with insane scrawlings on them blew around the room.

Yonder trotted over there and slapped his flapjack tongue around on her sweaty troubled unconscious face a bunch of times. Maybe he thought it was a bowl of milk. Naw, I guess he missed her, hadding almost expired on the mountain, never to see her big round sarcastic mug again. It failed to awaken her. All she did was go, "Louisious Betts, you bad Ambo boy!" When Yonder had enough, he strutted out to the kitchen where you could hear water sloshing around from him and his bowl, likely to wash out the taste of Shane's face.

"Hey, Shane," I say. "Snap out of it!" I gave the couch a good swift kick. "You're not making a very good first impression on Mabel here."

Shane came to and jumped up. "Where am I? What day is it?" Her hair was flat as a pan on one side and sticking up like turkey feathers on the other. "Ooo!" She had a frantic itch on her backbone she couldn't reach. "I-yi-yi!" She grabbed the TV antenna to scratch it. "Hey, where have *you* been?"

"February Mountain," I say.

"What were you doing up on that god-forsaken alp?"

"I went up to confront Strangitor and find out what Yonder is doing in the attic, but I ran into Mabel here, that I thought was Strangitor's impostor, but she's actually our step-cousin-in-law, not blood. Get this—Unc was married and had a wife that invented the turniloupe. Then Mabel and me got in a awful tiff, Yonder's externals disappeared, came back when we smelt Unc's pipe, and here we are."

"Turniloupe?" Shane says. She plunked back on the couch and got a snooty sidewise look that meant another gal's in the house. I should of knewn. She rudely pointed right at Mabel like she wasn't even there. "Step-cousin-in-law, you say?"

"But no blood. She's been meditating and fasting for her bad past and world peace. Mabel, Shane. Shane, Mabel."

"Enchanté, to be sure," says Mabel. She curtsied out of nervousness. "I like your outfit."

Shane looked down to see what she had on. It appeared to be pink long-johns and a lime cashmere chemise, with peds on her tootsies and a red cowboy bandana around her neck backwards.

"Oh, this old thing," Shane says. She caught herself getting flattered, looked Mabel up in down, then squinted back in forth between me and her, grinning sacreligiously and nodding. "Aha," she mutters.

"It's no aha," I say. "There ain't no aha."

By then Yonder had returned and sat there blatantly eavesdropping on us like we was a public access TV show.

"Where's she supposedly from, anyway?" Shane asks me.

"Greater Pertelote," says Mabel.

"Oh, *Greater Pertelote*," snorts Shane. "Hmph." She sniffed the air, made a face, and faked choking. "Boy, your whole wild bunch could use a hosing off." Then she caught the clock and blurts, "Oh, no! I missed the next debate with Shuffleboard! On foreign policy, my forté! I slept right through it! I'm finished!"

"Shane's running for mayor," I explain to Mabel.

"Oh, congratulations. I'm sorry you missed your debate."

"I bet you are." Shane sneered openly at Mabel. "You're not one of Shuffleboard's spies, by chance." Before Mabel could respond, Shane started crying. "Oh, what do I care. Spy till the cows come home. My candidacy is kaput. Look at all these original jokes I made up for the debate." She meant the scrap paper all over the floor. "I was going to clobber him with one-liners." She grabbed one and read: "It's good you take bribes to spend on dope, shady tarts, and offshore bank accounts, or else you'd have drained the Hmm treasury even faster than you did."

"That's a five-liner," I say, "in search of a punchline. Do you have solid proof of all them foul rumors?"

Shane snorted. "I only need flimsy proof of *one* of those foul rumors, then everybody will believe the rest. Oh, why am I talking to you and your new hussy about the nuances of democracy? I missed the debate. I'm ruined. I'll be lucky to get my *own* vote now."

At that, Yonder ceased eavesdropping, took off out the window, and's gone.

"My own staff is jumping overboard to get away from me," says Shane.

"Now that's a one-liner," I say.

Shane flipped on the TV, flopped on the couch, and grabbed a soggy leftover bowl of New Little Doughnuts Cereal with Free Extra Vitamins and Minerals from the coffee table, droobling it down her chemise as she drowned her sorrows.

I shook my head out of compassion and disgust. "Me and Mabel are going up in the attic now."

"Who cares?" Shane says. Tears built in her eyes as she watched "The Lost Dinosaurs of Egypt" on the History Channel. She mutters, "It's back to fortune-telling for Shane Washington, trounced mayoral candidate." Then she broadcasted a belch, long and mournful.

I'd had it, even for her. "Could you control your manners once and a while?"

"I'm in no mood to control my manners. My lifelong dream of being mayor of Hmm just crashed and burned like a sack of dog-doo. So lump my manners, you and your fancy little gal pal from Pertelote there."

Ooo, boy, I thought. Have a little mercy on your numbskull sister and her burning sack of dog-doo dreams. But I'm afraid I couldn't help myself. "You know, it might not be a good time to bring this up," I say, "but it turns out Uncle Leonard was quite the malty-millionaire through various investments after inventing a certain polish out of treebark and termites. Stocks, bonds, diamonds, oil fields, stamps, horses, baseball teams." Mabel raised a eyebrow at my embellishments. "He even owned the Unconscious

Forest! He had millions and billions! Who would of reckoned, eh? In other words, that measly pittance he left you—the one you keep rubbing my nose in—that weren't nothin' but chump change to the old rascal. What do you think of those raspberries?"

"I never heard such bilgewater in my life," says Shane. "Who told you such bilgewater?"

"Never mind who told me such bilgewater. But since you insist, Mabel told me such bilgewater." I pointed at Mabel with my thumb. "His step-daughter."

Shane looked Mabel over like a rattler looking over Minnie Mouse. "Is that true?"

"Yes, ma'am," says Mabel.

"Who got it?"

I started to say Mabel inherited the whole kaboodle, but the gal pinched my elbow. She was right, I had almost went too far. Shane would hate Mabel forever more, and might even try and sabotage me from scrounging a date out of this travesty.

"Oh, some distant old pal of his nobody heard of," I say. "Lucky bum."

You could see the injustice sinking into Shane like a old car into a swamp. She sqwuck her tears back into her eyes, and started chomping her cereal and peering knives at "The Lost Dinosaurs of Egypt."

I felt sorry for her suddenly, but I wasn't about to look wishy-washy in front of Mabel. I decided to feel sorry for her after Mabel left. Then I thought about missing Mabel and started feeling sorry for myself, and that made me feel better.

# 27.

I gathered up some good condensed reading material, including *Gopherwood: The Miracle Material, From Birdhouses to Arks*; *The Cloud of Unknowing*; *Gargantua and Pantagruel*; *Dictionary of Problem Words and Expressions*; *Don Quixote*; *The Kingdom Within*; *Waiting for Godot*; *Collected Nancy and Sluggo*; *Myth and Method: Modern Theories of Fiction*; *House of the Seven Gables*; *Fix It Now or Never, or Tomorrow*; *A Good Man Is Hard To Find*; *Heraclitus: Half-Thoughts on Flux*; *The Flag the Hawk Flies*; *Confederacy of Dunces*; *On God and Dogs*; *Zen and the Birds of Appetite*; *Little Red Riding Hood*; *Oranges for Magellan*; *Go Tell It on the Mountain*; and *1,000 Pancake Recipes*, placed them in a stack in the bathtub, and me and the appealingly dextrous Mabel clambed up on them into the attic through the trapdoor.

I lit us the lantern and Mabel gasped at her first sight of Yonder's audacious, sprawling enterprise.

"Land sakes alive," she says, strolling from mound to remarkable mound. "Land sakes alive." Then she got a load of the blueprint on the table. "Splendid," she whispers, scratching herself here and there. She puzzled over that conglomeration of signs and symbols, peering, going, "Hmm. Hmm."

It didn't take her two minutes to come up with a outlandish theory about what the animal had been building. She kept studying and tapping the big YONDEЯ at the top of the blueprint.

"*Yonder*," mummers Mabel.

"What about him?" asks me.

"He's trying to build Yonder."

"He *is* Yonder."

"He's building *another* Yonder."

"No, no, no, no, no," I say.

"That's what this blueprint is—Pop's comprehensive formula for Yonder, for the creation of the mixed animal. And this astounding array," she says, sweeping her nubile arm over the throng of objects surrounding us, "is Yonder's artful if deranged interpretation of Pop's hieroglyphics from the blueprint. He's trying to duplicate what Pop did. Yonder is attempting to invent a second himself."

"That's outrageously unacceptable! I thought he was trying to build a space ship, or make gold out of odds-in-ends. Why in tarnation would he build another one of *himself*?"

"A wild guess? He's lonely."

"Lonely? He is not lonely!"

"He just wants a companion, one of his own kind. You know, to hang out with."

"He hangs out with me. He don't need no companion of his own kind."

"Apparently he feels different."

"I wouldn't invent another myself if it was the last thing I did. One of me is already twice as many as I asked for."

"But you have many other fellow creatures to keep you company—people—who are just like you, more or less. All he has is himself. There's nobody else like him. Imagine that—the only mixed animal in an unmixed world."

Every time I learned something new it was like the first time I ever learned anything, so I liked to put up a fight if I could. "He's trying to build another hisself," I mummer. I took a brand new look around the attic. Each and every preposterous item was now imfused with Yondy's pitiful yearning for a second himself. What poignant self-centered gallantry!

Then the dangers of Yonder's project sprang at me like lions and tigers. I declare, "We got to destroy this madman blueprint."

Mabel slapped her hands on it and give me the eye. "As if it were ours to destroy."

"Whose is it? He stole it from Uncle Leonard, and Uncle Leonard's dead. This whole project is imnormal, abmoral, and unlegal as you can get. You need fifty science permits to clone anything, much less yourself. And what if evil forces got holt of it and recreated a army of him to spew across the countryside?"

Mabel nodded at me like Professor Socrates, meaning she weren't buying it. "As far as cloning goes, the resulting creature would turn out to be a different specie each time, depending on where you retrieved the sample chromosome from. I asked Pop how many species were in the animal. He said he lost count at thirty-three. You could clone him and come up with any one of those thirty-three, or more, but never another him. Yonder defies quality control. Besides, would it be so bad to have countless Yondies running around? It sure would make—would have made my ex-job of world peace a lot easier."

"It'd make my job as the owner and protector of the only Yonder around a lot harder."

"But nobody would bug you about your one and only Yonder because he'd be everywhere."

"There's only one Yonder, there's only suppose to be one, and he's mine."

"Mmm," Mabel says. She ran her hand over the blueprint. "Who could ever make sense of this? No, the secrets of this venture went to the grave with Pop. If Yonder thinks I could help him interpret this, help him recreate himself—because I'd been there at the beginning—he's sadly mistaken. All the scientists in the world couldn't put another Yonder together. Although,... unless,... if..." She touched her forehead, says, "It's warm," swayed, keeled over, and I caught her in the nook of time.

With my bum back it was no way I'd get even her fragile figure down from the attic without seriously damaging us both. I did manage to get holt of her in a decent manner and drug her over to the trapdoor.

"Shane! Help! Mabel fainted from the heat and the fuss!"

I expected my angst-wallowing sister to ignore me or dilly-dally. To my shock, she came running like Florence Nightingale and commandeered the entire rescue operation. Maybe she was hopped up on New Little Doughnuts Cereal.

She mounted the stack of books and lifted Mabel down easy as a balsa doll. Hoisting her over her shoulder, Shane lugged her down the hall to her own room and dumped her in her own dang bed. Then she got a whiff of the gal's mountain scent and toted her back to the bathroom, slammed the door in my face and turned on the shower full blast.

After a minute, Shane opened the door to issue orders: "Change the sheets on my bed! Pillowcases, too!" That's a gal's job, but I did it, so grateful was I that she had rented a heart from someplace.

After while they come out with Mabel bedecked in a fresh wool nightgown of Shane's, the one with the bunnies hopping around carrying tommyhawks and the Bill of Rights all over it in red script back and front. Shane led her patient to her room, tucked her in, and dashed to the kitchen.

I had the opportunity to observe Mabel from the doorway. She was already about 72 percent inside Dreamland. She sparkled clean. Shane had brushed her long red hair back and it looked like a strawberry waterfall going over the pillow. She tried to open her sleepy eyes to look back at me. "Your sister's nice," she mummers.

"Yeah, getting clobbered for mayor has sweetened her up like punch." I was acting the tough guy to keep from making a fool of myself by expressing the wrong romantic notion too soon.

Shane came charging back in with a fresh bowl of New Little Doughnuts Cereal with Free Extra Vitamins and Minerals and pulled up a chair next to the bed.

I protest, "You can't feed that garbage to a gal that just fainted."

"Hush," Shane says. "I added tofu chunks to it." She proceeded to spoonfeed the slop to Mabel until the pale redhead gal that stole into my life and cottage fell asleep and started snoring like the sweetest little brook that ever babbled over pebbles since time began.

Shane and me snucked quietly out of the room, leaving the door open a crack like everybody likes it in that situation.

"What's wrong with that gal?" says Shane.

"She's wore out. She's got a barnful of ideals she's totin' around."

"That's no good."

"Somebody's gotta do it. Thanks for being so unexplicably nice to her."

"Just thinking ahead."

"To what?"

"Voter registration deadline day."

"She don't even live in Hmm."

"She does now. That means I'll get at least three votes."

"You, her, and . . . Yonder can't vote."

Right then who came throwing hisself against the front door but the very animal. I opened up and he charged past me like he seen a ghost. He had on a red vest, he stunk of cigars, his fur was full of burrs, bugs, and sawdust, and he carried in his mouth a big old paper bag packed with something lumpy. He ran around in circles, dropped the bag at Shane's feet, leaped up in the bookcase and sat there watching the front door, jumping like a mouse trap at every noise.

"I smell trouble," Shane says. She peeked in the bag and gasped. Reaching in, she pulled out a fist of one-hundred dollar bills. New one-hundred dollar bills. Brand new one-hundred dollar bills.

"Where did you *get* this?" Shane asks Yonder. He pointed at the door with the top of his head.

We dumped the bag on the floor and counted it with building unbelievableness. It came to 80,000 dollars on the nose.

Just as I noticed there was some sort of green stuff on my hands, Shane goes, "What's this?" and pulled out a piece of paper from underneath the dough. "It's a receipt. From that stuck-up Marvin Wopper over at the *Hmm Gazette*, made out to 'Mayor Buck Shuffleboard Humphrey.'"

"Receipt for what?"

She read: "For . . . 'Eighty thousand dollars.'"

"Shuffleboard *bought* eighty thousand dollars? For how much?"

She looked at the receipt again. "Five hundred." She slapped her forehead so hard I felt it myself. "You know what this is?"

"One heck of a deal," I declare. "How could they sell money at such a discount?" I was using my kerchief to try and rub that green gunk off my hands. "What the dickens? This looks like stinkbug juice."

"It's the ink, stupid."

"Ink? From what? The money? Well, it must be *really* new if the ink's still wet."

Shane wore a starry look like her ship had just come in. "So, the publisher of the *Hmm Gazette* has been churning out funny money on his printing press and Shuffleboard's been funding his whole campaign with it. Bingo, baby. Bingo."

"What? Why, that would be so illegal nobody would even think of it."

She gave me a look of contemptuous awe. "Bro, you are the perfect ideal voter every politician dreams about."

Before I could protest with false humility, we heard a gang of footsteps clamoring up the stairs, followed by a rude pounding that about knocked the door off its hinges. I was afraid it would wake up poor Mabel.

We peeked out: on the veranda stood the very aforementioned duo, *Hmm Gazette* publisher Marvin Wopper and ancientarian Mayor Shuffleboard Humphrey. They held onto each other for support, sweating and wheezing from climbing the stairs. It was the first honest work either of them done all year.

Shane whispers to me, "I'll hide the dough, you hide the animal." She did and I started to, but the bookcase where Yonder had been was already full of his no longer being there. Burrs, sawdust, flailing insects, and wisps of fur drifted to the floor in his wake.

I answered the door. "Marvin! Shuffleboard! My favoritest people on the whole porch."

"Lemuel," pants Shuffleboard. "Our favorite fix-it lad." Shane popped up behind me. "And Ms. Washington, my worthy little adversary. You're a living tribute to your family and the female race, Sugarplum."

"Say," says Marvin, "did that dear sweet pet of yours happen to accidentally bring home a certain paper bag that he may have mistakenly stolen in broad daylight from under our table at Elroy's Bar & Grill & Dentistry?"

"Why, let me go check, Marvin," says Shane. "Hmm, a certain

paper bag, a certain paper bag." She gave me a wink and headed for the hallway. "Invite our upstanding friends in, Bro." I heard her dial the operator and whisper, "Sheena, get me the police, pronto." That meant old Constable Boris Drake, that his wife Hazel would have to pry out of his hammock first.

"Come in, amigos, come in," I say.

They entered waryily. They wore vintage golf outfits that village hotshots had took to donning. It consisted of spiked faux leopard saddle shoes with gilded curb feelers, Gaelic thigh socks, rather unfortunately snug citrus-colored Bermuda shorts, polished black patent belts, Hawaiian muscle polo tops, imitation suede rainbow caps with fluffy dice at the crown, and numerous large gaudy pieces of golden knickknacks sprinkled about their pasty limbs.

"Swanky duds!" I say, and I meant it. I liked to dwell on the edge of fashion faux pauses myself.

"Thank you, Sonny," says Shuffleboard. "We ought to get going, Marv." In the confusion of my appreciating their apparel, the mayor had lost track of their mission. He turned and bumped into the door I'd just shut. "Where'd that come from?"

Says Marvin: "Eh, Mayor, we have to reclaim our personal bag first."

"Sit down, Gents," I say. "Make yourselfs at home."

Shane returned with fresh beet floats for our guests.

"Where's mine?" I say. Shane made rude funny eyebrow gestures at me.

The Mayor sniffed his float. "Smells like dirty socks."

"I think I'll pass," says Marvin. "Where's our bag, if you don't mind."

Shane cast them a lethal pout. "A good guest drinks the refreshments before getting down to business."

The boys held their nose and choked them beet floats down, bringing muffled insane giggles from Shane. Marvin starts to repeat, "Where's our—" but his head flopped back on the sofa like a pumpkin, immediately followed by Shuffleboard's. It turned out Shane had dumped a double helping of valerian root in their floats, and they was snoring like rusty oil wells by the time Constable Boris and his tractor come puttering up the lane to set right political corruption in Hmm at long last for a little while.

# 28.

The first edition of *The New Hmm Gazette* came out the next day
with a banner headline:

CORUPPTION IN HMM COORIDOORS OF POWER:
MAYOR AND PUBLISHER JAILED
ON FELONEY COUNTERFEETING CHARGES;
MIX ANIMAL "YONDER" HALED AS HERO;
ELECTOIN CALLED OFF;
SHANE WASHIGNTON SWORE IN AS NEW MAYOR
BY SECERT CITY HALL COLIATION,
VOWS TO LOUNCH "NEW MORNING IN HMM"

There was so much headline on the front page there wasn't
no room for the story, but if you have a good headline, you don't
need no story. The "secert city hall coliation" turned out to be two
night janitors. Rudy Twogood, the hard of hearing night reporter
at the *Gazette*, thought the janitors was big wigs working late on
the crisis. Through the locked city hall front door, Rudy asked
them about the counterfeiting scandal, the arrest of Shuffleboard,
and what they thought would happen next. The janitors discussed
it and said "It's a damn shame!" Rudy thought they said, "It's that
dame, Shane," wrote it up in the *Gazette*, and a new mayor was
born in the name of representative democracy.

Shane threw a big fancy mayorial victory press conference out
in the backyard but left in a huff when every question was about
Yonder the hero who found the counterfeit dough. Launching

the podium into the pond, she stormed off to the Mayor's Royal Cottage. She hadn't no idea what she would do when she got there, but that was just what the village needed—fresh leadership in the total dark from a sarcastic fortune teller.

Mabel slept through the whole parade of events, from counterfeiting to coronation. Yonder took up a station by her bedside, guarding her in all her unconsciousness. I went in there and felt her forehead, reeled a few sweaty strands of hair out of her mouth. She was clammy but peaceful, still snoring like a little babbling redhead brook. I started getting a touch of romantic naushousness. Yonder watched me with a curled lip the whole while.

*

I made a Things-To-Do-Today list:

1. Nurse Mabel back to health that we might go on a date, forget world peace and fixing things, and have some old-fashion fun spending her money that I should have gotten my fair share of in the first place.

2. Help Shane be a good mayor so the village don't throw her out and make her move back in here and poke a stick in my personal plans.

3. Work on the Yond-O-Lator so the animal will be able to express his feelings and schemes clearer to me and therefore not have to build another himself.

4. Ask Mabel out.

*

I put asking her out last because the more you thought about it the less you felt like doing it. You didn't mind the date so much as the asking out. If the asking out went bad, you didn't even have the memory of a lousy date to keep you company afterwards.

*

At my invite, the village quack, Ernie "Transplant" Anderson, dropped in to give Mabel a check-up. She had come around a little but wasn't anything near the vivaciously annoying gal I come to know on February Mountain. I took a chance on Transplant because I needed a second opinion. The first opinion was mine and it wasn't good. Although Mabel hadn't uttered one word about that kooky bus tour lately, I had a feeling she was still stuck on world peace, and that worrying about it had her wore down and blue.

When Transplant was sober and in the money, you couldn't find a better doctor this side of Silent Tony's Barber College. But if he was sloshed and poking a scalpel at you with one bloodshot eye closed, or needed cash for roulette and wanted to remove some vital organ to cure your indigestion—head for the hills.

Transplant played the wheel at Leaning Clotilda's Roulette & Launderette Junction. Not only was one of Clotilda's legs longer than the other, she ran her joint on a lopsided houseboat on Nervous Pond. The bobbing water jimmied her roulette wheels so nobody could win except by blind luck. Accordingly, Transplant required a constant stream of organ patients. First, he overcharged you to remove the thing, then turned around and sold it to a yokel in another village, then took the yokel's out and rotated it with yours, making four killings with two organs. And neither of you needed anything in the first place except a new doctor.

Hiking down the mountain with Mabel, I had made the mistake of gossiping about various village oddballs, including Transplant and his organ proclivities. As soon as Mabel heard him tromping up the stairs singing the fight song from East Lumpston

Diploma Mill Junior College, she ducked under the covers and refused to come out.

The quack not only looked and smelt sober but claimed to had sworn off roulette. I heard it before, of course, but today was a new day. We haggled the fee in the living room out of Mabel's fragile presence.

"Twenty dollars," announces Transplant, holding out his beret.

"I'm broke," I announce back.

"Now, now. I'm sure your sister is siphoning a portion of her mayoral spoils your way."

"Ha. Yeah. She's siphoning not even answering my calls my way."

"Five dollars, then," bargains Transplant.

"Ten," I say, way ahead of him. Hmm currency was being devalued so fast due to economic unstability and leadership chaos, that it was actually cheaper to pay *more* for things now.

"Let's see it," he says. I slapped a big ten coin in his paw. He bit it and slipped it under his beret. I led him into the bedroom. He scoped out the situation and orders Mabel, "Emerge immediately from them blankies."

Mabel popped the top half of her red head out and declares, "You just do whatever it is you do right from there. And by the way, you're not harvesting any of *my* organs."

"Certainly not," Transplant soothes. "None that don't need harvesting." He winked at me, opened his bag and pulled out his heart tube, mallet, hand-crank generator, and other medical accessories, and commenced the check-up, except for one minor obstacle named Yonder.

Straining to hear Mabel's heartbeat through stratums of cotton, wool, flannel, and mothball vapors, Transplant got a sidewise gander at the mixed animal. Yonder gawked down at him from atop Shane's corner walk-in concrete vault, which I built for her to stash her diaries in. The animal lain up there pointed at Transplant like the sphinx, a combo of missile radar and a Buddhist owl. He had his mouth ajar to show off his pearly pointies, and his unblinking gleer locked on old Doc.

"Does Yonder know you from somewheres?" I say.

"I assure you not," says Transplant.

"He's certainly looking at you like he does," adds Mabel.

"Well, he certainly does not. Who are you going to believe, a mixed monster from the Unconscious Forest, or a sophisticated physician with impeccable roots in the community!?"

"Don't blow a gasket," I say. "He's just being protective of Mabel. He wants to ensure you know what you're doing."

"It's a little late for that," Transplant says, winking facetiously at the gal. "If I knew what I was doing I'd own five housepitals and be drinking Neapolitans on the beach in South San Itanicnic. Now, how's about shooing that aberration out of the check-up facilities. I prefer not to be ogled by a horse-monkey while I'm at my art and craft."

I say, "That horse-monkey *lives* for the sort of attention you're currently lavishing on him."

Transplant glanced at Yonder like a hot dog glances at a glowing bar-be-que. He took his dark glasses off the top of his beret where he had suavishly tucked them, and trode over as if to put them on Yonder.

"I wouldn't try that if I were you," I sing.

But Transplant slipped those sunglasses on Yonder like he was a manikin, and Yonder deigned to let him, for no other reason than that I just said I wouldn't do that if I were you. The animal's perverse streak was so thick that if you removed it there wouldn't be nothing left but a pile of whiskers, toenails, earwax, and bugs.

"There," Transplant says. He tried to resume the check-up but proved unable. "I can feel his mouth looking at me." Yanking a red handkerchief out of his back pocket, he hooked it to the corners of the dark glasses so it hung out over Yonder's entire facial protuberance. The animal, to spite me, had allowed Transplant to turn him into a cross between a bandit, a beatnik, and a harem gal.

The quack begun his check-up of Mabel in earnest. He proceeded to tap his mallet on her knee through the covers and her foot replied by kicking all the blankets up to the ceiling. As they came floating back down, Transplant asks, "Was that your right knee or your left knee?"

"What difference does it make?" she says.

He shrugged. "It's your knees."

"It certainly is," she says.

Transplant saw himself as quite the lady's man, but he wasn't going to breeze to victory in any conversations with Mabel. He pulled a old envelope out of his pocket and began to take some rather urgent notes.

"What is it, what's wrong?" Mabel says. He shook his head. She sat up. "What are you writing!"

"'Soy hot dogs, zucchini, and candy corn,'" recites he.

"What's that got to do with my knees?"

"Not a thing. It's my grocery list."

"Oh," Mabel says. She appeared quite took by the quack's inability to focus. "You certainly have eclectic dietary tastes."

"Thanks, Mademoiselle."

"You and your wife," she mummers inquisitively.

"Divorced, separated, forgotten," the quack asserts.

"You don't say," says she.

This exchange was not only irrelevant, it was inappropriate to medical ideals and rude to me. I say, "Let's all remember a little thing called the Hypnocratic Oath."

Transplant openly snorted in the face of the Hypnocratic Oath. He begun to tap Mabel's skullbones with his mallet here and there, which she was not quite so took with. Then he poked at her tongue and tonsils with the eraser end of a pencil he found on the table, peered in her ears by matchlight, studied her nostrils at questionable length, scraped under her fingernails with his own fingernails for a DNA test, hand-cranked the generator and ran a Geiger counter test on her toes, so forth.

Then he issued Mabel's diagnosis: "Exhausted, underfed, squirmy, thinks too much, but above average reflexes."

"I could have told you that," says Mabel, kneading her headbones.

"Why didn't you?" says Transplant.

"I don't recall you asking."

"You could have saved me a trip."

"I doubt you had anything better to do," says Mabel.

At which he shot her a flagrant wink. I expected outrage from her, but she responded with a couple sassy clicking noises in the side of her mouth like you'd do to get a horse going.

"Hey," I protest. I had drug Transplant over there as a favor to him and her both, and now I was getting backstabbed from the front and hoodwinked from behind. "This is a medical inquiry," I say, "not the Tunnel of Love."

All the sudden Yonder started growling on low voltage from atop Shane's vault. I hoped he was warning Transplant about his flirteries with Mabel. However, I lifted the dark glasses and kerchief and found him sound asleep sitting up. He was growling in his sleep, perhaps at the Mystery Police. I replaced his disguise and he begun snoring like a little paddlewheel, the kerchief flapping and shimmying in rebuttal.

Look, Mabel was about half irresistible, so you couldn't blame old Transplant for putting a move on. He himself was a mile of bad ditch in a beret and would of swiped a pancreas from his grandmother if he needed the cash. I wasn't worried that Mabel would find him ideal romantic fodder, but he had a air of uncouth confidence about him that a certain kooky type of gal might go for.

Mabel sat up against the pillows and linked her hands behind her head in a rather foolhardy posture. "Lemuel," she says, "I hope you didn't pay good money for my so-called check-up by Doctor *Hamhands* here." She looked at Transplant even though she was talking to me.

Transplant tells her, "Checkin' up on you is all the pay Doctor Hamhands needs for checkin' up on you."

My own ears looked at each other. "Gimme back my ten dollars, then."

"I'm Mabel," Mabel says, wiggling her freckley hand at Transplant like a swinging porch light at a June bug.

"Call me Ernie," says Transplant, planting a big gruesome smooch on her dainty hand.

"*Enchanté*," purrs Mabel.

"*Au revoir*," Transplant intones.

I knew enough French to know when I heard enough. "You suppose to be *leaving* when you say '*Oh, revoar*.' You diagnosed her as exhausted and underfed from pursuing world peace, so scram and let us launch a new regimen."

"I never got as far as what from," says Transplant. "Pursue world peace, do you, Punkin'?"

"She used to," I say. "*Punkin'* is looking for other hobbies at the moment." I grabbed holt of the heart tube around Transplant's neck and dragged him to the front door.

"Toodle-oo," Transplant calls to Mabel over his shoulder.

"*Auf Wiedersehen*," calls Mabel back.

I slammed the door and marched back in there. "You're in no shape to be flirting with a brazen quack like that!"

"Oh, I was just pulling your leg, silly. When I saw you were jealous I couldn't resist pretending I was sweet on the debonair old goat."

"Transplant don't know that. Anyhow, jealous of Transplant? Me? Hardly har. Never!"

"Oh," Mabel says with a pouty puss. She began coyly winding one of the chartreuse tassels on Shane's bedspread around her little finger. "It would only be the polite thing to do."

"It would be *polite* to be *jealous*?" The mysterious ways of gals was written in a book of shifting sands. "Is this part of your plan for world peace, toying with my village heart?"

"I'm sorry, Lem. You're right. World peace is world peace, but feelings are feelings."

"Is this what you call leaving your old bad ways behind? I thought you gave up meanness and everything years ago."

"Not exactly years ago. More like solstices. Like . . . two solstices."

"Two solstices!"

"Let's see—I gave up my old bad ways right before I went into Sister Waymaker's convent. I was in there for two weeks before she kicked me out—"

"Two weeks!"

"—then I went straight to Pop's and met Yond, and that was when my crusade began. One and a half solstices, I guess."

"Well, no wonder you still got a mean streak—them bad old ways ain't that old."

She pulled the sheet over her dishoveled head. "Don't be mad at me, Lem. It's hard being laid up in a strange village while your dreams are deferred. I'm doing almost the best I can."

I saw it was time to fire off a romantic shot across her bow before it was too late. I pulled up a chair by the bed and got my decisive voice out. "Okay, look here. What if I was to say, 'You know what, let's just go ahead and get this over with once in for all'?"

She popped out from the sheet big-eyed, like it was Christmas morning. "Get *what* over with?" she asks. She glanced with incongruous delight at the masked and snoring Yonder. "Does it have to do with travel?"

"A date normally does, lest it's a stay-at-home."

"Oh, a date," she says, keeping her excitement well-hid, then, "A *date*? You're asking me out on a *date*?"

"I said *what-if*. It's conjeculatory hypothecation."

Mabel giggled in my face and sang, "Lemuel asked me out on a da-ate!"

"Stop being too silly. We're conceited adults having a theoretical conversation."

Right then, bless my stars, Yonder jerked awake, fell off the top of the vault, hit the bed, bounced off, landed on his feet, sashayed out to the kitchen, and started banging his food pan against the radiator pipes like a jailbird. He was raring for lunch after a hard day's morning of staring at Transplant, laying like the sphinx, wearing a disguise, dreaming about the Mystery Police, and snoring.

Seizing the distraction, I excused myself to slap together a pile of sweet potato sandwiches and fennel pudding. Mabel continued melodilizing from afar: "Lem asked me out on a da-ate!"

I took lunch in and set down and we dined a deux. In the middle she looked up and says, "Yes, by the way, yes," and resumed chowing down. Afterwards, while I rubbed my satisfied belly and popped fleas on Yonder, Mabel conked off into a deep nap with her head still propped up, her winsome mouth open, and a petite thread of drool hanging off her sweet lip and swaying in the breeze of her dainty snoring. I wished I had my camera there to take a picture of it for the Home Snapshot Section of the *New Hmm Gazette,* or for her scrapbook if she had one, or for our grandkids or somebody.

# 29.

The next day Mabel finally got tired of moping around convalescing and reading Shane's old *Confidential* and *Modern Screen* magazines. She marched out in the living room and announced she was going to go explore Hmm. She had on a family-size shiny red purse slang over one shoulder, a red barncoat, a red shawl wrapped around and around her neck, and a flouncy red hat the size of a elephant's ear.

"Wowee," I say. "Where'd you come up with all them pretty red duds?" On the mountain all she'd had suitcase-wise was a old duffel bag.

"A girl knows how to pack," she says saucily. "So, any special sights I ought to see in this charming little burg?"

"One place I'd steer clear of is Lucy Ferdal's bull pasture. If I may, I'm none too thrilled at you wandering around in your still feeble condition, especially dressed like a mix of a stop sign and Bette Davis. These village roughnecks never laid eyes on nothing like that before."

"I'll manage. Or do you think your roughnecks will take advantage of little ol' Mabel?"

"Well, I guarantee you're not dumb enough to win any conversations. And if you still got that million-dollar check on you, don't go near Clotilda's, it's liable to slide right out of your pocket. By the way, that business about Unc leaving you loaded, that's on the level?"

"It most certainly is," she says. "I hope it won't interfere with our date."

"Why should it? Long as you don't insist on paying for more than half."

She laughed, thinking I was pulling her leg, but I kept a serious face as long as I could, then she stopped laughing, then I started laughing, then we laughed together. I didn't know if I was pulling her leg or not, but it was fun either way. I hoped she had millions and we had to wonder if it made any difference, rather than her be broke and not have to wonder at all.

*

While Mabel explored Hmm, Yonder and I packed a basket and set off to visit Shane at the Mayor's Royal Cottage, affectionately known as Mount Gasbag.

It was a handsome structure, the only two-story building in Hmm; namely, there was a tent on the roof to throw drunken luaus for visiting dignitaries in. Downstairs boasted five of everything—windows, doors, toasters, record players, washrags, compost buckets, mice, forks. You might not need them, but they were there just in case. Plus miles and miles of moth-eaten royal purple drapes hanging everywhere to remind you that you were deep inside the seat of power.

Around the Mayor's Cottage lain a 20-foot-wide moat filled with bottled European water from Ambo, and in the moat was moored a one-person submarine for the mayor to ride around in after a hard day of doing nothing with as much obfuscation and expenditures as possible. The sub boasted four loudspeakers attached to its periscope, allowing the mayor to submerge and deliver a real-time travelogue to tourists regarding the flora, fauna, bottles, tin cans, and tires that dwelt in the depths of the moat.

In short, the mayor's residence featured all the modern accoutrements that everybody else's money could buy. However, due to shady construction contracts, it was built on a methane bog, hence its nickname. It weren't even a mount, but only a big bubble from the pocket of gas trapped in there that held the cottage up to its proper prominence.

Therefore, the Mayor's Royal Cottage was like many of my past gal friends—good-looking with lots of interesting stuff, but highly expensive and unstable.

I figured Her Honor had gotten homesick as a barking loon by then. Under her hardened municipal exterior lurked the heart of a sensitive little girl weeping into her Doughnut Cereal. I pictured her banging her pleasantly flat head against the mayorial throne and crying out, "Lem! Bro! Yondy! Come save me from my own forsooken self!" That throne was a immense priceless antique red porcelain heirloom passed down through the centuries from Founder Lula Seeque herself, and I hated to picture the damage my sister's head was doing to it.

The trick was to keep her from throwing in the towel or getting impeached, because then she would have to move back in with me. I planned to put a quick end to her sentimental applesauce, get her to buck up, mayor forth, keep on trucking, and stay out of my hair.

It was a whole block walk over to the mayorial grounds. Half way there Yonder swerved off Mudpit Lane into Bud Rooney's gum grove and plunked hisself down in a bed of clover and bluebells. You'd think he'd been digging ditches all day instead of watching "Good Morning, Hmm!," fiddling around in the attic, and walking half a block. I knew better than try to dissuade Prince Lazybones from a rest break, so I joined in, careful not to get any grass stains or dog-doo on my three-piece faux tiger-skin terrycloth suit that I had donned in honor of my first mayorial visit.

Leaning against a cool, calm gum tree, Yonder and me enjoyed a snack we packed for the walk—a ration can of jujubees. They were refreshing and interesting, like little cherry-flavored rubber teeth. To wash them down we took a slurp of grape Nehi from my thermos, which has Low Stu riding on a buffalo on it, hand painted by Clare Cee, the child that also pulled the rose trick on Yonder.

Before long, sprawled in the shady bluebells and clover, I dozed off, only to be awokened by some sort of a gently burburing interlude. I looked: it was Yonder, crouched close to me in the grass and mummering a series of doodling jazzist inscintillations. It closely resembled his previous effort to communicate with me in the attic.

I sat up and yearned to find familiar language in it, but there was nor a tot or a jittle you could quite put your finger on. I tried to hear how close any of it could be called letter sounds. It was so quick and silky it was easier to say what letters *wasn't* in there. I counted no X, Z, Q, F, J, V, D, P, or W, to be sure. I wouldn't say I heard the other letters, only that I couldn't say I hadn't. I did note that he wouldn't be much of a Scrabble partner.

I had to be addled to think the animal could utter even a letter. Then again, the widow Lottie Engram was once headed to the kitchen during a commercial break and heard her dead husband Rudolph ask, "Could you grab me a snickerdoodle while you're up?" What was more addled, dead Rudolph talking to Lottie, or live Yonder talking to me?

As the animal's pleasant if mystical blithering washed over me, a number of busybodies noticed us tucked into Bud's gum grove. They clomped over to see what we was up to. The last thing I needed was a mob of jealous chatterboxes getting wind of Yonder trying to talk to me. To be sure, Hmm had tooken the mixed animal and his questionable ways to its heart, but they were still superstitious oaves and would not take as kindly to me and him having a conversation, especially if they thought we was gossiping about them. Around there it was still a man is a man, a gal is a gal, a mixed animal is a mixed animal, and never the twain shall meet.

"Shoo," I command the squad of meddlers. "Mind your own business. I'll tell my sister the mayor you're bothering me if you don't watch out."

"What was you two talking about?" Irka Nelson says.

"Talking?" I say. "We're not talking about nothing. How could a animal talk, Irka? And if it did, I would plug my ears out of decency. What a revolting, abnormal idea. Shoo! Shoo, dad-blast it!" They departed reluctantly, back to their rustic errands and chores. "Talking. What cheek! Don't forget I'm the Mayor's brother now! Shoo! I'm watching you!" I made a gesture with my elbow, knee and eye.

The animal lain back down. He placed his red gold chin against the cool grass. I could tell I had disappointed him once more by not being able to decipher his indecipherables. With a sigh as deep and torn as all of Gnosis Canyon, he stared off over the top of the bluebells. His distant eyes, presently silver, gold, and green, misted up with memories of the past, or yearning for the future, or perhaps a bittersweet acceptance of the present.

"Breaktime over," I announce.

Yonder popped up from his melancholy in the bluebells like a big piece of silver-orange toast and we galloped together out of the gum grove toward Mount Gasbag, just as if nothing had never happened before.

# 30.

As we charged around the corner of Mudpit Lane, Yonder jammed on his brakes and skidded into the last person standing in a long rowdy line—none other than Clare Cee, the artist child that painted Low Stu on my thermos—and I skidded into him. Yonder, not Low Stu.

"Yondo and Lem!" says Clare. "How's Lao Tsu?" I held up the thermos. Clare frowned. "He could use a touch-up. His fu-manchu has lost its fu!"

"What do you suppose this here line is for, Clare?"

"To see Mayor Shane," she says.

Indeed, the column of excited villagers snaked all the way to the Mayor's Royal Cottage, which sat in the distance atop the methane bubble like a big smug white frog atop a toadstool. Folks in line flocked around Yonder and gave him the usual wary lovey-dovey. Meanwhile, I put two in two together and it came out one.

Namely, my sister in her misery must of barricaded herself inside the Royal Cottage, and these fiends was lined up to peek through the window while she banged her poor thick skull against the throne or other royal things. Her lust for power and laziness had come to a bitter end. Carrying the village on her plump shoulders had worn her down to a grisly pulp. She had been mayor for three whole days and now her tragic descent into public disgrace had began.

I curdled my loins and raced to the front of the line. As I neared the drawbridge, I was met with widespread resistance. Everybody begun to shout rude synonyms and poke me as I passed. They didn't care that I was going to rescue my sister from the abyss, they only cared that I was butting in line. Meanwhile, they patted Yonder and babytalked him as he pranced alongside me, and he drank it up like he never heard of me.

Merle and Pearl Eh, the Chinese weightlifter ex-scientist couple, stood crossed-armed on the drawbridge like a wall of muscle. Their pomaded hairdos stuck up like fingers in the disconcerting international fashion of the time, and they liked to drench themself in after-shave and perfume that smelt like wet rust, old pillows, and pineapples gone wrong.

"Nuh, nuh, nuh," says Pearl, tapping my chestbone with her hot-dog-like thumb. "Who are you, butting in Mayor's Favors line?"

"You know who I am. I'm the Mayor's brother slash adviser. And I'm going to advise her you been jabbing her brother with your baldfaced thumb. What do you two aromatic mumps think you're doing anyway?"

"Mayor protection," says Merle, flashing some phony cardboard badge.

"Then protect her from mistreating herself for these lumpkins' entertainment. In fact, step aside, you fragrant coxcombs!" I tried to sqwuck between them but they was like two meat buildings dunked in rotten fruit.

"Where ya figger *you* is going to be going, Sir Fix-it-kins?" inquires Merle.

"I is going to be going to save my sister, *Pearl.*" I deliberately used bad grammar and called him by his wife's name in order to get both their goats.

"Oh, we think your sister's name were *Shane*," quips Pearl. Her and Merle laughed like musclebound donkeys, and the whole line joined in their idiotic merriment. Never try to outsmart a moron, because (1) they never realize they're losing the conversation, and (2) they're smarter at being dumb than you are at being smart. Meanwhile, Yonder continued soaking up the petting and cooing of the very mob that was braying in my face. His eyes rolled around in his head like pinballs from the mass love.

I whispered to him, "How can you lap up their babytalk while they're hating me for my freedom and lifestyle?"

Yonder shrugged, bared a few teeth, and raised his eyebrows, as if to say, "Though you have a point, it's not a very sharp one," then pretended to ignore me, not necessarily in that order.

I turned back to Pearl and Merle. "You two dinwits will be lucky to get run out of town on a wagon of corn cobs when my sister hears about you waylaying me like this!"

"*Dinwits?*" Pearl says. "We was top scientists in China."

"Two class 5-A software genius," says Merle.

Tears of injustice twinkled in the Ehs' eyes. I always suspected they had made up that whole story, but their tears forced me to express compassion: "Too bad a hamlet of doofuses turned you from scientists into hired mayoral bodyguards."

Merle ignored my understanding. "Your sister said you will butt in line when you smelt favors getting passed out. She knewen you'd scoot over fer yer favor quicker'n a sidewinder grabs a biscuit." The Ehs inconsistently affected a travesty of a Hmm accent in order to blend in better.

"Favor?" I say. "I'm here to stop her from banging her lonely head against things, not to wait in line to gawp at her with this ruffian mob!"

Which mob began to laugh in a fake uproarious way to try to

hide their hurt feelings from themselves.

"Why would she bang her head for," says Pearl, "except for not thinking up 'Mayor Favors Day' sooner."

"OK," I say, "what the Sam Hill is this Mayor Favors day."

Everybody pointed at a big cardboard sign hanging over the mayorial front door, handmade in crayon:

MAYOR'S FAVORS DAY LINE!!!

ONE FAVOR Per Hmm Denizen & ONE FAVOR Only!

NO GUARANTEE for Getting It Granted!

But Guaranteed NOT to Get It Granted If no GIFT FOR MAYOR!

Keep Favor Asking to No More Than FIVE (5) WORDS!

Also!

NO Talking or Muttering!

NO Rambunctious Behavior!

NO Eating, Drinking or Flip Flops!

Eyes Front at All Times!

NO Barefoot! NO Playing!

NO Electronic Gizmoes!

NO B.O. or Stanky Breath!

NO Butting in Line!

NO Crying, Complaining, or Pouting!

OBEY Orders of HmmLAND SECURITY FORCE At All Times!

PUNISHMENT for Breaking Rules Too Awful to List!

!!!!!!!!

The sign suggested that this event had nothing to do with Shane banging her head against anything after all.

"If you don't known," says Merle, "denzin means pissant."

"Peasant," says Pearl. "That sign," she says to me, "is so even some fix-it johnny could git it and behave like everybody elset."

Says I: "Are you kidding me? Look at this entire rambunctious barefooted eating drinking muttering mob. Not one person is obeying a single rule on that dumbbell sign."

"That only proves what a nice forgiving mayor that Mayor Shane is," says Merle. "Now back of the line with youse! Pronto, cowhand!"

"Cowhand!" I'd had it up to here and beyond. "Listen, my fellow clodhoppers—step aside or I'll have my sister ride you and your provincial biceps out of town on the nearest water buffalo."

At which Pearl and Merle sput on their hands, hoisted me off the ground, and hurled me wholesale right in the moat. Everybody in line got a hoot out of my dunking but Yonder. He jumped in and dragged me by my tiger-skin terrycloth collar onto the bank where I sat sputtering with that European Ambo water bubbling away in my sinuses. "This is a gargantuan outrage!" I declare. "I'll have Shane thrash you two knurls within a inch of—"

"What in the name of Communist revolutionary threat to social order and democracy is going on out here!" booms somebody that sounded familiar, namely, Mayor Shane. Rather than beating her flat head against things, she was being toted in the throne out the doorway by a retinue of Hmm's finest citizens. Her carriers included but was not limited to Dr. Ernie Transplant Anderson, Red Bond the Chief Burrocrat, Max Pica the Minister of Nap Hour and Silence, Sheena Axminster the telephone operator, and hello and behold even Shane's vanquished foe, ex-Mayor Shuffleboard Humphrey! He must of broke out of jail!

Shane clapped her hands and the gasping entourage set her down. "Hot! Hot!" she cries, and her weary minions begun cooling her off with purple velvet hand fans. "Here I am granting favors left and right," pronounces Her Mayorness. "Must I contend as well with some yahoo insurgent howling and splashing in my royal moat like it was the village plunge?"

"It's no insurgent, Your Sistership!" I say. I kept slipping down the moatbank in my waterlogged terrycloth suit.

"Oh, it's *you*," she sneers. "Who told you you could swim in my moat? Shouldn't you be home fattening up your wanton peace train lovebug Myrtle?"

"It's *Mabel*, Your Mayordom."

She called to her legions in line, "Helloo-oo!" and waved a hanky at the squealing rustics.

I spoke out of the corner of my mouth. "Psst! Shuffleboard escaped from prison. He's one of the dopes carrying your throne." The poor old culprit was leaning against the cottage with his mouth open, wheezing like a sack of piccolos.

"I pardoned the precious simpleton," says Shane.

"You never," I say. "What for?"

"A good leader would rather be loved and feared than never loved at all."

"How is anybody going to fear you when you let a guy out of jail that counterfeited a bag of fake money to try to subvert democracy?"

"Because it confuses them, and confusion is the first step to both love and fear."

"It's also the first step to a box of baloney. Did you notice that they're all listening to you right now as you describe how you're playing their feelings like a toy xylophone?"

Shane turned to the wrapped mob. "Who wants a mayor's favor?"

"Me! Me! Me! Me! Me!" cries the village.

"Who wants me to play your feelings like a xylophone?" says Shane.

"Me! Me! Me! Me! Me!"

"Who wants a box of baloney?" says Shane.

"Me! Me! Me! Me! Me!"

"You ought to be ashamed of yourself!" I say to Shane. "You're worse than Shuffleboard. At least he had the decency to try to hide his corruption from the light of day!"

"Don't yell at Mayor Shane!" Sheena Axminster yells at me. "If you can't respect the woman, at least respect the mayor."

"Look at you people," I rebuke the riff-raft. "Trading your dignity for a box of baloney. You're no better than a bunch of wild monkeys jumping around in a kuklaberry tree!"

Shane hollers, "This ingrate is disrupting Favors Day with attempted nepotism! Security!"

Pearl and Merle grabbed holt of my suit and got set to re-moat me, but Yonder puffed up, snarled and swayed his hiney like a depth charge. Merle and Pearl saw he meant business and unhanded me.

"Shane, I demand that you personally flog these meatbound hoodlums for flanging me in the moat and treating me like dog-doo."

"Balderdash," says Shane. "They gave you a much-needed bath. Besides, as my Hmmland Security Force and cyber-geniuses in exile, they're designing an anti-terror balloon-camera spy system that allows me to watch every villager to make sure no terrorists are attacking them." She turned and asked the crowd, "What do you all think about my New Balloon-Camera Happy Spy Safe Warm Anti-Terror Milk Security Cookies Program?"

"We love it!" cries the village. "Happy Safe Warm Milk and Cookies, we love it!"

"Thank you, Dear," Shane says to the village. "Now," she says to me. "Cease inciting ruckuses. If you wish an audience with Her Mayorship to request a favor, toodle to the back of the line and wait politely like my other law-abiding subjects. No one will ever accuse Mayor Shane Washington of letting her self-centered brother and his self-centered pet butt into the favors line. Speaking of which, I notice that your hands are empty. You would be wise to exeunt and return with an appropriate tribute to persuade Her Meship to grant your measly wish, whatever it may be."

At which she clapped her hands and her wobbly legged escorts struggled to lift her throne and lug her back into the Royal Cottage.

I hollered at her, "You only got secretly appointed because Shuffleboard got arrested because of *my* pet that found that bag of fake cash!"

Shane clapped her hands and her slave detail grinded to a halt on the front porch. Over her shoulder Her Sheship says, "Speaking of your undeniably valuable animal, watch your mail. You'll be receiving a hefty but fair inheritance tax bill on him shortly."

"Inheritance tax? On a so-call animal? Since when?"

"Since the new secret Constitution."

"What new secret Constitution?"

"The one I'm writing. Homeward ho, and make it snappy!" she commands her staff, and they dragged her throne the last 18 inches inside and slammed the door.

The village begun throwing their mayorial tributes at me as I fled the premises, including various produce that had overripened in the long hot wait, softboiled eggs, window treatments, soccer balls, whole honeyed hams, potted flowers, footstools, bags of punch, homemade girdles, gift certificates, candy corn that stuck to the punch and begun to dissolve in my hair, small toys that stuck to the melting candy corn, and the like. All the way home, Yonder was trying to lick my face to soothe my jangled nerves, or to consume the tribute food that was stuck to me. Either way, I appreciated the positive attention that I wasn't getting from nobody else, even if who knew where that tongue had been.

# 31.

By the time me and Yonder got home, Mabel had returned herself, hadding survived her excursion into Hmm's back country wonders. She was sprawled in her red outfit right on the dichondra grass with her elephant ear hat over her face. I sauntered over to see if she was alive and strike up a conversation. She peeked out at the favors' gunk and moatmoss all over my hair and suit, then looked plum through me as I recounted Yonder's and my adventures in the Mayor's Favors line. She showed no inclination to give me a reciprocal travelogue of her exploits in the village. Perhaps she was preparing mentally for our big date, getting in a zone.

\*

After a well-deserved shower, I ducked in the garage to resume inventing the Yond-O-Lator. To be honest, I never tried to invent anything so intricate and mysterious. I feared I might be over my head, maybe messing in territory you shouldn't mess in, like the Tower of Babel, only at a sub-atomic level. Uncle Leonard had been poking in similar territory, and look what happened to him.

Nevertheless, if I did invent it, I would be one happy man, at least for a while, and I believed a certain mixed animal would prove to be happy, too, in his way.

Yonny stretched out on the work bench to observe my progress up close, which he had every right to. After all, the invention carried his name and involved his inalienable pursuit of improved conversation. Whether he understood a word, he had exceptional listening skills, when he felt like it. He possessed a whole parade of facial expressions, contemplative throat acoustics, and body English galore to ambiguously punctuate what you said. He made you enjoy your own bunkum just by the way he listened to it, and he never interrupted with one-upsmanship, except when absolutely necessary. I often found myself confiding in him, just to see what I had to say.

As I tinkered with the electron wobbler aspect of the Yond-O-Lator, I and him got a conversation going. I like to think of myself as a gentleman of the laconic school, but sometimes talking gets my creative beans a-jumpin'.

"May I run something by you," I ask him, "concerning the philosophical framework of my project? Or, rather, *our* project?"

He raised his left eyebrow in piqued intrigue, but curled the right side of his mouth with coy agnosticism. In a conversation he trode the Tao path: he goosed you forward while simultanuseoly holding your beltloop from behind.

I say, "Now, a smidge of the following is borrowed from your Jung, your Sontag, your Einstein, your Mead, your Laurel, and your Corey, but the bulk is original yours truly. You see, Yond, communication is kin to a iceberg. Ninety percent is hid in the subconscious. Our subconscious contains the inert desire to give away our emotions and thoughts to people and animals, and to receive in return love, understanding, and dialectics. Capiche?"

He squinched a cheek, held out a paw and teetered it back in forth.

"Good enough. Now, our feelings and thoughts yearn to be expressed more than we yearn to express them. Think of your hidden feelings and ideas as jackrabbits multiplying in a cardboard box. The box is us as we toodle around town minding our own business. On the one hand, if rabbits are coming out of you as you shop, it causes social problems. On the other hand, the rabbits want to get out of the box a lot more than the box wants to let them out. Although it's good for the box if they get out, because if they don't, soon there won't be no box. So, we forget about the rabbits at our own apparel, and the box gets burst or ate. That's why people say something and then go, 'I can't believe I said that.'"

Yonder wiggled his ears and nodded plaintively in understanding.

"I know this sounds more complicated to me than it does to you," I add, "but communication involves us hearing our own words, too. If we couldn't hear what we said, later on we wouldn't know if we said it or just thought it to ourself.

"Second, *all* spoken communications is composed of sound atoms colliding in the air. Nothing more, nothing less. Now, the ingredients of every sound atom is rhythm, nitrogen, curiosity, sonar, chaos, habit, starlight, and the magnetic desire to connect with other sound atoms and become words. Different amounts of these ingredients produce different letters and accents. Incidentally, I discovered many of these secret facts by studying bubbles in the bathtub. Find big worlds in little worlds, that's my and William Blake's motto."

Yonder spied a cavorting shadow from my hands that was perpelled onto the garage wall by the work light as I fiddled with the invention. The enchanted, calculating look on his face as he studied the shadow made me think of Plato in the cave watching his own silhouette from the campfire and thinking he was a caveman in the birth pangs of Western Philosophy.

"Just like human beings at a party," I continue, "sound atoms have a social nature that leads them to bump into one another for a larger purpose, and also a anti-social nature that drives them to go home and put their feet up on the coffee table.

"Sound atoms arrange themselves into audular patterns that the eardrum interprets into words, based on a sub-cellular, lexico-musical thesaurus acquired from the historical genes of the village that determine what sound atom shape means what word."

Yonder made a pained face, which I read as disagreement, but then his tummy muttered like a bad transmission and he emitted a amiable and rather lazily doodling fart. After which he sighed, smiled, and nodded sidewise with a hiked eyebrow, meaning to me, Please continue.

I was enjoying my own explanation, which I had never heard out loud nor in such confident detail. "A illustration will suffice. Picture when we speak that weightless ping pong balls are perpelled out of our mouths and float in the air with etymological insignia, or letters, and a drop of otherworldly glue on different sides. These self-adhering projectiles spell out words in the air, but in invisible mathematico-chemistrific terms somewhat abstract for your stage of development."

In response, with meticulous thoughtfulness, Yonder employed a hind digit to scratch his ear and concluded with a prodigal yawn full of portent.

"Fortunately, atoms are too small for the naked eye to see. To give you a idea, the tip of one feeler of one bug has more atoms in it than there are stars in all the universes of the world."

Yonder lowered his eyebrows, crunched his forehead, and slowly but blatantly shook his fat head.

"If you have a question, please raise your hand. Now, if atoms were big as ping pong balls, the room would be too full of them for us to see each other or the furniture. We would have to go outside to talk and even then the sky would quickly fill up. In every cubular inch of air in every room there is hundreds and hundreds of atoms of every kind, including silence atoms, pollen atoms, darkness atoms, smell atoms, vision atoms, thinking and feeling atoms, crumb atoms, definition atoms, so forth. So imagine if sound atoms got big as ping pong balls, or better, bowling balls, for purposes of illustration. You would have to watch your words or get crushed by your own bowling balls before you even finished a sentence. However, sound atoms are soaked up by silence atoms and dissolve into sugarwater vapor, leaving room for other sound atoms. Silence is like the very woods where you come from, a realm that consumes every sound that happens in it as if it was never there."

Yonder twitched and stared off into the lonely distance of the workshop. It was a lot of information to take in all at once, and he looked properly overwhelmed. The student must be knocked off his feet by the teacher in order to learn how to respect facts he don't know, whether they're true or not.

"Now, all species use different sound atom patterns worked out by their members through the centuries, as here in Hmm. Every species speaks in a different language, but a certain common denominator makes my invention possible. Namely, every living thing has the same basic desire to express their feelings and theories in a way that will get themself listened to, understood, loved, agreed with, and petted.

"In conclusion, all that is required for one specie to communicate with another is for there to be some gizmo in between the mouth of one species and the ears of another species, a gizmo that interprets one species' invisible, self-adhering, sound-atom bowling-ball word patterns into the word patterns of the other species. In other words, a *translator*.

"And that's all I'm going to say. Except that it involves the unchartered frontier of post-molecular technology, a pinch of ESP, mountain water, popsicle sticks, recommended DNA, pinpoint timing, bird calls, fifty dictionaries, silver glow-in-the-dark paint, secret space-age polymers, a tuning fork, luck, Morris Code, impatience, and a mile of nylon cosmic string."

Yonder made a shoulder dip, a tilt of head, a scrinch of left side of lips, and a glance down sidewise with eyebrows up, that I took to mean, "Sounds simple enough."

"Nothing's half as simple as it sounds," I hasten. "Remember what Marshall McKuen said: 'The meaning is not the message.' Accordingly, I left out several ingredients from my narrative, in case the walls has ears. Tempt not, want not."

If Yondy's thunderous purring and blatant eye-batting was any indication, he seemed comforted by my narrative. He whinnied with happiness as I petted his big head and worked various items out of his shimmying fur, including a yo-yo, a hunk of coral, a U-No Bar, and my missing condensed copy of *An Elementary Treatise on Determinants, With Their Application to Simultaneous Linear Equations and Algebraic Equations*, which was Lew Carroll's best-selling sequel to *Alice in Wonderland*.

I reflected that while my *theory* of the Yond-O-Lator was state-of-the-art, the ice under some of my actual *facts* might of been a little thin. Nevertheless, there was only one piece of connectory data I needed in order to complete the invention, and it involved a special chip that I was trying to imagine into being, when the telephone rung.

Before the ring had done rang, Yonder took off and's gone. In his wake a top that shook loose from his fur set to spinning on the workshop floor with a clatter and a hum. Something in the way it was going both fast and slow at the same time gave me the inkling that it was spinning for me, personally, and I couldn't take my eyes off it till the phone rung again.

The last telephone call we received had been five years earlier, a wrong number for Shane from the South Pole. When people in Hmm have something to say, they get up, throw some clothes on, and hike over to your house and say it. It's old-fashioned but it saves you the trouble of saying a lot of things you mistakingly thought you had to say.

"Hello?" says I tentatively to the telephone. Then it rung again. I had forgot to pick it up, so I did. "Hello?"

Sheena Axminster, village telephone operator, says, "You have a call, Lemuel."

"Is that so?" I remembered Sheena taking Shane's side in the Mayor's Favors' fracas and being rude to me, and I still didn't appreciate it. "Whom from, if I may?"

"The gentleman declined to state."

"South Pole feller?" I say.

"Negatory, northwards," says Sheena. "Sir, go ahead, Mr. Washington is on the line."

"Hello dere," I says.

Silence responded, the pregnant kind.

I tried to think of some South Pole words, in case it was the same wrong number as five years ago, when a hissing noise come from the other end, like somebody trying to sarcastically suck a kernel of corn out of their dentures.

"Who is this?" I command. "Or should I come over there and find out for myself?" There ensued more misanthropic sucking, which struck me as vaguely familiar. "Can you hear me?"

Whoever it was grumbles, "Reception great."

At that bucket-of-rusty-nails voice, my blood stammered and my brains slammed on the brakes. I'd heard it utter maybe a hundred words in all the years, but I known that voice to the bonetips of my big toes. And then the poke at that ribald joke I had told him.

"What are you doing here?" I say stupidly to the phone, then:

"This isn't you."

I felt him leering through the line, with curled lips, sparse yellow pirate teeth, and the glean of the fiend in his Peter Lorre eye.

"If this is whom I think you are," I say, my voice strange to me, like I swallowed a clarinet reed, "then you ain't dead and buried in the Unconscious Forest after all, is you."

He sniffed and sput lackadaisically off to one side in the telephone. "You got sump'm a mine, Nephew, 'n' I'm comin' to claim it," and hung up.

"He's gone," says Sheena the Nosy. "Friend of yours?"

"My Uncle Leonard." Just saying it made my blood go slushy.

"You know what he told me? 'Get that kid Lemuel Washington, that halfwit.' I stuck up for you. I told him you were hardly a halfwit."

"Thank you."

"Your uncle don't sound well."

"He's been dead and buried a while. Did he say where he was calling from?"

"Nope. It was such a racket in the background, I thought he was at a party of imbeciles. Crows, it was. Sounded like a thousand drunken devils cheering him on. He had to turn away and shout shut up, several expletives deleted, and they did, them crows, shut right up. Dead and buried a while, eh?"

I nodded and hung up with the room going clammy and spinning like a loop-de-loop.

I hadn't no idea how happy I been before the call, but now I did. It couldn't be him, but if it wasn't, who was it? What sump'm of his did I have that he wanted? It sure wasn't that bike or them drums. What could it be but the animal hisself? What would Unc do to get him back? Now I knew why, when the phone rung, Yonder had took off like a cannonball out of hell.

# 32.

On the other hand, what damage could Unc do even if he *had* returned from the grave? He was a slow, shuffling, grumpy old man to start with. It stood to reason that stewing in the ground for a few months would of further slowed him down. If he did get holt of Yonder, you could just push him down and grab the animal right back. Why would Unc even want him, except for spite? Was spite a good enough reason to go to all the trouble of coming back from the dead? On the other hand, perhaps he had degraded into a zombie. He could try to eat Yonder, I supposed, although it would be one uncooperative little snack.

Then there was the philosophy angle. If Unc *had* came back, it threw a real monkey wrench in your whole theory of life, death, etc. Sure, you had old Jesus pulling a U, but there was a moral back of that—if they knock you down, get up and have another go. This here was *Uncle Leonard*—rude, mean, self-centered and no moral in sight. It did not help the reputation of the universe.

Did Unc's soul simply climb back in his body and take it to a phone booth to call me? Or was he a ghost-type spirit that rung me via mystical short-cut? Did he borrow a dime, or did he have change in his pants? For that matter, did his pants come back with him?

Before I could solve these sublime riddles, Transplant Anderson dropped into the workshop. Just as cosmopolitan as ever, he plopped his doctor bag on the workbench and peered at the Yond-O-Lator. "What the hell is this contraption?"

"It's a new mouse trap/bread slicer/can opener."

He raised his eyebrows and frowned. "I'm here to give Mabel her free follow-up." That little "free" meant his intentions were devious. And it reminded me to get going on my own devious intentions if I wanted to beat him to the punch with that gal.

I led him to the kitchen to stop him spying on the Yond-O-Lator and to test out another invention-in-progress, namely, tumbleweed tea.

"So," I say, "I saw you helping tote the mayor's throne around. Quite a comedown for a semi-educated man like you, cowtowing to my blockhead sister."

"Community service," he mummers. "Plus, she made me Official Hmm Organ Engineer. Speaking of, where's the patient?" He looked around like I had Mabel in a cupboard.

I peeked over Transplant's shoulder through the window: there Mabel was, getting her red duds all muddy, happily splashing with the frogs and ducks in the pond, while Yonder paddled around in his yellow water wings. I was not about to fetch her for Transplant to get his scoundrel paws on again. She was in the process of restoring her natural sassy and didn't need no free follow-up from the likes of that quack.

"She ain't here," I proclaim. "She went home to the North Pole."

"*North Pole?*" He plopped down in a chair I'd been fixing and it half fell over. He was so crestfellen from the news that he continued leaning in it at a crazy angle against the wall. "Well, *that* explains a few things," he mummers.

How could it explain anything when I just made it up? I wanted to tell him, which would win me the conversation, but also undermine my successful lie. "Yep, Mabel's in the North Pole," I say, "but *Yonder* is here. You want to give *Yonder* a free follow-up, Ernie? I'll go get him."

"Leave that heartless monster be!" To distract himself, Transplant tried his tea and spat it out on the floor. "Ptui! What is this, *tumbleweeds*?"

Transplant was a conceited slyboots, but I decided to bend his ear. Unc's telephone call sat on my heart like a fat cat on a mouse. I needed a man-to-man about mortality, the Afterwards, how a spirit could make a telephone call, and such like. As a medical fellow, Transplant had attended plenty of death-related festivities. Also, conceited people grew pleasanter when you picked their brains and gave them a chance to show off. I anticipated from him a practical and worldly outlook that would brang me down to earth, but when I inquired as to his appraisal of death, I was amazed at his preferential extremism.

"*Death*?" he snorts. "Lem, death is but a quaint theory, a hobby that disinterests me. However, if you rustics prefer to believe it exists, be my guest."

"Huh? Are you saying you don't believe that death exists?"

"It's not a matter of belief, it's a matter of preference. I prefer that death doesn't exist, and so it doesn't. However, since you're weaseling a free consultation, how's about rustling up some proper vittles to take the taste of this chemistry experiment you call tea out of my mouth."

I obliged with a batch of leftover fried turnip slices with guava mustard, and threw some fine unsweetened lemonade in a pint of Shane's homemade eggplant cognac.

As Transplant dug into the grub, I say, "The idea of dying, disappearing forever—leaving behind my body, brains, books, workshop, snacks, rhythm and blues records—it naushates me."

"As it should, if you're simple enough to prefer it."

"You think not preferring it is going to stop it from getting you?"

"It's worked so far."

"What if *everybody* frolicked around preferring there wasn't no such thing as death?"

"It'd get crowded, because nobody would die." He smacked his lips. "Nutmeg?"

I fetched it. "You couldn't sell a philosophy like that to a bunch of idiots."

"I prefer to give it away free to one idiot at a time."

"Well, I know one idiot that won't take it even for free."

In response, Transplant forked a mustard-drenched turnip slice into his yaw, shook a clud of nutmeg in after, chewed contemplatively, washed it down with lemonade eggplant cognac, and nodded at himself in approval.

"If I didn't prefer gravity," I say, "I suppose I'd float up in the sky?"

"If you dispreferred it sincerely and in ample quantity. I happen to prefer gravity. It keeps my hat on." He patted his beret with his fork, splashing mustard and nutmeg all over.

He was beginning to make sense, so I changed the subject. "I don't see how Old God could of invented death on purpose in the first place. It had to had been a dab of bad luck that snuck in at the last minute, like a fly in the flapjack batter just before you pour."

"Except a fly is real. Death is not. Death is make-believe, like a *ghost*, and you certainly don't believe in *ghosts*, do you, Lem?"

"I prefer to abstain at this time." I wondered if he had found out about Uncle Leonard's telephone call. If Sheena Axminster knew about something, odds was everybody in town did. "Now, come on, Ernie, you're the village sawbones. You see everybody drop dead all the time."

"That's them, not me. If I'm a beekeeper, am I a bee? If I'm an anthropologist, am I a caveman?"

He winked at me and took a big slug of that sauce. He was a good arguer and used intriguing but shady parallels.

"You know, there's a couple people and a animal that I know," I say, "that learned how to hang around and not bug me every second of the day. I don't care to think about them getting dead and leaving me alone to mope, wail, putter, and groan."

"Try preferring to imagine they moved to London and forgot to write or call, forever."

"What's to stop me from preferring to go to London and visit them?"

"Nothing, but by then they would have preferred to move to Paris."

"I don't see why following them around the world and never finding them is preferable to them being dead. In fact, it's worse, because you'd run up travel bills."

Transplant shrugged. "Sooner or later, you prefer what you become. I mean, you become what you prefer." He was blotto from the cognac. It was a crying shame I had to rely on a conceited drunkard skunk to reveal the secrets of the universe. "Death, ghosts, God, Heaven—all mist for the grill. Don't worry about a thing, just get paid up front." He burped like a bullfrog, pushed away from the table, removed his beret, and patted his sweating forehead with a corner of the tablecloth. "Ooo." He looked slightly green, but satisfied. "That's what I call a load o' leftover turnips."

At which he leaned forward and fell asleep, bonking his forehead on the walnut table. His beret tumbled into the mustard bowl and he begun to snore soft as a turtle dove.

It's funny how people, when they're sprawled out asleep, snoring and drooling and helpless, seem nicer than when they're awake and acting like they know what they're doing. The asleep certainly make better listeners. Transplant never met Uncle Leonard, couldn't of cared less, didn't believe in nothing, and was out like a light, but I felt less nervous and lonesome just talking to him about it anyway.

"Oh, speaking of ghosts," I say. I stretched out and relaxed because now it was impossible to lose the conversation. "My Uncle Leonard apparently returned from the beyond. Can you imagine? Chuck the woodsman claimed Unc had died dead, and he himself buried what remained. But who could say anything for sure about going-ons in the Unconscious Forest, where strange wonders congregate and conspire against all of human so-call common sense?"

# 33.

I lain a throw rug over the snoozing Transplant and went to set and meditate. My soul had gotten itself bedeviled by worries and could use a good settling down. Plus, I was way behind on fix-its. For example, Bing and Serra Nilap kept bugging me about when was I going to get going on their project. They had seen on the Outdoors Conveniences station where you could put your whole vegetable garden on a lazy Susan, sit at your umbrella table and pluck fresh vegetables as they swang by. Ever since that animal arrived, I had been barely able to mind my own business any more at all.

I was meditating pretty good, omming in time to Transplant's snoring, and about half a chakra from nirvana, when my mind swerved into a spiritual ditch. I just could not banish worrying that Unc was going to shuffle back and snatch Yondy.

I never asked for that animal, nor wanted him, nor known he existed, but Unc bequothed him to me, and now he was mine legal and moral, Mabel's will notworthstanding. I had grown admittedly fond of the critter, and I believed the big little fellow had cultivated some feeling for me hisself, despite his general ho-hum philosophy of life. Therefore, I would not stand for anybody grabbing him, neither Mabel nor her stinking miserable Pop. Couldn't *nobody* in this whole buttinski world mind their own business, including a dang dead man?

If he did try to reclaim Yonder, he would be in for one heck of a rumble. I was not a violent nor heroic man, but if it was unavoidable, and a just cause, I was certainly capable of pommeling a dead man to within a inch of his life.

I saw what I had to do, namely, zip out to the Unconscious Forest. If needs be, I would grab a shovel, march to Unc's grave, and find out once in for all who's dead and who ain't.

*

Yonder wanted real bad to accompany his beloved carekeeper. Every time I pulled him out of the Henry J he jumped right back in. Did he know where I was going? Did he want to flee Hmm because he knew Unc was on the loose? But if he was scared of what lurked in either Hmm or the Unconscious Forest, he didn't show it. His face was a portrait of non-nonsense cool—big tranquil unblinking eyeballs, earnest watchful lips, serenely palpitating nostrils, and ears sitting up like fur-robed, lemon-orange buddhas. But who could be sure? His looks were living parables. Again I determined to finish that confounded Yond-O-Lator so to hear what was on his mind any given moment, if anything.

I booted him out of the Henry J one last time and had Mabel hold him until I got out of there. She sensed something was up, but I wasn't about to inform her her Pop had come back from the dead, nor that I was going to make sure his corpse was in its grave properly rotting away. Info like that could throw a pall over your upcoming first date. So I lied: "I must go away and do some deep thinking about me and you." That was about the fourth most interesting thing in the whole world that you could say to a gal.

"So," she says, "when is this so-called date you asked me out on supposed to occur?"

If only a date was over once they said yes. "I thought you could use some gal space to get your feet on the ground."

"Speaking of feet, you're not getting cold ones, are you?"

"Oh, the contraire. The date I got planned will be a romantic hotfoot, if I may. Get ready!" I tore out for the Unconscious Forest before she could accidentally trick me into lying any more.

*

All the way there you could sense a big, glum force of bitter smugness named The Spirit of Uncle Leonard hovering around the jalopy. I put the radio on WNDR and kept it turned up the whole way. Luckily, it was Etta James Day, who made you think of sweet hopeless romance and not no taunting ghosts nor corpses in the woods rising from their graves.

*

Before long I re-entered the Unconscious Forest where everything begun. I pulled up in front of Chuck's cabin and clumb out. It was quiet and still as anything. You could hear the hairs twanging in your nostrils as you breathed the cold forest air. Smoke doodled out of Chuck's chimney. I was wondering what direction Unc's body was buried in from there, when I noticed on the ground where I was standing a strange raggedy shadow was beginning to grow around me as I stared down. All the sudden a scream tore the sky and I looked up—a immense old crow barreled out of the sun straight down at me, spinning and cawing like a torpedo all the way. Before I could move, who leaped out of the jalopy rumble seat and up on top of the roof but Yonder hisself! who catapulted over me into the air! and cracked skulls with that kamikaze crow like two wooden cantaloupes! KUH-RACK!

The mixed animal then did a reverse-flange and landed on his feet. The crow crashed into a handy clump of ferns, waddled upright, pranced around in circles shaking its head, took off clumsily, and didn't look back, but once.

"Boy!" I say to Yonder. "Stanley Stowaway! Close call! Thank you, bud!"

He was busy giving the stink eye to that retreating crow, and then to a profusion of others hanging around in the trees, who took his non-verbal hint and departed en masse, clamoring and ungainly.

"Did that old crow lose his mind?" I say. "What did I ever do to him?

Yonder insisted on remaining outside the cabin while I went in to see Chuck. He actually snarled at me when I tried to pull him inside. He stood there scrutinizing the sky and woods.

Good old Woodsman Chuck was happy to see me, once he remembered who I was. He served me some pine cone turnovers and peanut juice and we pleasantly shot the breeze about the price of tea, the future of the planet, that case of apricot rotgut I'd promised, so forth. Then I got down to business.

"Chuck, I gotta ask you something. How certain are you that Leonard was dead when you buried him out there wherever?"

"Sure as I could get, short of poppin' the fella open for a nautopsy."

"Ipso facto, he had stopped breathing?"

"I believe he done had."

"Hmm. How exactly deep did you bury him?"

"Understand, that ground out there's hard as a sidewalk. You don't dally in the woods diggin' holes at night, buryin' folks. Mighty untowards events transpires out there. I done what I said I'd do, I done it reasonable, I done it quick."

I thought people that lived in the woods would be more comfy around dead bodies, or woods for that matter. "Six feet or so?" I ask.

"Let's say none of his body parts was stickin' out."

"Chuck, no offence, but you might have threwn some leaves on him and say the same."

"Might."

"Could animals of got to him?"

"I put rocks on top the dirt enough to keep critters out."

"Enough to keep him in?"

"How's that?"

"Did you happen to take the man's pulse by any chance?"

"I figured Doc already would had. I don't get paid to pernounce nobody dead."

"Who was this 'Doc' person anyway?"

"Had to been a vet, what with Yonder's transplant."

"I wonder how a vet would be traipsing about pronouncing human people dead?"

Chuck shrugged. "Nobody else 'round. You make do. Myself, I did good just haulin' him off in the wheelberra, layin' him to rest. Pulse takin' weren't part of it. 'Sides, Doc wrapped him up tight in a old tarp."

"Tarp, eh? Did you ever lain your eyes on the actual body?"

"I seen the actual feet stucken out. Smelt 'em. It was your Unc all right."

The more I heard about the night in question, the more it sounded like one gruesome botch after another. That Unconscious Forest was the very picture of uncivilization. It was a miracle Yonder made it out of there alive. I ask the woodsman, "You feel like strolling out there and showing us the grave?"

"Hells no." Chuck gave a manly shiver. "But I'll drew you up the best graveside map ever drewn." Which he did, and it proved both simple, accurate, and picturesque.

Yonder and me took off and sprinted the whole way to outpace our fear, or at least mine. I read the directions by dusk light as we galloped through the trees, hurtling past startled critters big and small. The mixed animal was all around me the whole way growling, snapping and roaring at spirits and beasts in the charismatic foliage.

It was dark by the time we come upon it and skidded to a halt: End of the World Bluff. It was no mistaking the simple, dreadful, magnificent scene: the mound of rock-covered dirt in the middle of the clearing, a cliff overlooking a abyss of total darkness below, and up above, as you never seen it—the Rorybory Alice, in immense violet and lime phantom shapes that reminded you, in case you forgot, that something beyond was going on. We stood there froze, the Lights blazing and that mystical bee-like buzz from the Lights that Uncle Leonard listened to whilst meditating Yonder up. Me and my mixed animal paused a moment to eavesdrop on the universe.

Then he went straight for that grave with nary a twitch of fear. He stood by it just looking down, cool as a 90-pound cucumber. I crept over sidewise inch by inch until I was standing safely behind him. The long mound appeared undisturbed.

I sniffed the air and whisper, "You figure he's in there?" Yonder kept looking down at the grave. Every twig snap, every beast step, every leaf twiver reminded me of my mortal impertinence. "Could you do me a favor and find out?"

At which the animal set upon the grave like a wild boar after a buried crate of apples. In about a minute, to my simple horror, Yonder emerged from the dirt holding cross-wise in his mouth what could only had been a huge Uncle Leonard legbone.

It was every bit of all I needed: Unc was in there, and I was gone. I broke the Olympics record for leaving a graveside, squawking over my shoulder for Yonder to catch up or get left behind.

He must of took a short cut because he was already in the front seat of the Henry J by the time I jumped in—still holding Unc's legbone in his mouth! Thank Old God that Yond let me have it without a struggle and I flang it out the window accidentally onto Chuck's porch swing. I turned the key and we were on the highway roaring home before I noticed that the beast now had something else in his mouth. I abhorred to think it was a handbone or ribbone until I realized it was Unc's corncob pipe. Unholy smokes! He must of found it in the grave and kept it as a souvenir. He bounced it up in down on his lip in the Unc manner, sucking on it with a hideous whistling.

"O, Yonder, most loathsome!" I grabbed it from his lips and hurtled it out the window into the underbrush as we sped away. He didn't even look fazed or that he missed it one bit, proving that he did it for one reason and one reason only.

"That is unacceptable," I say. "That's not something friends do to friends, even in fun. If you act like a fiend, you'll become a fiend."

He put his head back and howled at the top of his lungs, meaning that was his idea of a fiend, or that he was sorry, or that we had confirmed that Unc was dead and buried. He curled up on the seat and poked my arm with his wet bear snout until I started petting his big self-centered beanpan. I ran across a fat throbbing knot on it that had to come from knocking skulls with that crow to save my life. I recalled the mystery telephone call, and them crows Sheena claimed she heard behind the caller. With Unc now proved ironclad guaranteed dead, that whole phone call was looking like a cruel hoax, pulled off by one or more of the many Hmmites that were jealous of my freedom-wheeling lifestyle. What a far-fetched way for them to retaliate, but jealousy is a far-fetched mistress.

After while Yonder fell asleep from my petting and started snoring what sounded like a rendition of "Little Drummer Boy, A Rump A Bum Bum." I put on WNDR and Etta James to drowned him out.

# 34.

Making sure that Unc was dead and disintegrating in his grave, minus the legbone on Chuck's porch swing, freed me up to start planning the date with Mabel. She was nowhere to be found upon our return. I thought she may of been out getting primed for the date, perhaps spending some of her millions downtown on a touch-up at Gertie's Mugs, Pinkies, Piggies, and Savings & Loan.

Meanwhile, Transplant continued dozing his life away. Who said the wicked don't get no sleep? As a matter of fact, I was a big fan of sleep myself, and I decided to go grab a much needed chunk of it. My motto was: Sleep makes a king of every man. I drunk my lullaby tea, popped my earplugs in, donned my Roy Rogers and Dale Evans and Trigger pajamas, piled my pillows on top of my head, closed my black velveteen funeral parlor curtains, turned the sound machine to jungle noises and sawing logs, and sailed away.

At some point a strange high-pitch near-music from somewhere pierced my dream perimeter. I thought it was the drunken keening of Shane's elephant-trunk tea kettle, but then it begun to develop into the most wondrously mournful whining and moaning that ever invaded my eardrums.

I sat up and tried to identify the eerie tune. It had the quality of feeling familiar yet alien at the same time. The sound was as a human vioella from the fourth dimension, or music made of spinning mercury.

The beautifully wretched din was coming from around the

house. I rose and searched for its source. Appearing to derive from several directions at once, it sounded like the saddest person in the world that was having their longing translated by a musical saw from Mars.

The melody was so weird, terrific, shameless, and faithful to the suffering of existence that it made me lose track of where I was. I had to sit down. It were as if the mysterious disturbance had alchemized my guidance system into warm putty.

I wondered if it could possibly be Mabel in the garden madly pining for me, but I looked out and she was nowhere to be seen. I noticed it was that time of day where you can't really tell what time of day it is.

Transplant continued to slumber on the couch right through the song, his turtle dove snoring providing a soft bass underpoint to the soaring, exorbitant tune.

Finally I realized that the sweetly grievous sounds was coming not from outside but in, namely, the attic. That was all the clue I needed.

I grabbed the stack of pots and pans from the hallway and mounted it in the bathtub to peep through the trapdoor.

Sure enough, there was Yonder himself, an ominous silohuette in the veiled light.

All the arcane fragments of his self-recreation project had been shoved ingloriously out of the way. That left him sidewise in the middle of the attic, with his tail risen up and fluttering about with a grace and mindfulness of its own, like the living fur baton of a conductor leading a orchestra from eternity.

However, looking closer in the twilit attic, it wasn't no orchestra, but rather a small oak box on thin legs. Further, two antennas stuck up for his tail to dance eerily betweenxt. It was from a speaker on top of the box that the keening refrains of sorrow and longing coursed forth, fearless and unabridged.

In other words, Yonder had discovered the Thereamen Electromagnetic Oscillator Box that I had stuck up there, that I built for Shane to give to her dream boy friend that she never met.

I had tried a few times to play the baffling contraption myself. You were suppose to wave and wiggle a special transmission wand in between the two antennas (one for amplitude and one for frequency). For the life of me, I never got the hang of it. I figured I must of left out some essential ingredient in its manufacture.

Now, standing on a stack of pots and pans, with my head stuck through the trapdoor and my chin resting on the attic floor, I learned from Yonder's artful tail that I didn't leave out any ingredient at all. He taught me what a vortex of lilting anguish the Box was intended to express. It was a otherwordly experience for me and any passerbyes that got insnared by the Thereamen sound atoms as they tumbled forth from the cottage attic.

It sounded like a hundred heartbroke nightingales on laughing gas, wailing as one for their missing beloveds.

Suddenly Yonder spotted me. His tail stopped mid-wiggle. A single poingnant chord hung in space like a ten penny nail being pulled lingeringly out of wooden air. He stared, exposed and meek, as if, "Should I feel caught doing what I shouldn't?"

Somehow I found the words to assure him: "Oh, please continue, Sirrah. Your tail is tearing my ribcage open like French doors to my heart."

Yonder winced at the beauty of my metaphor, and resumed playing.

I needed to get closer to that infiltrating song. I boosted myself off the pots and pans into the attic, with tears leaking down my cheeks. The high-pitch nature of the music must of oscillated my eye ducts, inducing my tears reservoir to grow unstable and overflow.

As I stood there, five feet away, in the spiritual hands of the animal's tail, the long wispy sonar arms of the Thereamen reached into my deep past and hauled up a terrible parade of the saddest, hurtfullest times in my life, one after another. I remembered my mom and then my pop passing into the Afterwards from the Arctic Croop that wiped out half of Hmm, and Shane and me having to raise each other like two sweet little idiots against the world, and the Halloween Sunspot Drought, and the Terrible Depressing Recession we thought would never end. I remember falling down Dingo Rudeheart's well, and catching my big toe in Gingham Moony's wringer, and Shane when the fire ants invaded her bloomers, and me and my first fix-it failure, the Applegates' dishwasher that they accidentally used cement in instead of lye. I remembered my girl friends flying by like a freight train of big wild weeping faces, all the people I hurt, or shortchanged, or didn't feel like saying hi back to, or wished was dead, or lied to, or got revenge on, or didn't help when I could of.

"Oh, Yond," I snurfled. "Music so splendid, music so tragic."

The maestro glanced sidewise, regarded me with the sad purse of his mouth and a conceding bob of his big head, and with a sweeping flourish polished off the uncanny symphony just as sudden as he had began.

Immediately a new head popped up in the attic trapdoor, namely, Mabel. Her face like mine was wet and wrung out in a emotional avalanche from Yonder's Thereamen passion.

"Goodness gracious," she says. "I thought the sound was coming from the clouds." She blew her nose and almost fell off the pots and pans. "Yondy," she says, "you *must* repeat your performance on our world—on the *big date*, with Lem and me, for the *world* of Hmm to hear."

I didn't want to disappoint Mabel in our shared moment of miserable musical bliss, but Yonder, amazing Thereamenist that he was, would not be included on no date of ours, and nor would that Thereamen. It would be crowded enough as it was with just us two.

# 35.

I and Mabel descended from the attic, leaving Yonder to snooze off his symphonic exhaustion. We paused to take in Transplant tossing in turning on the sofa. He had slept through my round trip to the Unconscious Forest as well as the animal's entire performance. He was slumbering away his many troubles. Plus, undeniably, Shane's eggplant cognac packed a wallop. The medical gambler's mustard-smeared beret was all mushed up on one side of his big rumba-shaped head, and tufts of salt in pepper hair stuck out like crazy passengers about to jump out the portholes of a sinking ship.

"There's the feller you're jealous of," Mabel says, wiggling a finger in my ribs.

At that, Transplant begun to sleeptalk: "Organs, organs, who's got the organs? If I don't transplant, who will? Beware to do people favors. No good transplant goes unpunish!"

Mabel and my hearts was already softened up by Yonder's masterpiece, and now this. How much pity could you stand to have? "Transplant, wake up," I say. "You're having a nightmare about your rotten in corrupt life."

He jumped up and stood there like a abandoned building. He looked like he'd been shot out of a cannon. His snazzy hipster clothing was all askewn. "Oh, bad, bad dreams," he says. "But waking up is worse!"

"Take it easy, Transplant," Mabel says.

"*Ernie*," he corrects. Then he saw it was his would-be. "You!"

He grinned daffily and tried to straighten his clothes that were on half-sidewards. "You're back from the North Pole already?"

"Pardon me?" says Mabel.

"Go home, *Transplant*," I say.

His eyes glazed with self-pity. "They're after me, Lemuel!" He fell to his knees before me. "Don't make me go home. I have no home. Help me! They're cold, they're ruthless, they take no prisoners."

I feared who his organ dealings had entangled him with. "The Mob?"

"Worse. The HMO."

He meant the Hmm Medical Oligarchy. "Ernie, dang it, you can't go around swapping organs like you're rotating tires. Didn't I tell you?"

"You told me, Lem. I did not listen." He hugged my legs. "I thought you were a sniveling paranoid imbecile. I deserve no mercy from you. None!"

"Arise. You're getting drool on my Sansabelts." I lifted him up. "Snap out of it, man. Where's that famous disgusting vanity of yours?" I took him by the shoulders to shake some sense into him and was dismayed at his surrendery rubberishness.

Mabel asks him, "What can they do, revoke your license? Arrest you for larceny? Moral desecration? Mayhem?"

"No, they just want their cut of the pie. I neglected to slip a few envelopes under their door." He got a phony pouty shy look. "I thought Lem might front me a loan, then I'd multiply it at Clotilda's lickety-split."

"You'd multiply it by subtraction. How much do you owe?"

"Fifty big ones."

"That's all I've got to my name, fifty bucks."

"That's *grand*."

"Grand for me, because I'm keeping it."

"Might I at least hide out for a spell?"

"I just got rid of one sarcastic conceited oddball around here, I don't hardly need another. Especially one that's being hunted for unpaid bribery, if not crimes against humanity. It would betray all my ideals to help you, plus you couldn't even chip in for groceries. Wait a minute, don't you own the Hmm Drugstore & Casket Company?"

"The HMO confiscated it for graft past due."

"Oh, let him stay," says Mabel. "Couldn't you scrape together a little something to tide him over?" She gave me a wink. "Do the right thing and problems work themselves out." I wanted to ask her, why didn't *she* scrape together a little something from her malty-millions? Not in front of him, of course—I didn't want that grifter to know she was a moneybags. On the other hand, if I yielded to her compassion for him, it might grease the wheels of the date to come.

"You can stay for a very brief nonce," I tell him, "and I'll lend you a few bucks for snacks. But don't take no parts out of nobody. In fact, don't even touch nothing!"

# 36.

Well, guess who ended up tagging along on our date? His name ends with R and starts with Y and rhymes with trouble. The main problem was that animal vaccums every bit of love and attention out of any room he sashays into, and the whole point of a date is to vaccum all the love and attention for yourself. Yonder was in the mood for travel and entertainment, and Mabel couldn't say no to him, so I was outvoted.

At least I refused to let him bring the Thereamen Box, which he attempted to. He had fell in love with that contraption. It allowed him to musically jettison his emotional luggage on anybody in the area. I anticipated first-date obstacles with a gal as stubborn as Mabel, without us sobbing from the animal's tunes. I was taking her to Jinx's Pawn & Putt, and it would be rude for the customers to have their most painful memories dredged up by eerie music while they're trying to sink a 20-footer.

Also, the bicycle would be crowded enough with me, Mabel and Yonder, plus I had to bring that drum set Unc left me. I hated to do it, but recent neglect of my fix-it art and craft had forced me to hock them drums to pay for the big night out.

We got ourself pretty spruced up. I wore my plum pin-stripe canvas four-piece, and Mabel slipped into some kind of pink, faux-buckskin, Annie Oakley ensemble that was fetching and robust. She was a darn good sport. She hopped right up on the handlebars like a true cowgal, and I got us a-going after a wobbly start. Yonder the chaperone loped alongside until I got some speed up, then leaped on the back fender and held onto me awkward and grabby.

"Settle down," I say, giggling against my will. "You're tickling me, I can't drive!"

Did I mention I tied the drums to the bike's rear bumper? Because I did, and we drug that whole bouncing apparatus behind us all the way over to Jinx's. Boy, you ought to hear a full set of drums being drug over cobblestones behind a bicycle with so many people on it the rims are grinding and screeching and flurring off sparks. Some fun. It was almost like Unc was banging on the drums back there. Crowds run out to cheer us on, but with the drums and the rims going you couldn't make out what they were screaming. A bunch of them had on their pajamas so it must of been pretty exciting to get out of bed and wave your arms and jump up in down and cheer for.

"Not to beat a dead cymbal with a stick, but what have I been snared into!" Mabel giddily hollers in my face. Bad puns are against my literary religion, but it did me good to see her loosen her petticoats. We was thrilled by the live drums accompaniment and it got the date off to a real butterbing.

Jinx, however, was not thrilled at the ransacked mess them drums was in by the time we got there. But he owed me for the fog-funnel-vaccum irrigation system I devised for his quinceberry crop, so he agreed to pawn them for a half hour of putting.

Mabel and me had ourself a wild swell time. She proved to be a excellent putter, sinking one after another from most every range and angle.

"You was born to putt, Gal," I say. "Who'd guess you was recently on your death bed?"

"Love is the great healer," she says.

I wondered did she mean me lovingly taking care of her, or her felling in love with me, or her and golf. I say, "Oh, thank you," which covered two of the three. She laughed. "Maybe when you forgot about that big exhausting world bus peace tour," I add, "it took a load off your weary mind and ailing body."

She didn't laugh at that. In fact, she missed a putt bad for the first time that night. I suspected if she had truly dumped that Yonder tour dream of hers or not. She changed the subject with a ten-foot pole: "One thing I like about you, Lem—you don't let my vast inheritance affect how you feel about me." That didn't have nothing to do with anything, but right then she sunk another long putt. Aha, so when she was winning the conversation, she putted like Babe Zaharias at the British Open.

I say, "Even if I did let it affect me some, out of chivalry I wouldn't show it."

"A lot of boys couldn't help but show it, chivalry or not."

"Unlike a lot of boys, I don't mix greed and chivalry." I hadn't no idea what I meant, but it sounded like I did, which is even better, so I went and sunk my longest putt of the night.

To tell the truth, nobody can't not be moved by a gal having untold millions, especially if you liked her plenty before you found out. If it was 50/50 that I could fall for her, maybe untold millions would of led me to try to win her heart. But with Mabel, I already cared for her into the 70s at least, or high 60s, so the riches was only a slab of butter on the biscuit, not the biscuit herself.

As far as Mabel went, who known how she saw the big picture of me and her. With gals, all you did was watch your front foot and don't step off any cliffs. If you looked up at the big picture with a gal, you just went right over. Gals was born for the big picture. A gal not only had her own mind humming away on new methods to outsmart you, she also had all other gals' minds since time begun built into her mental molecules to advise her along. Whereas a fella's mind was pretty much on its own from beginning to end with no help in sight.

Meanwhile, there was something about a gal sinking one nice 20-foot putt after another that got my socks a-going. Even though I suspected Yonder was doing some sub-sensory trick to help her out. Every time she putted he was standing right next to the pin and his fur swole up and went in different directions while the ball took circuitous routes and rolled into the cup, clunk. I couldn't prove nothing, so I decided to take my drubbing with dignity.

"Where'd you learn to swing a club like that, Mabel?" says I, husky like.

"TV." I noticed she gave a little wiggle before she sank them putts.

"You play golf on TV?"

"No, I watch golf on TV."

Once I'd daydreamed about dating a golf pro gal. They were tidy and reasonable, strutting around the greens. I found that assuring and attractive. Not that Mabel was a slob, but personal grooming and mental orderliness was important in the single game. I decided to kid her. "I watch brain surgery on The Learning Channel, but I wouldn't fiddle around inside somebody's head."

"I don't blame you," she says, "if you fiddled like you putt." She laughed and sassily plucked at my earlobe. I liked it when she laughed and goofed off, because her doors of stubbornness flang open then and her true her shoned out in a splay of dramatic playfulness and simple gal mystery.

# 37.

After our puttfest, we bicycled over to Little Jimmy Sammy's Snacks & Cakes for a sweet or two. It was a popular Hmm nightspot and packed like a tin of candy-famished sardines. I was perusing the menu when Mabel returned huffy from the ladies' room. She had discovered a rust spot on her faux-buckskin backside. "Look at this," she says. "It's from that bicycle of yours."

"What? Where?" It was a big nasty blotch that I pretended not to see at first, particularly since you didn't want to linger your eyeballs on your date's rearwardness any longer than you could get away with. "Oh, that little thing? It'll bleach right out."

"It would have been thoughtful if you had taken an S.O.S. pad and scrubbed the rust off your bicycle before the date."

"Frankly, I was too blinded by your beauty to notice the stars in the sky, much less the rust on my bicycle."

She stopped futzing with the blotch and squinted at me like I was a wet painting she was working on. "You oily tongued *devil*, you."

"In fact, I might need to put out a S.O.S. just to keep from drownding in the high tide of your sweetliness."

"Unless you drown in your metaphors first."

I pretty much had her where I wanted her, so I pretended not to hear that last part. Ignore a compliment now in then to look aloof and careless, traits that are attractive to women on the prowl. Of course you never *act* like you had her where you wanted her.

Oh, the contraire, I gave her a occasional glance like I never seen her before and wasn't much interested in seeing her again. It gave you a air of the forbidden and nebulous.

"Is something wrong with you?" she says.

I thought she meant my tummy, that was gurgling. "Maybe hunger spasms."

"Do they make you give me faces like you don't know who I am? Because I don't appreciate it one bit."

We squabbled affably over the menu, settling on a item I'd never tried but heard plenty rumors about, namely, "Little Jimmy Sammy's Blindfold GrabBag of Mystery Sweets Delight."

What Jimmy Sammy did was wrap a couple of his old neck-ties around you and your date's eyes and slap XXX-size bibs on you. Then you took turns reaching in a large paper bag stuffed with different pies, cakes, donuts, cookies, creampuffs, and so on. You just pulled a fistful out and chowed down. You could try to guess what it was, or simply enjoy. Jimmy Sammy provided a big stack of warm fresh moist towels, too, to wipe off as you went.

I and Mabel resumed our engrossing conversation as we dined.

"What do they do," she says, "take us out back and hose us off afterwards?"

I thought she meant later in the date, which I took it as presumptuous. "Afterwards *what*?"

"Dessert. AKA, gluttony incarnate."

"Oh, I see," I say, relieved and chagrined both. She giggled for a unknown reason, being blindfolded, as I savored a combination of boysenberry pie and chocolate éclair.

"Ooo, yum, cherry cobbler and pineapple mousse," she declares.

I felt like my common sense was getting fermented by the heady moosh of mystery sweets delight, not to mention the dreamy blindfoldedness and brushing arms with Mabel as we reached in in out of the sweets delight sack.

In fact, I had the sensory impression that she was licking the cake off her arm and sticking it right back in again. Also, I was alarmed because her arm felt rather larger and hairyer than I remembered. "You know what?" I say. "Could you maybe wipe your arm off with a towel before you shove it back in the bag all wet and smeary like that? It's kind of bad for my appetite."

Mabel gasps, "I thought that was *your* arm!"

We ripped our blindfolds off and found Yonder had his entire head stuffed inside the dessert bag clear up to his shoulders. We managed to pull him out of there, got mad, then naushous, then laughed at the animal and ourself—our arms, faces, head, fur, and bibs was all stuccoed with a mush riot of happily devastated mystery delights.

*

I and Mabel wiped down with Jimmy Sammy's complimentary towels and were partaking of our after-dessert coffee and cupcakes. We crossed our legs in the continental style, refreshed and proud of our successful feelings. Yonder busily lapped up a bowl of Sparkling Mackerel-Flavored European Ambo Water du D'Eau.

At which perfect point who dropped over to our table to pay their respects but Merle and Pearl Eh, the spike-haired ex-genius weightlifter scientist thug security couple. The last time I saw them they was hoving me into the mayorial moat.

"Hey, Lemuel!" says Merle, like we was long lost broes.

Pearl adds, "You're the feller Mister Washington we want to looking for."

The Ehs stood there spry and resplendent in hers and his fuchsia silk jump suits.

257

Yonder, my own thug security, hopped up on the table, bristled twice his size, bared his beguiling chompers, aimed one eye at Merle and the other at Pearl, and snarled low and smooth as a new chainsaw on idle. He sunk one saber claw in the tablewood and drug it slow across, raising seven long oaken curlings as it went.

The Ehs noticed. "Hey, no, whoa, now, Yondol, no, hey, whoa, ho," says Merle.

Pearl says, "We come in peace in toleration for animals and stranger others."

At which Yonder deactivated all his devices, jumped off the table, and resumed lapping the flotsam of cakes and pies off himself.

"Whew," says Pearl, and her and Merle slipped each other a wink.

To be honest, I didn't mind them two, even with the dunking. There was something about that scientist thug duo that was both bewildered, gladdening, industrial, and one of a kind. They had such a unusual character composition it wouldn't surprise me if they actually had been geniuses and came up with a big fancy idea way back when.

"However," I say, "if you don't mind, how about a apology for that dousing, for old time's sake?"

"Oh, sure, sorry," they say, "old time, no problem, oops, douching, sorries, heh."

I made godfather gestures of forget it and sit, sit, and they did. I introduced Mabel and them.

"Très enchanté," Mabel says.

The Ehs didn't know no Italian, but was polite enough to pretend they did. Mabel impetuously extended her hand for Merle to kiss, but it was Pearl who took it. She inspected the somewhat gnawed fingernails, nodding scientifically. The table bucked as Yonder shifted position underneath for a new angle on his cleaning business.

Merle gleered around the eatery, then leant toward me until his head was a inch from mine, big as a moon drenched in lemon-lime after-shave. "Pssst," he says. "We are to come in fortwarm you of a plans for the soon throwing of your mayor sister secret over."

"You soon *what*?" I say.

Pearl says, "They will to coo."

"There is a revolting palace in the future of delivered for her mayor bloodly," Merle says.

"Cootie, tot," says Pearl.

Mabel says, "I believe they're foretelling a revolution to oust Shane," and disconcernedly nibbled her cupcake.

I splutter: "The hell you say! Revolution! On what basis? I thought these rubes couldn't get enough of her Shanetocracy."

Says Merle, "She ronned up village inflation on the non-stop party; imports foreign shoes and socks to crushing trade deficit; sold off spare mayor throne, drapes, silverware; rising taxes on everybody twice, including dead peoples; installs bowling alley in royal hallway using non-union animal husbandry; new Constitution make Shane permanent mayor and rename Hmm Shane; heating moat to ninety degrees; bowling all hours of day in night—"

Only a mooncalf would have been surprised at this uprising. Shane had played the village like her own private gumball machine. Truly, a good coup dé-tat was just what the doctor ordered. The only problem was she'd be moving back in with me. "It will be no revolution!" I declare. "No muddy homespun tyranny shall trample the robes of freedom and privacy in my hometown."

I peeked at Mabel, who raised her eyebrows and pursed her plump lips in quizzical admiration for my decisiveness in a crisis. "If I may intrude," she says to the Ehs. "Why are you tipping Lem off? I.e., what's in it for you?"

Pearl teared up. "I.e., to not get stuffed in no rain barrel and rolt out of town like Mayor Shane going to get!"

"Yeah, we didn't do nothing!" squeals Merle. "We was just following you sister's orders to muss people for her royaltainment. Stuff *her* in barrels, not us Ehs!"

I decided that bodyguards who were so carefree about their own fear and selfishness couldn't be all bad. "What knockabouts is behind this cockamamie coup anyway?"

Says Pearl, "A secret knit group of businessmen, peace activists, defense contractors, lobbyists, consultants, real estate brokers, media personalities, trade unionists, folksinger/songwriters, and other sorted neerdools."

"Defense contractors?" I say.

"Dirk and Sid over at Dirk & Sid's Hardware," says Merle. He proceeded to name the entire secret group from top to bottom. It included pretty much the whole population of Hmm, including a number of children and newborns, plus a few long-dead folks that must of signed up to the coup before Shane was even borned.

Mabel says. "What are peace activists doing in a violent revolution?"

"Peace activists protesting Mayor Shane's invasion," Merle says. "Defense contractors want bigger invasion."

"Invasion?" I say. "Of what?"

"Ambo," says Pearl.

"Ambo! Why invade that cornburger?"

Says Merle: "To distract from bankrupt Hmm, open up new capital markets, and exploat natural resources."

"Are you kidding? Ambo's worst off than Hmm. They got no resources except them mutant warthogs in Old Phosphorus Cave. Besides, invade them with *what*?"

"Me and Merle," says Pearl, tearing up. "See, we look tough but don't care for rough stuff. We perfer to prance and shine. Well, beside horling you in the moat, Lem. But that was orders only. Nevermore, we quit, so she fired us."

Adds Merle: "And she took our Hmmland security badges, village credit card, and basketballs. But the cooers don't care, they want to clean house, and that means us in rain barrels, too. Oh, how we mighty is fellen."

Pearl nodded sadly. "It's a long way from the head to the bottom."

"Not in politics," Mabel says. She seemed rather blasé, as if she was thinking of something more important, as usual.

"We need counter-coo, Lem," bursts Perle.

"And how," from Merle.

"Well, first," I say, "we've got to inform the citizenry of Hmm and get them involved against this outrage to my personal privacy, or, I mean, democratic ideals."

"Everybody already know about coo," says Pearl.

"What? All these people know?" I meant the half of the village that was in Jimmy Sammy's right then cramming themself with sugar slop.

"They knows," says Merle. "They perfer to not to get involved."

"They perfer what!" I stood up and smacked the table like a four-star General. Forks and spoons jumped all over the place in terror. "Attention! Citizens and dinners! Oh, you prefer to not to get involved, eh? Let me ask you this: where is your patriotism and dignity, my dessert-plastered chums? Look at yourselfs. Are you too addicted to your cake to stop this revolution against my sister before it reeks total havoc on our shining hill?"

Most everybody pretended to ignore me, but a few folks glanced up and smiled coquettishly, then returned to their dining experience.

I sat back down, burned out on politics.

Jimmy Sammy come up and asks Merle, "Get you and Pearl something?"

"I wouldn't mind an Rhubarb Freeze," says Merle.

Pearl bumps him with her ample shoulder.

"Oh, two."

"It's not what I mean. We have buttered fish to fry." Pearl shook her head at Jimmy Sammy. He winced and departed with a put-off curtsy.

"Perhaps," says Mabel to me, "we should gather our wits and help your unbodyguarded sister with the same generous spirit in which she recently helped me."

"I wouldn't worry about it," I say. "Villagers is fiery, but their memory is short as a drunken hamster in a sailor suit. Shane can lay low in the woods a couple months, then wander back home and nobody'll give a dang, except me."

But Mabel continued arraigning me with her furled up eyebrows. "I think we can do better than that."

"Okay, okay," I say. To the Ehs: "So, when is this top secret coup that the entire population is either a part of or don't care about suppose to commence?"

"Tomorrow at one," says Merle, "after Nap Hour."

"Oh, good. Mabel and me can go for a stroll at Bygones Lake as per the date itinerary, then I'll devise a appropriate counter-coup at some later moment." I had no hope of such, but a good leader keeps his people deluded and relaxed as long as possible.

Merle and Pearl stood, declared, "I! I!" and saluted me smartly.

"Don't do that," I hissed. "Sit down. Never say 'Aye, aye!' to your leader or salute him in public. If the revolutionaries saw that, they'd start fitting me for a rain barrel, too."

Merle says, "If you need security as counter-coo leader, please hire I and we, who is currently interemployed."

"If I may," says Mabel, "you folks seem a little nervous for the bodyguard game."

"No, thank you," says Merle. "We're in the natural-born free-lance innovative software programmer game."

"Free-lance innovative software," I mummer.

"Once we were top five-A computer engineers, in China," a rueful Pearl says.

I say, "Let me run something by you two, on the outside chance you were who you say you are. What if I happen to be stuck in a certain microchip dilemma? Let's say I'm building a gizmo to translate the inscrutable sounds of Yonder into decipherable human language, let's say, English."

Merle and Pearl perked up, and Mabel's eyes got big as lumps of green coal. Yonder looked out from under the table and made a echoey chittering like a box of chipmunks, as if to say, "No gizmo could capture my inscrutables."

Delighted, Mabel says, "You never mentioned such a gizmo before."

"I'm mentioning it now only in the strictest confidentiality. I'm going to patent it as the Yond-O-Lator. Now, I envision said chip connecting the de-moleculized input manifests, namely, Yonder's various non-verbal orals separated into basic sound atoms categoried by size, color, spectral identity, mood, intention, sub-text, etc.; the vaccum limbo terminus of the silence chamber where the sound atoms are purified of extraneous background remnants; the voltage gated ion motives; and the reversular lexical yield reconstituted into general English, if that's of any help."

Mabel appeared impressed, while Merle and Pearl launched into a brisk Chinese tet-o-tet, both whispering at once. They grabbed a napkin and began making doodads, diagrams, typographies, pictographs, coats of arms, tableaux vivants, and such like, which spilled off the napkin and took over the tablecloth.

Finally, Merle clears his throat and announces, "We conclude you need very special connector chip. Based roughly on mechanics of spinning top."

"Spinning top?" I say. "I knew it!"

From Pearl: "Chip *might* be called 'Special Cosmiversation Enhancement Beam Transmo-Reversaloid Linguistic Field Capacitance Chip.'"

"Wait a minute—such a chip exists *already*?"

"No comment," Merle says, "but if so, it probably don't work in this case. Would need overwhelmed adaption conversion workings. Never used on animal kingdom. Only used on very little pre-talk babies and very old post-talk oldies."

"And it works with them?" says Mabel.

"Iffily," says Merle. "Extra experimental. Involves cosmic distance ladder framework. May cause disruption of human spoken communication worldwide if improperly abused."

"How could that be?" says Mabel.

"How could everything be?" Pearl says. "Also, chip only made in China. Exports banned under penalty of you don't want to know, we don't want to say."

"There's no way to get our hands on one?" I ask.

"Legal, no," Merle says.

"What about not legal?"

"I and Pearl know nothing of not legal. We leave China empty-hands. No contrabands!"

"Well, damn," I say. "The chip don't work to start with, and there's no chance of getting one anyway? Why'd you get my hopes up?"

"Perhaps," says Pearl, with a uncalled-for coyness, "you may show us the Yondon-O-Translator just to see it for our curious."

"No, perhaps I may not." I stood, and to Mabel and Yonder declare, "Let's go to the lake and walk off our grabbag of delights, not to mention this rude and untimely disillusionment."

# 38.

While I and Mabel strolled up the moon-smacked shore of Bygones Lake, Yonder threw hisself around the beach to burn off his Little Jimmy Sammy sugar high. He ricocheted in and out of the woods and up in down the sand like a 120-pound combo of meerkat, gazelle, and ball bearing.

Mabel starts us off: "You know, Lem, you're the first man I ever knew who was more interested in me than I was in him."

"Oh, thank you." I knew how to appreciate the nice half of a backwards compliment.

"Men in general aren't interested in me as me, rather than . . . well."

"Rather than your millions?"

"I didn't have my millions until recently. I meant—"

"Oh. I get it. Well, I like you as you. Even if you had no money. Even if you wasn't a gal."

"Is that so?"

"Well, I like you *more* now that you're a gal, but don't forget, I known you when you *wasn't* a gal, namely Strangitor."

She laughed, meaning I won that inning of the conversation. We moseyed along in quietude, with that old Hmm moon so fat in the black sky it could of been hanging three inches above the water. Each of us nursed their or her own thoughts. I mainly thought about what she might be thinking about behind that slightly cockeyed face of hers that I had gone fond over. Boy, was she ever complicated with ideals and things. It was like she was sitting on a bluff inside of herself, gazing out upon an inner Grand Canyon.

"So," Mabel says, "how do we put the kibosh on that uprising against your sister?"

"Oh, that." Dang Shane, dang democracy. Even though she was accidentally appointed by two janitors. "We have till Nap Hour tomorrow to come up with a counter-revolution."

"Maybe we ought to start planning it now. I'm kind of looking forward to it."

Why was she looking forward to planning a dang counter-coup instead of enjoying our sensitive walk under the low shimmying moon and nighttime scents of pine and éclair? The worst that could happen from the revolution was that Shane would have to come back home and get in my way again. And then it hit me like a brick Aha—Mabel wanted to keep Shane in office so she could claim the cottage, me, and Yonder for herself! So, she had as many devious designs on me as I had on her. Well, well, well.

Yonder continued to sugar bounce about the entire beautiful area. As the gal and me strolled along, I picked up a nice flat black stone from the beach and nonchalantly sidearmed it over the surface of the lake, sending chips of moonlit water hurtling at each skip. I got swept away on the beauty of it all. "Instead of planning a counter-coup," I say, "maybe we ought to start planning our—gee—*future*?"

"Oh," she says, both a sigh and a groan.

My heart hit that "Oh" like a tugboat hit a iceberg. "Boy, that ain't exactly summersalts."

"In my heart I'm doing somersaults, but they're bittersweet. For now, Lemuel, other plans call."

"Like what other plans?"

She glanced up sidewise at me like, "You know what other plans."

"Oh, no, that dad-dang peace trip! You said you give that up!"

"You said I gave it up."

"Well, you should of said you hadn't gave it up when I said you did. This just flangs a sack of stinkbugs right in the middle of everything sweet we been building up."

"I know," she says. "But world peace would be pretty sweet, too." Sadly, she reached over and drew her very intelligent fingertips along my neck and give me one of them eerie flutters in your inner face that you stretch your mouth and rub your jawbone to try to get rid of.

I edged us past the little rickety pier and down to the maple bench that watched over the water. We sat us down. Under the suddenly plommeting circumstances, we certainly didn't neck or nothing, but we was right next to ourself and you could feel the hair on your arm and the hair on her arm bashfully sniffing each other. Her reviving the peace tour made me want to go, "Where do you get off!" or else grab her by the shoulders and smush a kiss on her mouth like some jerk in a Western.

Soft as can be, Mabel says, "Why don't we drop these weighty matters and try to enjoy the dwindling embers of a lovely evening together?"

"Now you make it sound like you're taking off in the morning." She didn't say nothing again. "Not with Yonder, I'll tell you that."

"No," she says. "Not with Yonder."

"That's right. Although, how can you give a Yonder peace tour without Yonder?"

"I'll just have to play the cards that God and . . . others have dealt me."

I grew blue and darker blue thinking of Mabel going back into the cold world from whernce she come, abandoning me and Yonder to our own heartbroken devices.

I decided to be completely honest and trick her into staying. I would work on her pity and guilt by spinning the true story of my sad and lonely life. I started with Mom and Dad passing on to their Maker from the Arctic Croop, leaving me and my little sis wanton orphans fending for usselves, Shane picking up fortune-telling from a passing carny, and me self-learning to fix things like yo-yos and eyeglasses for pennies and nickels. From there I rolled on through the most poingnant facts, that I already listed in Chapter 34.

Like mice into a cherry pie, the tender, naushating memories of my life story wormed their way into Mabel's heart. Peering in my face, she cooed, her eyes grown damp, and she took my hand in hers. Yonder skidded to a halt to listen to the part about him, but his sugar bonfire blazed up and he tore off again. He veered onto the shaky little pier and chucked himself off it like a ragdoll end over end into the lake and begun paddling around like a Mississippi steamboat in the moonshine.

I could of told Mabel anything about me and it would of only opened her heart wider. I wished I had gone through more awful things in my life so I could keep basking in her emotional charity. I considered making predicaments up, but that would of defeated the purpose of being honest, and I couldn't think of anything anyway.

Afterwards, she leant over and kissed me mostly on the lower cheek but part on the lips. It was our first one-third of a kiss. My heart flapped like a flag in a storm. She whispers, "Thank you, Lem, for talking with me."

We watched Yonder swim further out in the lake, dropping out of sight, popping up here, slithering over the surface, submerging, reappearing slick as a whistle way over there.

"Wee otter," Mabel says.

"We oughter what?" I say hopefully, then understood. "Oh.

Yes. He's part fish. He has revolving seahorse hairs on his legs and tail. I first seen them activate when I gave him a bath in the rain barrel, right before we went and met you on February Mountain."

Mabel gave forth a big sigh for everything. The animal lazed on his back in the lake, la luna glistening on his ample platinum midsection. The thought of her going soon, the light on Yonder's tummy, our best and only date of all time about wrapped up—truth and sadness and beauty all mixed up together—conspired to loosen my tongue once again:

"Maybe I ought to told you this earlier," I say, "but I didn't want you upset on top of not feeling good. It's okay to say now, since I know it ain't so. Namely, Unc, or Pop, seemed to of momentarily not been dead after all."

"What?" She grabbed my wrist. "That's not funny."

"You can say that again. However, Yonder and me took a drive out to the grave, and Unc was in there all right. Frankly, Yonder unearthed a bone. I tucked it back in the grave, of course." That was a white lie. In fact, I could still see Unc's legbone bouncing up in down on Chuck's porch swing. "Yonder also took his pipe," I say, "which I thrown out the window, for sanitary's sake."

Her voice was like live wires: "Why would you think he was alive in the first place?"

"Oh, I got this dumb telephone call from him."

"Pop *called* you? When?"

"Uh, three days or so? But it wasn't Pop at all, of course. Or Unc. It was some village jughead that was jealous of my lifestyle. He had fake crows in the background and inside info he stole from Shane. Don't forget—Yonder and me saw Unc's bones with our own eyeballs."

"Have you ever heard of a ghost?"

"Well, village gossip is full of them, but how could a ghost call me on the telephone? How could they put a dime in the slot?"

"You accept that there could be a ghost, but not that he could call you on the telephone?" She stood and straightened herself as if something forward had been going on. "Yes, you should have told me sooner." She looked quickly out over the lake. "Pop said if I ever took Yonder on that tour, he'd stop me, even if he had to come back from the dead."

"Yeah, except for one thing. You ain't taking Yonder on no peace bus tour. Or did you forget?"

She didn't say nothing nor give her face away, but I could put two in two together. She was after Yonder again, or had been all along. You couldn't put nothing past even a normal gal, much less one obsessed with something wacky as world peace. She asks, quick and cold, "What exactly did this caller say to you?"

"Not much. 'You got sump'm a mine, Nephew, 'n' I'm comin' to claim it.'"

The blood drained from Mabel's face like the bottom fell out of a family can of tomato juice. She jumped off the bench and hollers over the lake, "Yonder! Come here now! Swim in right now! Where is he, damn it? Yonder! Where are you! Come now! Swim to my voice!"

He never came when I called, but at Mabel's summons he begun swimming to shore like a outboard motor was strapped to his back.

"You think Unc is really come back for him?" I say.

"Yes," she says, straight as a nail. Then, peering out at the thing charging over the water, almost to herself: "Is that Yonder?"

I tried to pick out my pet's dark golden red orange form in the splashing of water headed toward us. It was a Yonder-size splashing, but no sign of Yonder could be discerned in it. The water, that appeared to be swimming by itself toward shore, neared, grew, and burst from the lake onto the sand in the exact shape of the living Yonder, and immediately begun shaking itself off of itself.

"Oh, no!" I say, although Yonder himself took no notice of his crisis.

"He's water!" says Mabel.

He was water and nothing but, water standing on the shore, water shaking off water in sheets. In harmony with the lake, Yond had swam himself into being all-water.

"What do we do?" I say. "If he stays water, the sand'll soak him up!"

"Stop shaking!" Mabel says. "He'll shake himself away!"

Which did not appear the case. No matter how much he shook, the bulk of the water remained in the shape of Yonder. He personally believed everything was normal, so he begun returning to normal, just like that, transforming smartly from water back to his regular combination of elements.

In wild gratitude I and Mabel squeezed and smooched him, wet as he was. He shook supersonically a moment, after which he stood almost completely dry, fluffy, and warm to the touch, unlike us, who was now soaked.

"We've got to go, *now*," insists Mabel. "Pop could be anywhere waiting to pounce."

"The ghost of a old dead man can't be up for much pouncing. Worst comes to worse, we could push him around at our leisure."

"How could you push a ghost around? Boy, are you naive. Living non-matter that's on a mission is *relentless*. Even if you pushed him down a trillion times—" She peered intensely at the ground we had walked over. "Look."

I did. There were three sets of human footsteps in the sand where there should of been two. The extra set was barefoot.

"Ghosts don't make footprints," I say. "Could it be Yonder's?"

Mabel put a finger to her lips and mouthed the word "Whisper," as if ghosts had bad hearing. I wondered how she known all these ghost facts. She knelted and inspected the sand like a lead detective, then stood and took charge, grabbing Yonder's collar and my hand and rushing us toward the bike. Plopping herself on the seat, she urged the beast up on the handlebars and I hopped on the back fender and held on gingerly. My chin rested in the cozy crook of her neck as she got a-pedaling over the cobblestones, but it tickled her and she made me move it.

She drove right over a pothole to get my attention and yells over her shoulder right in my face: "Lemuel, you *must* give your unbridled permission before Yonder can go on the tour! If we went without your blessing, he'd be sad and spread gloom wherever we went!"

I wondered why she was yelling now if we was suppose to whisper before. Couldn't the ghost be trotting alongside the bike and eavesdropping? "He ain't going nowhere and he ain't spreading nothing," I say. "Is that why you were staying with me in Hmm? To wear me down till I give up and turned him over? Is that why you said yes to the date and sat along the lake and rubbed arms and pretended my life story was interesting?"

"No, no, no, no, no. Oh, Lemuel, why do I have to choose? Can't I have you *and* world peace? Just come with us!"

"I'm happy in Hmm and so is Yonder. We're happy together right here in village reality where we belong."

"If you're anxious about leaving Hmm, I'll help you. I know the scary world out there, I'm a survivor, so you don't have to be afraid."

"I ain't afraid of no scary world!"

She said nothing more but pedaled like our lives depended on it. In order to make her happy, I would have to make myself unhappy, either by yielding up Yonder, or by going with her on some beatnik bus tour that would take me a million miles from my home and private lifestyle. If I didn't go and didn't let her take the animal, or if she stayed with me and him and pouted and moaned for the rest of her unfilled life, we would both still be unhappy as ducks in sand.

The rumbling and bouncing of the bike over the cobblestones, plus my and Mabel's shouting had put Yonder sound asleep.

All the sudden I felt sick and tired of everybody trying to push and pull Yondy around from every direction. I realized I'd never asked him, and I doubt Mabel had neither, exactly what *he* thought about the dad-dang world peace jaunt, especially if he was going to be the heart and soul of it. I was sure if he had the chance to decide, he would stick with me, and thanks but no thanks to world peace.

"Yonder!" I say.

"Ghlrm?" he approximates, coming to.

"You don't want to go on that wild world beatnik so-call bus peace ride with this pushy redhead gal here, do you?"

The animal thrown his head back and let out a cry like somebody hurtling down a mineshaft.

"Is that a yes or a no?" I say.

He let out another, worst than the first.

"It sounded to me like maybe a no," Mabel says.

"I was thinking the same thing," I say.

"Mistletoe!" Mabel shouts, and pulled off the lane into the woods under a big old apple tree with dark clumps of the parasite plant lurking in its branches above. It was a peculiar time to think about kissing games. I doubted I could even get in the mood.

"Ghosts hate mistletoe," Mabel explained, as us three disembarked chaostically from the bike. "We're safe here." She parked the vehicle against the apple tree and we all set down beside it on a nice little grassy patch.

We put our heads together to see if we might ascertain Yonder's philosophy about the proposed world peace journey.

The first point we gathered, through thumb gestures back in forth between him and me, a paw on his heart, and a pouty face, was that he would simply miss me. That was about the best heart-breaking news you could get. Mabel reminded him that it wouldn't be forever. I told him we could talk on the phone and e-mail. "I ain't saying I'm signing off on it," I remind Mabel. "I'm just saying what if."

That left the more serious problem, which Mabel had in fact suspected on February Mountain. It took us a while to decode that him tapping himself in the chest, pointing at Mabel, making a big circle, putting his arms out, paws up, with a shrug and a frown and a shake of his head, meant that he was afraid he might not measure up to the great task before him, that he would let Mabel and the whole world down. His humility was a lesson to everybody that needed it.

"Come to think of it," I say, "that is one whale of a burden to dump on a little animal—bringing peace to that big crazy world out there."

Mabel patiently explained to Yonder that there was nothing special he had to do, because he was so special to start with. "Just show up every day, be yourself, and your wonderful beingness will automatically translate into every language and culture, and per-form its mysterious peace-making mysteries to perform, voilà."

You could tell from his pursed lips and eye rolls that Yonder was buying the old just-be-yourself bit about as much as me, and he didn't have half the rhetorics in polemics skills I did.

To join in the fun and wear down his good judgment, because I can't resist a good debate even when I'm on the wrong side, I threw in a few various irrelevant arguments of my own, full of illustrations and fallacies, about what a swell job he would do out there, how he was born to have his own big movement behind him, peace was at hand, so forth. He seemed to enjoy hearing our rationales, and before long he had indeed got his good reason properly wore down.

He looked up through the apple branches and mistletoe into outer space, as if consulting it, then looked at us and nodded somewhat trepidatiously, which brang hugs and cheers all around, and sealed our fates forevermore, for a while.

# 39.

What did we find first thing at the cottage but a special inheritance tax bill nailed to the front door. Scrawled in red pencil on a post-card that portrayed Shane in a gladiator outfit with a sword in one fist and a flaming torch in the other, it read:

> It has come to our attention that you owe the tax of one hundred dollars for inheriting bike, drums, and unlicensed animal of questionable origin from Uncle Leonard. Pay up.
> Yours truly, Her Royal Mayor, Merciless But Just, Shane Washington

Before I could express my outrage, Mabel begun darting around packing up, jamming things in my Henry J and calling the bus station for the schedule, while Yonder gathered foodstuffs and tucked them away in compartments in his fur.

I felt left out as a pig in polka dots. Oh, how lonesome I would be dropping off Mabel and Yonder at the Hmm Bus & Jewelry Station, then returning to a cottage empty but for shadows, echoes, and a tax bill.

Plus, there was that counter-revolution I had to draw up for the Ehs. I foresaw the cottage not being empty for long if Shane got overthrewn and waddled back home in a rain barrel to take it out on me, when who come busting through the door but Her Mayor herself, followed closely by Merle and Pearl.

"Hide us, Lem!" Shane squeals, locking the door. "They've taken over the Royal Cottage! They threw my throne in the moat! They're telling dirty limericks about me over the submarine loudspeaker! And now they're coming for us!"

Mabel, me, and Yonder peeked through the curtains. Indeed, a horde of Hmmizens bellowed in the distance, waving banners that proclaimed "Shane Is a Orfull Mayor!" and "Used Lawnmower Sale at Dirk & Sid's!" They were stampeding in our direction, carrying rain barrels and sack lunches. It looked like a bunch of neighboring Ambonians had joined in to thwart Shane's secret invasion plans. Our mere privacy wall would not long hold back a crowd so hopped up on freedom and loathing. Yonder hissed and growled at the approaching ruckus, and begun raiding his own fur for snacks, perhaps for battle energy.

"The revolution is on, Baby," I mummer.

"Do you has our counter-coo ready?" says Merle.

"I thought you said it wasn't suppose to be till tomorrow after Nap Hour."

Shane remarks bitterly, "A mob of surly bumpkins has no respect for schedules."

Says Pearl, "Save us, oh, Lem!"

I looked around and didn't see nobody that knew what they was doing, except Mabel, who was packing like a dervish to split the scene. I had to pretend to be in charge. "All right, all right. Let me think. Give me some elbow room!" Not only did I have a counter-coup to plan, I had to get Mabel and Yonder to the bus station on time so they could start saving the stupid world.

The first thing a counter-coup needed was a good slogan. I paced like a fiend, glancing at the bookcase, trying to remember one good saying I might of gleaned from the millions of books I'd read. What would Kafka say? "Look around and not have no idea what's going on," which I was already doing. What would Low Stu say? "Ride into the sunset on a water buffalo." Not helpful. What would all those other condensed authors say? They'd probably all sit around and write a book. I guess we could of thrown books at the charging, foaming riff-raft.

Finally, I remembered that some had history thrust upon them, some wandered around and bumped into it, and some were so surrounded by self-centered pandemonium that they had to invent history as they went. So, I plunked down on the couch, crossed my legs in a commanding, thoughtful, European way, and made a intellectual face, only to discover I had sat on top of the blanketed, snoozing Transplant.

"Ouch!" he says. "Who's on my head? Get off, doofus!"

"Transplant!" I say. "I thought it was one of our missing bowling balls."

Ernie caught wind of the hoot in holler of the advancing mob and went to take a peek. "Oh, no, the HMO! Hide me!"

I say, "I'd be surprised if the HMO *wasn't* a part of that bloodthirsty rabble."

"I'd be surprised if a certain undead Unc-slash-Pop weren't also!" says Mabel. She threw a tablecloth over Yonder, hoisted him on her shoulder and staggered to the garage.

"Where's *she* going?" Transplant says.

"World Yonder peace tour," I say, at which Transplant ducked off into the garage. "Where are *you* going?" I ask, but he was already gone.

Shane peeked out of her room where she'd been hiding.

"By the way, thanks for the special inheritance tax bill, Sis," I say.

"Oh, that. I guess I won't be doing any tax collecting for a while."

281

"Gee, I was just about to write you a check."

"Could you make it out to 'Shane Washington,' leave off the Mayor part?"

Merle announces, "Pearl and Merle will also be going on world bus peace, too, tour."

I say, "I'm sure Mabel will be happy to hear that."

"Who's Mabel?" says Pearl, then whispers, "Do you mind could we had a look at Yondery-O-Translator while we wait to the bus?" She winked and conspiratorially patted her tattersall purse.

"Huh? Oh, who cares. It's in the garage on the workbench. Welcome to it, another of my honorable flops."

Merle and Pearl exeunted, whispering and flexing. That left Shane and me to listen to the wretched multitude rather slowly approaching. It sounded out of breath. I looked out to see and hello and behold the frothing throng had paused for a snack down the road at Zim's 500-Flavor Slurpso & Mortgage Emporium.

Shane and me took a look around the old homestead. It might be a while before we could safely return. I dreaded the mess that swarm of unwashed rascals would make of the place by the time we got back.

I left the garage door down for a surprise exit, revved up the Henry J, with me and Shane and Mabel in the front, Merle and Pearl and Transplant in the back, and Yonder standing tall in the rumble seat on top of the ice chest. Plus somebody tied the Thereamen Box on one fender and the bicycle on another.

It was a cloudy night by then, so the solar panels on the Henry J were at low power and the cow poo gas was cold, meaning by the time we heard the caterwailing mob climbing on top of itself to breach our wall, we had got just enough steam up to crash through the garage door at about one mile a hour. We almost got stuck in the door but picked up speed from a slight downhill grade on the way to the bus station and kept about three arms' length in front of the panting serfen mass, who was almost out of gas themself, despite the Slurpsoes.

However, any carload of morons could see that if I stopped at the bus station to let passengers out and unload all that crap, the gasping rabid beatnik lump and proletariat would of overtook and done with us at their pleasure.

Accordingly, and without protest from nobody, I kept it floored right past the bus station and finally put some breathing room between our necks and the mobus populi. In the rearview mirror you could see them jumping up in down and tearing their signs in two and falling all over the boulevard, rolling around in the dust and coughing and throwing up in sheer revolutionary delirium, free of Shane's tyranny at long last.

As for us escapees, we gathered momenta in the Henry J and passed through the ancient crumbling gates of Hmm, just like Low Stu had long ago traversed the gates of the Great Wall of China on his water buffalo. Before you knew it, we were zooming along the open road, nothing in our rearview mirror but where we been and where we might not return to ever again.

# 40.

Time and space had a mind of its own out there where Hiway 3 rolled southwest forever between the undulant dunes of the Ruby Desert on one side, and the roiling high tide of the Barbell Sea on the other. After some breathless jabber about escaping with our skins, we sloppily decided our first destination would be Droplette, the nearest town in hundreds of miles big and civilized enough to kick off Mabel's and Yonder's World Peace Henry J Tour, which we also decided had already began, because we might as well do something useful as long as we were on the lamb.

Not that everybody was thrilled to be along for the tour, but it didn't take much convincing. If you were forced to pick between 1) a world peace tour, or 2) getting ripped limb from limb by the sticky hands of a mob of political idealists: Welcome to the peace tour.

Mabel, sitting snuggily beside me in that jam-packed Henry J, sighed to pass understanding. "That was not quite how I pictured the launching of my tour."

I patted her on the shoulder. "Well, the whole town seen us off."

Next to her, Shane was busy spit-polishing her crystal ball, upon which there splashed now in then a tear for the heartbreak of her four-day political career.

Next to her, or seven-eights on her lap, Yonder stuck his head out the passenger window, wearing Transplant's dark glasses against the star-slewn night.

The Ehs was busy in the back on both sides of Transplant, fiddling with the Yond-O-Lator that sat atop his doctor bag on his lap. He nodded in and out of sleep as they pushed his head out of the way in different directions.

Beyond that, none of us barely broke the silence, except the radio. Nobody complained nor groused much, odd for that lot. The starch had temporarily been took out of that bunch's moaning and groaning sails. We were in our own thoughts, the kind you get when you're leaving one chunk of your life behind and heading for another that you known nothing about.

As we hightailed it through the night, I, for one, harbored plenty second thoughts about what I signed up for. Events had transpired too swiftly for Mabel nor nobody else to plan stuff out. Where, beyond Droplette, was we going? What would we do when we got there? What if nobody in Droplette or anyplace else wanted peace after all? What if everybody couldn't make heads nor tails out of Yondy, or seen us all as ciphers in a pointless farce, instead of saviors of the future of the world?

And to think, as I captained us through the tunnel of darkness into the great veiled unknown—a lump and beatnik mob was that very moment lounging and drooling all over my couch, coffee table, TV set, bed, garden, workshop, attic, fridge, and I tried to stop myself before I got to my condensed books and the mob's crumby sticky paws sliding around inside trying to pick the letters off the page and eat them or something.

With the mood my passengers and me was in, there weren't no hope of but the dismalest of conversation, or going round in round with your own night thoughts. I put the radio on. Nobody stopped me. It weren't nothing to do but drive and drive and listen to "Sixteen Tons" by Tennessee Ernie Ford, "The Wayward Wind"

286

by Gogi Grant, "Singin' the Blues" by Guy Mitchell, "The Great Pretender" by the Platters, and a whole train of like songs that plucked your defenseless miserable heartstrings. Sometimes it felt better to feel worse.

*

Along the way we pit-stopped at various fleabit snack stands. At one such, wolfing stale exotic crackers and rattatwee, we and the stars drunk in each other. The Ehs tinkered non-stop with that idiot Yond-O-Lator on the fender of the Henry J, spilling rattatwee juice all over it and themself. Shane sat on a boulder marking her fortune-telling cards, while Transplant leant against the snack stand smoozing a flirty snack stand gal.

All the sudden a breeze kicked up out of nowhere and a whirlygig, a little dust tornado, came spuming out of the dark plain, circled the snack stand with a measure of deliberation, and lingered there swaying, as if giving us the once over. The thing lifted the hair on my neck.

"Dust devil," Transplant comments with a shiver. Yonder's ears perked up mid-chew, and Mabel gawked at the swirling object. As the whirlygig just as sudden lit back into the night, me, Mabel, and Yonder glanced at ourself, hoping it was only a whirlygig and nothing but.

Back on our way in the Henry J, the heater kicked and rattled, and Harold Melvin and the Blue Notes and Dinah Washington and Bill Withers and Lavern Baker and Jimmy Reed and Brenda Lee and Ivory Joe Hunter crooned from the little radio one by one for our pleasure and edification. I just hoped we were headed toward Droplette okay, much less world peace, having never been that far down Hiway 3 but once as a kid, and never at night. I didn't want to mention it, because what if we were lost on top of everything else?

Back out in the rumble seat Yonder let out a occasional howl of salvation or lonesomeness, a knowing and ominous call to rattle the bones of every living thing in range out there in those hinterlands.

We drove and drove until I saw a hand-wrote sign that said "Droplette 345 mials." I was glad to see we were going in the right direction, but we would never make it that night. We reached an unanimous consensus to find a spot to camp out in. After while I pulled off the road into a picturesque abandoned farmhouse clearing in a long gone wild landscape of cornflowers, kangaroo reeds, and acres of giant johnny jump ups.

I parked and we piled out. In the quiet you could hear distant waves from the Barbell Sea going "Shhh," and from the Ruby Desert came a coyote's chillful cry, maybe communicating with Yonder. Along with the little farmhouse a dilapidated swayback barn lurked with moonlight leaking in and out like rays of honey. Whomever lived there must of pulled up roots years before and couldn't have minded us laying low for a night or two.

As we stretched and groaned, that same eerie whirlygig or dust devil from the snack stand (at least it looked and acted the same, only maybe bigger) come toodling through the clearing and lingered there at a distance watching us, wobbling its hips back in forth rather mockingly, like a big flamingo dancer made out of wind and sand.

"We care for the dust divils not, do we?" says Merle.

"Us, no, never do, never did," says Pearl.

"Them's spirits," mutters Merle.

"Who says?" I say.

"China," says Pearl, and they wandered off with the Yond-O-Lator.

Transplant and Shane begun to unpack, while me, Mabel, and a skittish Yonder continued to observe the dust-up as it passed slowly away along the fringe of the kangaroo reeds. You had the feeling it was looking back over its shoulder at you. This whirlygig was acting fairly foppish for my tastes, if it was suppose to be who I suspected. I sniffed the air for tobacco stank, in vain.

"Did Leonard ever dance the flamingo?" I say.

"He did take a lesson or two from Mom," says Mabel. "Why?"

"Oh, a hip wiggle from the whirlygig reminded me of a dancer gal I once knew."

"Not knew well, I suppose."

"Not well at all, plus from a goodly distance."

As the dust specter passed into the night with a dramatic nonchalance, Yonder recovered from his skittishness and lickety split out to explore the new territory in the opposite direction from whernce the dust-up went. "Be careful!" I call after him. Mabel and me exchanged a quick worried look, but Yonder was Yonder, and what could we do.

Mabel mummers, "If it is Pop's ghost and he wants to grab Yonder, he's had plenty chances. Why wouldn't he just go on and do it?"

"Maybe he's buying his time," I say. "I never heard of no ghost doing a Spanish dance and flirting over their shoulder at you."

I wondered if we should tell the others that the ghost of a dead miserable hermit madman may be wandering around the campside, but I didn't want them to think I was crazy until I was sure.

*

We explored around in the farmhouse and found it spooky and stanky. It had developed into a unusually pleasant evening outside, so we decided to be comfyer camping under the stars.

Transplant and me got a fire going in the farmyard and the gals slapped some tofurkey sandwiches together, plus strawberry pop from the ice chest. Mabel had did a excellent job of packing. Yonder put in a brief appearance to gobble twice his share and somewhat ease me and Mabel's worries, but when we turned around he was gone again.

Merle and Pearl scavenged a run-down redwood picnic table in order to resume their hopeless twiddling with the Yond-O-Lator on. Shane got some coffee going, and her, Mabel, Transplant, and me sat around in a circle on buckets and fenceposts, chowing down. We worked us up a lively little conversation, which is nice to do in a situation like that.

"I can't believe my beloved peasant followers turned on me so quick," says Shane, quietly weeping and licking mayo and mustard off her fingers. "I was everything for them—mayor, queen. I was the Eva Peron of Hmm, giving them hope where none existed before. I gave them my *life*!"

"You gave them three days," I say.

"Three and a half," she sighs. You could see how bad she missed the trappings of power, even though they turned into a albatross on her prim and donna soul. "I believe my reign was a humdinger, but only history can decide." At that, she blew her nose, shrugged, and cheered up: "Say, who wants their palm read?" Nobody jumped at the chance. "Half price?"

Transplant says, "I can barely stomach what already happened, much less what's going to."

Shane says, "I'll let you all in on a little secret. Don't tell any cash-paying oafs we might bump into on this fool's journey, but I never give unhappy readings. A happy customer is a return customer. Oh, I throw in a mysterious item or two, but mysterious to a mark is just an eerie kind of happy. Even if I saw a safe was going to fall on your head tomorrow, I wouldn't tell you. Not that you're oafs or marks, of course. Come on, who's first?"

Everybody muttered and moaned, in no mood to hear even a guaranteed happy fortune. Shane humphed and started reading her own palm: "I see a journey, a long journey into strange lands full of coyotes and clodhoppers." In response to her prediction, she ohhed and ahhed to herself. I never seen her so jolly and upbeat. Maybe she was born to get ran out of town.

As for me, the only thing boringer than somebody telling you their dream was somebody telling you their own fortune. I decided to razz Merle and Pearl, that were still monkeying with the Yond-O-Lator. "Give up," I say. "Without one of them special experimental universal translator chips, that thing couldn't translate silence into silence. You're trying to pick cherries off a lemon tree."

They giggled in Chinese. Merle held up a computer chip and grinned.

"What's that?" asks Transplant.

"Cherry," says Pearl.

I gasped. "Is that the Chinese chip for babies and old folks!"

Pearl coyly shrugged. She slipped the chip into the Yond-O-Lator motherboard. Her and Merle closed their eyes, said something to themself, and made circles and triangles in the air. Then Pearl said some Chinese hogwash into the microphone, flipped the switch, and the machine said the same saying back, but in a mechanical Chinese voice.

The Ehs hoorayed and high-fived, bumping their muscled butts together like demolition balls.

"What are you celebrating?" I say. "All you did is turn it into a fool of a tape recorder."

"No fool," Pearl says. "It translate whatever into Chinese. Chinese chip, neh? So, Chinese translate. Then we tell you.

Therefore, I says, 'Do you work, Yondo-O-Translator?' and it say, 'Do you work, Yondo-O-Translator?' but in Chinese, then I tell you in English what it said."

"Come again?" I say. "It translates Chinese into Chinese? The entire point of this invention has flew like the Sputnik high over your pumpkin head, Madame."

The others fell silent and gathered around the picnic table to observe this travesty of a conversation.

"Let me see that we may dedensify you, Lem," says Merle saucily. "Here, say something now," and he held the microphone up to my insulted face.

I say into it: "You two Ehs are a couple major league nudniks. How's that?"

Pearl played back what I said, it came out in Chinese mechanical talk, and Merle says, "You said, 'You couple is very important two noondiks. How that's, Ehs?'"

Everybody laughed. I laughed, to spite myself. The fire even laughed. "You just heard me say that in approximately English. Stick to hurtling people into moats, my iron-pumping chums. The subtleties of science nor language don't become you."

"Here, Yondero, go come here," Pearl says, and Yonder trotted out of the cornflowers and hopped right up on the picnic table. Pearl tells him, "Place in this microphone the sample of personal mouth sounds."

Yonder grewn contemplative. He tilted his large head at a pensive angle and squinted up into the starry night.

"I gotta see this," says Shane.

"Me, too," I say. "A unreliable animal making nonsense sounds into a jimcrackcorn gadget that turns it into Chinese and then some biceps twosome supposively translates it into a ragtag bastard of English. That's sciencetainment."

Yonder elaborately cleared his throat and produced into the microphone a klatch of resonations that closely resembled the otherworldly uulations and trillings he had previously exhibited only to me alone in the attic and the gum grove. It made me feel special one moment because the others were mystified and never heard anything like it before, and then unspecial the next because now they had.

Pearl doodled with the Yond-O-Lator. More mechanical Chinese hoo-ha spat forth, which required a hasty conference among Merle and Pearl. Then Merle proclaims: "Yonda says, 'Thanks you for everything, Lemuel.'"

The whole gang sat and stood there froze, then slowly looked at one and another.

I say, "What's everybody looking at everybody for? I guess people will believe anything. 'Thanks you for everything, Lemuel'? Now I know you two are making all this up. Yonder would *never* say thank you for *anything*, Lemuel. That is the most spoiled ingrate mixed animal that gets whatever he wants and thanklessly demands more. You picked the one saying in the world that he'd never even *think* of saying if he lived to be as old as February Mountain."

"I have to unwillingly support my brother on that," says Shane. "As much as I like to see him outsmarted for his own good, words of gratitude and humility are not consistent with my experience of this supremely presumptuous creature."

Yonder pretended to be unconcerned with both my diatribe and my sister's rather well-put concurrence. He gave the Yond-O-Lator a couple big licks as if it was a ice cream cone.

"Why don't *you* ask him something," Shane says to me.

"Not hardly. Whose side are you on? This is a charade. It puts folly to shame."

"Ask Yondy something," Mabel says, and the whole outcast

rabble takes up the chant: "Ask Yondy something! Ask Yondy something! Ask Yondy something!" Yonder himself joined in with the combo of a taunting oriole and a horse laughing at the moon.

"Okay, okay, pipe down," I say. I tried to think of something wily to ask Yonder that would outsmart the lot of them. I remembered how in our rush to flee Hmm we'd forgot to brang a map. I say, "Come to think of it, Yonder, where the heck are we exactly anyway?" He was too self-centered to even care where *he* might be, much less anybody else. Therefore, any answer he gave would have to of been made up by the Ehs.

Pearl held the microphone up to the animal, who mummered a single meaningless but melodic buzzing noise, the machine translated it into Chinese, and Merle translates it into English: "'Here.'"

The others mummered and applauded as if a masterpiece had been unveiled.

"Okay, hardly har," I say. "'*Here*'? Once again, even if he really did say that, it doesn't prove a thing." I asked a fast question before Yonder could think to make up a trick answer: "What kind of sandwich did I pack for us for February Mountain that I kept leaving crumbs of to not get lost and you kept leading us in a circle and eating them?" Nobody but him and me knew it was garbanzo. "Quick! Either you know it or you don't."

Yonder made like he was trying to remember, then mammered more enchanting gibber into the microphone, the machine spewn it out in Chinese, and Pearl says, "'Guhbamzo.'"

"Holy moly mackerel," I blurt.

"Is that *right*?" says Mabel. "Garbanzo?"

"What if it is, so what," I say. "Anybody could of guessed that. You was on the mountain, too. On the way down you must of saw a garbanzo bean on the trail that Yonder missed, and now you just told Pearl by Morris Code eye signals."

Mabel laughed. "Even if I could, why would I do such a thing?"

I say, "To increase the mystique of the kingpin of your peace campaign, why else."

"Oh, who cares?" says Shane. "What kind of a stupid question is that to ask anyway? Here you have the first chance in history to actually communicate with an animal in English, and you ask him what kind of dumb sandwich you were throwing around on a hike? Plus you already knew the answer. Sheesh. Snap out of it, Bro!"

"What am I suppose to ask him, then, smart aleck?"

"I don't know, ask him the secret of life," she says.

"How would he know the secret of life?"

"I dare say he'd more likely know it than you."

"That ain't saying much," I say.

I glared at Yonder, who was trying to keep his smug nostrils from flaring because everybody was talking and wondering about him again as always.

"Did you hear the question, or what?" I ask him.

He looked at me blank faced as Buster Keaton. He was going to make me come out and ask it in so many words. "OK, Yonder, what is the dad-dang secret of life?" I looked at Shane. "Happy now?"

The blasted animal stared somberly up at the night riding stars again, blinked, and offered the microphone a rather terse collection of burblements and flummeries.

The Yond-O-Lator grabbed his folderol and sput it back in Chinese, which Pearl translates: "'The perfect square have no corners.'"

Everybody let that bilge sink in a moment.

"'The perfect square have no corners'?" I ask Pearl, even though somehow I looked at Yonder as I asked it. "That's your secret of life?"

As the goofy cryptogram kept sinking in, everybody but me looked at one another like children on the first day of class.

Pearl and Merle consulted, then Merle offers a alternate interpretation: "'There are no corner found in the best square of all.'"

"Oh, that's better," I say. "And there we have the secret of life according to Yonder. Who's laughing now? Me, that's who," even though I wasn't. I looked around to see if any saps had fellen for the square without no corners. To my shock, they just might had, if crinkled foreheads, squinched eyeholes, and slowly nodding noggins was any indication.

"What does a animal know about arithmetic?" I say. "How could there not be no corners in the perfect square? If you count inside and out, there must be ten or fifteen corners in there. You couldn't squeeze more corners in a square if you had a crowbar and a pound of butter. Animal, how is that the dad-dang secret of life?"

At which a jack rabbit tore through the clearing and Yonder took off after it like fur lightning into the cornflowers and kangaroo reeds, gone.

"I knew it," I say. "You can't pin down nonsense."

And just as sudden Yonder come tearing back through the clearing with the jack rabbit chasing *him*.

"Yonder!" I say. "Come here!" but he was already gone, jack rabbit and all.

"The ideal square admits not the impediments of corners," Transplant says plaintively.

Shane looked heavenwards and says, "Corners have no business in the consummate square."

"The perfect square," adds Mabel, "gives no corner onto which for the mind to hold."

"It was bad enough to start with," I mutter. "Wait a minute. You know what? I believe I heard that saying before. I did! That's from the *Tao Te Ching*. He stole that from Low Stu!"

"I wouldn't put it past him," says Shane.

"What if he did?" Mabel says. "An animal steals an epigram from a great work of spiritual literature? Think about it."

"I don't need to think about it," I say. "It's plagiarism!"

Mabel says, "Lemuel. He talked. He talks."

Could it be so? I mummered it out loud as soft as I could, to see it better: "Yonder talked."

Merle and Pearl was proudly dusting lint off the Yond-O-Lator like it was their little piglet who won a blue ribbon for squealing at the county fair.

Just then a terrific commotion emanated from deep in the cornflower stand, and it was a-coming our way. Yonder shrieked and blasted out of the stand like a bristling rocket chased not by the jack rabbit but by the *whirlygig*! the *dust devil*! And it was about three times bigger than ever.

Everybody else jumped back as the horrified animal flewn into my arms and almost knocked me over, but I held on, swallowed my terror, and command the charging whirlygig, "Halt, Sirrah! Cease thy charge! Now!"

The dust devil skidded to a stop, its whirling top wobbled, and it appeared to paw the ground with its lower funnel.

"These damn whirlygigs in these parts!" blusters Shane.

You could see now that the devil had plenty other crud and whatnots besides dust swirling around in it—a pair of mushy slippers, a old telephone, crow feathers, a dirty beaker, a stained and singed lab coat, a rusty can of tobacco, and the like.

"It *is* him!" Mabel shouts. "Those are his accouterments! It's his ghost! It's Pop's ghost!"

"It's whose *what*?" squeals Transplant.

"Uncle Leonard?" says Shane.

Mabel wails, "Don't let him get Yonder, Lem!" I held the poor beast tight and she joined in. I remembered the mountain clearing where her and me held onto him for dear life once before.

Shane and Transplant jumped around hollering blandishments at a safe distance, while the Ehs held the Yond-O-Lator as tight as me and Mabel held Yonder, who clove to my neck, slobbering with fear, digging his claws in, grrring and purring at once.

Uncle Leonard the ghost dust devil rose mightily up stallion-like to strike.

All the sudden I holler stupidly, "Take me instead, Unc!"

"No!" says Mabel. "Don't take anybody!"

I didn't know if I meant it, so to see if I did, I say it again, "Unc, take me instead!" I confess to mixed motives. I planned to put up one stink of a fight had it took my offer, but if we got out of it alive, Mabel would hand her heart over to me gift-wrapped for offering myself in Yonder's place. I was also working for sympathy, although what sympathy could you hope for from a dust devil ghost of a madman? Still, you never known.

In response to my offer, the whirlygig produced a sound like if you threw a armful of forks into a cement mixer.

At which point Merle twiddled the Yond-O-Lator, the machine sput out some Chinese razzmatazz, and Pearl announces, "Dust Divil says, 'No push luck, lemming.'"

"'No push luck, *Lemuel*,'" corrects Merle.

"That dust devil can't talk!" Transplant hollers from safety. "That was just whirlygig crap crashing together. That is not any Uncle Leonard! Don't listen to that Dust-Devil-O-Lator!"

After taking note of Transplant's uncharacteristic passion over anything but himself, I announce to the dust, "Lemuel push luck any time Lemuel feel like pushing luck." I had tooken on something of a whirlygig Chinese idiom.

Declares Mabel to the dust devil: "You're done here, Pop. You cannot have Yonder. Pass on and let him be. Pass on to wherever you're supposed to go. And go in peace, as in now!"

"If that *is* you, Unc," says Shane, "stop being the same damn belligerent mean old bastard *dead* that you were *alive*. Hasn't croaking taught you anything?"

At which the whirlygig broadcast a noise like a bucketful of gravel getting pitched into a tractor fan. Pearl activated the Yond-O-Lator, it gave a Chinese rendering of the gravel clamor, and Merle provides his outlandish take:

"Dirt says, 'Okay, okay! Jeppers crappers! Gripy whinin' yapper mobe! Take him! Take him! I gives!'"

Everybody stopped in a standstill of unbelief. Further gravel and forks tumult ensued, additional Yond-O-Lator, and more Merle:

"Divil states: 'Take him damn bleedy hearts peace tour! Fats lot of good its do you!'"

Mabel gasped with global delight. "Do you mean it, Pop?"

A longer bloviated clatter of silverware and rocks bespoke, then the O-Lator, then Pearl:

"Whirlygig claims, 'I mean what do, say what say, do what mean. But me be round, eye you like hawk eye sack o' hamsters. One hair harm in mix beast head, Unc fix ever last one you! Go take him tour!'"

You could of filled a stadium with our cheers, hopping around, and general celebration hoohaw.

Once more the devil clattered and crashed, Yond-O-Lator spoke, Merle translated: "Whirly Pop says, 'Holt it! I still got me bidnis with *sawbones*!'"

At that, a arm-shaped segment of the dust-up poked forth in the lab coat and pointed at Transplant.

Shane discreetly inched away from the pinpointed doctor.

"Me?" says Transplant. "Heh! Why, there must be some mistake!"

The whirlydevil resounded like ten garbagemen dumping cans, and Pearl translated from the Yond-O-Lator: "'You suppose put me ice, *Doc-tuh*.'"

"Who, me? Ice? Heh! You certainly have me confused with some other physician, Mr. Dust."

Unc—as I felt safe to call the phenomenon by then—produced a tumult like a train wreck as it advanced on Transplant, who backed up a few steps, then collapsed to his knees and clasped his hands. "I confess! I confess! Oh, forgive me, old man. Forgive me, you poor dead bastard!"

At which Unc not only ceased his advance on Transplant, but instantly calmed, quietened down, and even diminished sizewise. It was as if the plea from Transplant had been the main goal that all his ruckus had aimed to reach, and not the grabbing back of Yonder at all.

Nobody but Transplant and Unc had a idea what was going on. We gathered around the stricken, knelting Transplant, who commenced to unfurl the astounding details of his confession: "I was afraid. The HMO, the IRS, and the FBI were after me. I could hardly let it be known that, under less than sanitary or legal conditions, I was forced to transplant a human heart into a wild animal for a thousand bucks."

Yonder roared in my and Mabel's arms, and Unc made a turmoil like a zooful of cages rattling.

"Okay, *ten* thousand bucks," says Transplant. "Which by the way I lost at Clotilda's that very night out of grief and regret, if it's any consolation to my accusers."

Says Shane, "Whoa, back up."

"Human heart into wild animal?" I say.

"Leonard's heart into Yonder!" Transplant shrieks, and begun to moan and weep and smack himself all over in retaliation.

This news hit me like a runaway taxi. Mabel fell back and sat on the ground. The Ehs jabbered hysterically, and Shane for once was strucken mute.

I demand, "Cease the sobbing and explain yourself, Ernie."

"Water, water," coughs Transplant.

As Pearl fetched him a glass, Yonder broke my and Mabel's grip and ran over and started jouncing around the perimeter of Unc the dust devil with a monkey-like jocularity. It was as if he missed the old cynical hermit, but wasn't sure it was safe to show it. Unc responded with light kicks of his dust feets out towards Yonder, who playfully nipped at them and coughed from the dust. This rough tango of theirs was another bead in a growing necklace of inconceivables.

Transplant gobbled a whole glass of water and resumed: "It all started with a call from the Unconscious Forest, from this Leonard fella. He had a job for me. I didn't know him from a monkey's uncle—no offence, Lem—but he says it's cash up front, and lots of it. Long story short, he wants a fresh heart put in his dying animal. According to a vet up there who's not up to the task, the animal has a bad ticker and not much time. But I can't even get out of Leonard the species of the animal. He gives me some impossible cockeyed story. But I'd done a mess of human transplants—so to speak— why not animal, whatever the mix? I came up with a, frankly, not too damaged ticker of a recent roadkill, bless its heart, got it on ice and headed up there. Zero chance of success, but I could always use the practice and the cash. I told him, No guarantee. He says get up there."

Mabel caught my eye and indicated with her chin behind me.

I turned, fearing Yonder was listening and reliving the night of terror. Instead it was Unc the Dust chasing Yonder around the clearing, and then Yonder skidding to a halt and turning and chasing Unc back around.

"Problem was," says Transplant, "I grabbed the wrong cooler going out the door. Grabbed my lunch instead of the roadkill heart. I arrive, get the animal ready, pop the cooler, there's my egg salad sandwich. Leonard's ready to cut *my* heart out. Animal's open on the table, life fading like light out of a evening sky."

Mabel couldn't help but wail, "I helped put poor Yondy at death's door by screaming with Pop about him right before you got there!"

"Hey, there you go," says Transplant. "Spread the blame around, I don't mind. Although, ahem," he says, pointing at the chase between Yonder and Leonard in the near distance, "the aggrieved appears somewhat alleviated."

Everybody noted it and evidently approved. "Do go on, Doc," says Mabel, alleviated herself by her outburst of shame.

Transplant complies: "There was no time to get another heart. Leonard rants and raves a minute, then stops and says take *his*. Put *his* heart in the animal. I remind him he might need that himself. He doesn't want to hear it. He threatens me. He offers me double, triple, ten times the original thousand. Ten grand! Under threat and temptation, I make a lot of crazy promises. I swear to put his heart in Yonder, put Leonard himself on ice, run and get another human heart, slap it in him, take care of both him and the animal till they recover from surgery. In case he didn't make it, I vowed to take Yonder, a bike, some drums, and his pocket change to Lem and Shane here, after burying Leonard on some damn bluff. Most of which tasks I pawned off on his good neighbor Chuck. Even if I'd had any ice to stick Leonard in, I had no heart to stick *in* him, not on short notice. There's limits even to my harvesting skills. Basically, he was asking for a death sentence, which he had to have known, although we always hope, right to the end and maybe beyond. I figured it was all out of blind affection for his pet anyway, so it would be a great time for him to go. He did unfortunately pass, as we know, but the transplant proved a resounding success, to my amazement. I have no idea how that animal didn't reject that heart. Part luck, like roulette. Somehow the old man's DNA must have gotten swirled into the original batch when Leonard was mixing up the beast, maybe a cut, maybe a tear. Who knows? One of those events we physicians don't like to call a miracle. Who knows how anything works? It's a crapshoot. Of course, because of certain moral and legal reasons, I chose to forego any personal fame about what turned out to be a breakthrough masterpiece of experimental transplantation surgery."

"Well, I never," says Shane.

"I thought you preferred to not believe in death," I say.

"There's an exception to every preference," says Transplant. "And then, of course, I set the fire to cover my tracks, but I did drag Leonard's body out first, and wrapped him up nice so Chuck didn't have to see the muddle when he buried him out in his favorite spot." Transplant hung his head. "And now I throw myself on the mercy of the court of my peers."

"If that's what Uncle Leonard wanted," says Shane, "that's what Uncle Leonard got. The customer is always right. You saved that animal, Ernie, and that animal got me the mayorship, if briefly. I, for one, have no beef."

The Ehs nodded in general forgiving approval. Pearl says, "Confucius says, 'To be wronged is nothing unless you continue remembering it.'"

Mabel, whose very father it was, agrees, "Unconditional mercy.

For Transplant, for Pop, whatever he was or is, for everybody. For everything. After all, we are embarked on a world peace tour."

That left me. In my view, Transplant was getting off the hook mighty easy. But he had told his story so quick and smooth, with such rich emotional details, addressing most all extant questions with flair if not plausibility, that I couldn't be the only hold-out. "Okay," I say. "Guilty of plenty, but forgave of all."

"Look!" barks Shane, and we turned to see Yonder leap head-long at Unc the dust devil and Unc vaccum the critter completely into his whirlygig self. The whirly span him around and around and then spewned him out to crash furlong into the cornflowers. Yonder staggered forth, wobbled woozy a moment, then wiggled his hiney and ran and flang hisself right back in Unc's chaostic spin.

Shane declares, "Are they playing?"

"I believe they are," mummers Mabel, "and I believe they're having fun."

Uncle Leonard the whirlygig ghost hurtled Yonder out one last time, snorted, retched and snarled for old time's sake, stuck one dust hip out, then the other, and tore off across that farm clearing, up the road toward Droplette, gone like he was never there, except for one old floppy slipper that flewn out like as from a open dryer. Yonder ran and grabbed it and brung it back to me, laying it at my feet like it was the stanky grand prize for everything he put me through since the very beginning.

Mabel and Transplant and Shane and Merle and Pearl started yapping all at once about the whirlywind and Transplant's confession and what everything meant, all the while drifting naturally back toward the campfire.

I needed to be by myself a while and not think about nothing. I was all jammed up. I went and lain in the car, with my feet sticking out the window. Yonder jumped in to join me and seemed to want to chat, gesturing at the Yond-O-Lator out on the picnic table. Frankly, I had too many feelings and thoughts to start putting them into words, or to listen to what anybody else might have figured about anything yet. I petted him a little against my will and pretty soon he got restless and jumped out the window for another pasture.

*

I fell asleep some, then got up and listened to my fellow exiles plan the itinerary of the tour while they roasted marshmellers. Transplant found a old jackknife and got busy whittling a wood object. It looked like some human inner doodad, a pancreas or sacroiliac. Finally, I decided to go off on the far edge of the clearing by myself and try and meditate.

I figured I was way too flummoxed by events to get much going, but surprise—my flustered chakras lined up and cooled down, and a nice karmic vibe got to brewing along in there. I even glanced at the future once or twice and considered how maybe it wouldn't turn out so rough as it might ought to.

After while I thought somebody started the Henry J to make a getaway, but it was just Merle and Pearl asleep in the back seat, snoring so powerful you thought the car was idling.

I fetched myself a root beer popsicle from the ice chest and strolled out in the meadow. Laying by a old gingko tree, I enjoyed the crispy night, the sky so deep and dark and thick with stars.

I gnawed on the popsicle and gratituded about things. Like Merle and Pearl finalizing the Yond-O-Lator (because sometimes you need help with something), and Yondy finally getting across some of what was on his mind, including thanking me for all I done for him, which I agree. Although, in my opinion, the whole "no corners in no square" saying was far too curt and coy for anybody's first words.

I hoped old Uncle Leonard's ghost would take a more tidy form if he did keep his threat to visit us later on our world peace journey. What if Mabel spent a bit of her millions on a nice hotel suite for us now in then, say? You didn't want a big whirlygig charging through the lobby and up the elevator to your suite to see how you were treating Yonder, with gravel and forks and old slippers flying out, disturbing all the other guests.

I thought how it was good to have Transplant along for the ride, a bon vivânt doctor on a perilous voyage, now cleansed by confession—as long as he didn't get any big ideas about Mabel.

I even admit I was happy Shane filled her lifelong ambition of being mayor of Hmm, even though the results was mixed at best. May history be kind to the disastrous blip of her administration.

I even hoped the lump and proletariat in Hmm was enjoying their revolution, not doing too much damage to our cottage, and that the stability, justice, and corruption of the village was beginning to settle down some in the post-Shane era.

And of course I was grateful as could be to Old God that brung me Mabel out of the blue when I least expected it. I hoped the peace tour turned out okay for her, and that I might prove a good influence in helping her continue to undo her bad old ways, although perhaps not totally entirely, if I may.

Right then I happened to glance up at the roof of that old ramshackle barn, and guess who was up there but Yond, eating a big fat orange from the food cooler. He had got hisself silohuetted right at the peak of the gable. The sky lay so dark behind him you could see moonlight from the opposite direction tingling off his fur, and gleaming in his many splendored eyes. He sat there pure-perfect, self-centered as could be, peeling and dining on that orange a slice at a time, rather casual for the likes of him, as far as food goes. He regarded the tarpit of the night sky and the signals from the constellations and whatever else his mixed heart desired to regard.

Watching him munch away on that orange as he studied outer space, serious as a child at play, you would never known all the obstacles and sufferings he had underwent since getting hisself created in the middle of the Unconscious Forest, all which left him up on top of that swayback moon-stang barn in such a moment of peaceness and orange slices and astronomical rumination.

I thought about calling him down to come be with me, but I couldn't remember one time he did, come when I called. I don't think he never meant nothing by it. It was just his way of showing me that he liked me so much he couldn't stand to get any closer.

Right then he turned my way. Behind his eyes I could sense the wheels of cogitation moving big and sure as old wagon wheels over the prairie. He blinked once, real slow, and all the sudden, for what felt like the first time, I understood him. Or didn't *understand* him so much as just plain *give* him my understanding, free of charge, for that peculiar moment, as simple as passing a platter of potatoes to somebody before they had to ask, and he give it back to me, easy as could be, with another blink, and a smerl, and a potato or two missing. Whatever unknown things was going to happen next on the tour, I reminded myself to be sure to stop in wonder every once and a while about that mixed animal, that Yonder, and all our other exile companions, including myself, and, in fact, to be fair, while I was at it, to stop in wonder a little bit about you, too, now in then.

# Acknowledgments

Thanks to all those who helped me in any way with *I Inherited a Mixed Animal from Uncle Living in Woods*—the good folks at Democratic Underground (where Lemuel and Shane and Yonder et al. came to be); Paris (my dear wife and blessed first reader); Barry L. Young; Bill W. and my Higher Power; and Kevin Atticks, Jack Stromberg, Abby Szypula, Becca Thompson, Mac Ferrone, and all the good and talented people at Apprentice House. I heap thanks upon you all.

# About the Author

*I Inherited a Mixed Animal from Uncle Living in Woods* is Richard Martin's second published novel, following *Oranges for Magellan*. His work has appeared in *Virginia Quarterly Review, North American Review, Chicago Review, Greensboro Review, Night Train, Adirondack Review*, and elsewhere. He lives with his wife Paris and their cats Marvin and Slim in Santa Monica, California.

Apprentice
House Press
*Loyola University Maryland*

Apprentice House is the country's only campus-based, student-staffed book publishing company. Directed by professors and industry professionals, it is a nonprofit activity of the Communication Department at Loyola University Maryland.

Using state-of-the-art technology and an experiential learning model of education, Apprentice House publishes books in untraditional ways. This dual responsibility as publishers and educators creates an unprecedented collaborative environment among faculty and students, while teaching tomorrow's editors, designers, and marketers.

Eclectic and provocative, Apprentice House titles intend to entertain as well as spark dialogue on a variety of topics. Financial contributions to sustain the press's work are welcomed. Contributions are tax deductible to the fullest extent allowed by the IRS.

To learn more about Apprentice House books or to obtain submission guidelines, please visit www.apprenticehouse.com.

Apprentice House Press
Communication Department
Loyola University Maryland
4501 N. Charles Street
Baltimore, MD 21210
Ph: 410-617-5265
info@apprenticehouse.com • www.apprenticehouse.com